LR

NOBLE DEEDS

CHRISTINE MARION FRASER

NOBLE DEEDS

HarperCollins*Publishers*

The characters and events in this book are entirely
fictional. No reference to any person, living or dead,
is intended or should be inferred.

HarperCollins*Publishers*
77-85 Fulham Palace Road,
Hammersmith, London W6 8JB

Published by HarperCollins*Publishers* 1995

1   3   5   7   9   8   6   4   2

Copyright © Christine Marion Fraser 1995

The Author asserts the moral right to
be identified as the author of this work

A catalogue record for this book
is available from the British Library

ISBN 0 00 224103 X

Set in Linotron Galliard

Printed in Great Britain by
HarperCollinsManufacturing Glasgow

To the memory of Commander John Douglas, OBE,
An officer and a gentleman

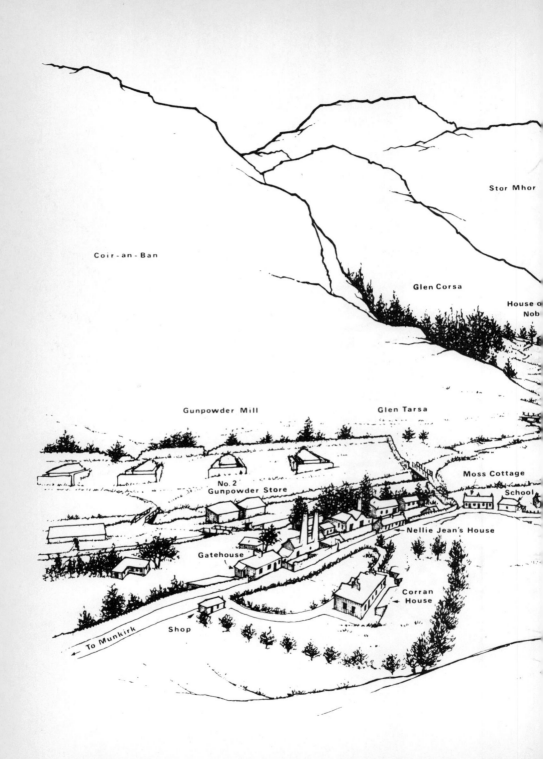

Stor Mhor

Coir - an - Ban

Glen Corsa

House of
Nob

Gunpowder Mill

Glen Tarsa

Moss Cottage

School

No. 2
Gunpowder Store

Nellie Jean's House

Gatehouse

Corran
House

To Munkirk

Shop

Paddy
Stool
Hill

Knock Farm

Corran Kirk

Coach House Inn

McDonald's
Cottage

River Cree

Clachan of Corran

W

S   N

E

NOBLE DEEDS

CHAPTER 1

Memories

Glen Tarsa, Argyll, 1893

Anna sat easily on Knight's broad back as he trotted steadily down through the heather-clad slopes of Coir an Ban, making for the bridle path that skirted the River Cree.

It was April and spring was everywhere: new green leaves were popping out on the bog myrtle; fat, yellow catkins hung from the hazel branches; the gorse bushes were almost ready to burst into golden bloom. The sun was rising higher, dispersing the mists of morning, and it was warm enough to feel that winter had finally kicked off its traces.

Anna inhaled deeply, delighting in the sweetness of the air, elation flooding her being at the feel of the sun on her back, the perfume of springtime in her nostrils.

Down below, the tall chimneys of The House of Noble rose into the sky, surrounded by the rolling green meadows of Leanachorran. Beyond the fields, the wild moors of Glen Tarsa stretched, merging with the blue haze of the distant hills where the sun glinted on burns tumbling down through the corries. Little white cottages and sprawling farm buildings dotted the glen, and men were busy in the fields, sowing, ploughing, tending the animals.

In one of the fields two Clydesdales plodded, unhurried and calm, adding to the serenity of the morning. Behind them was Magnus, Anna's brother, guiding the plough, striding through a sea of rich, dark earth that fell away from the blades in steady waves.

Anna urged Knight to go faster. The tall figure that she knew so well was nearer now, clad in a faded green serge shirt and brown tweed trousers, tucked into heavy boots.

She felt a pang of guilt. While she rode idly about on a horse her brother toiled in the fields. He enjoyed his work and was more a son of the earth than many who had been born to it – yet, still, she felt guilty. Her life had changed so much in the past few months, ever since she had become Lady Pandora's companion.

It had been the start of a new life for her. She was still the daughter of Roderick McIntyre of The Gatehouse – she could never escape that label – but now Nora McCrae came in three times weekly to 'see to the house' and Anna's days of drudgery were no more. In just a short space of time she had tasted more freedom than in all her sixteen years.

Those wonderful trips with Lady Pandora for instance: the town house in London, theatres, ballet, opera, parties, dances, shopping in stylish fashion houses, meals in fashionable restaurants. Then Christmas at the Nobles' family mansion in Devon, Wheatley Manor, a lovely old house surrounded by gardens and lawns, rolling fields, peaceful glades and rambling woodlands.

Anna began to daydream. The glitter and glamour of Christmas at Wheatley had been overwhelming: parties every other night, beautifully dressed women, handsome men, servants with sweating faces running at the snap of a finger. Huge log fires had burned in the grates, tables had groaned with food, the wine had seemed ever flowing, the singing and the laughter seemed never to stop.

Privately Anna had to admit that the womenfolk were overdressed and overloud; that the menfolk were supercilious and condescending; that the food would have been better appreciated on the tables of more deserving people, like those in Glen Tarsa for instance – ordinary men and women who worked hard to feed and clothe themselves and their children.

Anna had loved coming home to Glen Tarsa; this was where she really belonged, here were the people she had known all her life.

In the old days it might have been different, the days when she had been little more than a drudge in her own home. Now there was Nora to look after things so that Anna's life was one of comparative ease. Yet she never fully relaxed, was never completely sure of what was going on in her father's mind . . .

As it was he hated Nora 'snooping into his private affairs'. He had forbidden her to go near his bedroom and Anna still had the job of cleaning it. She had never grown used to the idea of another woman lying in the bed that she still thought of as 'Mother's'. The heavy smell of Nellie Jean, her father's woman, never failed to repulse her and she found it hard to be nice to a woman with so little regard for the feelings of others.

Lady Pandora had wanted Anna to come and live full-time at Noble House but Roderick had objected strongly to the suggestion. 'The lass must bide where she belongs,' he had stated firmly. 'You can have her with you as your companion every day but the big house isn't her home. She has enough notions of grandeur as it is and I won't have a daughter o' mine getting to feel she's above herself.'

Anna sensed that he wanted something more out of the deal, something he might never get if he allowed her out of his jurisdiction completely. He was biding his time, waiting to make his next move. Roderick had always been an opportunist and never more so since 'her ladyship' had first started to show an interest in his daughter.

Anna drew in Knight's reins, feeling the need to be still and quiet for a while. She gazed dreamily over the landscape, her eyes travelling the length of the valley and up to the hills that she loved. It was all so familiar, so dear: the river rushing along, the dark, mysterious woodlands, the

3

orderly march of the drystone dykes, the patchwork colours of the sylvan fields, the russet of the beech hedges softening the hard lines of the road that snaked its way through the glen.

In those fields she had walked with Peter, Lady Pandora's nephew; together they had wandered through the woods, talking, laughing, looking for wildflowers as they went along . . . those little flowers . . . wild and free. He had said that, his blue eyes gazing into hers as he handed her the dewy posies he had gathered.

She had pressed the tiny blooms in her 'book of memories'. Such precious memories of herself and Peter – the love, the laughter, all written down so that she could remember the sweet and lovely hours she had spent with him.

Anna's breath caught. Their time together had been so brief. She remembered the snow-filled wonder of their first Christmas together, the fun they had shared, the love they had discovered for one another. Then had come spring, a season filled with flowers and magic, one that had merged into summer when the sun had shone every day and the skylark's song had been never ending . . .

So brief – her breath caught in a sob – before that summer had ended Peter was dead, killed in a fruitless attempt to save the life of his tutor, Andrew Mallard, hung from a tree near the Rumbling Brig . . .

Anna's thoughts turned to her father and the things he had said after the bodies were discovered. He had more or less implied that he didn't give a damn about Mallard but, 'Too bad about Peter, it wasn't meant for him, I know how much he meant to you . . . ' Words that would live in her memory for all time, words that woke her from nightmares and made her feel sick in her waking hours. Over and over she asked herself what they meant and she always came to one conclusion . . .

Anna had vowed to find out the truth, somehow, sometime. Peter should never have died, he should be here with

4

her now, warm and dear in her arms, not lying cold in his grave in that lonely spot in Corran kirkyard, the moss and the ivy already creeping over his headstone. He had been sixteen, only sixteen . . .

A sob escaped Anna; it was too painful to remember. Dashing a hand over her eyes, she flicked the reins and Knight moved on.

Anna had gone to Noble House that morning with the intention of working on the portrait she was painting of Lady Pandora, but her ladyship had said she was suffering from a headache and had shooed Anna out of the house, telling her to go and enjoy herself and not to return till lunchtime.

Anna had been glad of the excuse to get away from the painting for a while. Lady Pandora was a restless sitter and Anna often wondered if she could do full justice to a beautiful woman like her employer.

But Miss Priscilla McLeod, her old teacher, had taught Anna well. Her guidance, combining with the girl's natural talent, had produced results that neither of them could have visualised three years before, when Roderick had made his daughter leave school at the age of thirteen.

Miss Priscilla had taken the girl under her bony wing. In her own home and in her own time she had set out to teach Anna all that she herself knew about art.

These visits to Knock Farm had been the start of a new life for Anna. She had grown to love the cosy, welcoming atmosphere of the old house. She loved the homely ways of Kate McLeod, Miss Priscilla's sister, and the sly good humour of Ben, their brother.

Every room in the house was filled with interest of some sort but, best of all, Anna liked the book-lined den with its wonderful, fusty smells and its sense of timeless tranquillity. In this room she spent as much time as she could, poring over the art books with their pictures of paintings by the old masters.

Over the years Miss Priscilla's matchstick body had grown more sparse; her squinting 'mightier than thou' expression had become almost permanent; her large, sensitive mouth smiled even less than before – except when it was curving with pride as she watched Anna's talents blossom.

News of Anna's artistic prowess had quickly reached the ears of those in high places. A number of the local gentry had commissioned her to paint portraits of their children.

Their attitudes towards her had been varied: some were merely curious, others were condescending, often they displayed a mixture of both feelings. They told one another that she was 'a sweet little girl, so clever with a paintbrush. Where did she pick it up, one wonders? She is, after all, just a simple country girl.'

It had been a novelty to have their children sit for her but as time wore on, the novelty wore off, but they began to take genuine notice of her and vied with one another to employ her services first.

Her landscapes were different from other artists of the day, filled as they were with gossamer light and colour that was dewy, yet throbbed with rich and vibrant tones.

Even Roderick was surprised when he saw her paintings, and being Roderick he was quick to exploit the situation. To one and all he boasted about his daughter's artistic skills, he bemoaned the sacrifices he had had to make in allowing her to pursue her ambitions, he basked in reflected glory and savoured the scent of future riches.

Declaring that it was demeaning for a young lady to take money from 'her betters' he made it his business to collect it for her, his big, meaty fist closing over the guineas with dignified reluctance, his expression one of resigned sufferance as he spoke about the expense of keeping his daughter in 'the manner she had come to expect.'

Anna's thoughts took her backwards and forwards as she rode on. Rays of spring sunshine poured over her, shining on her mane of flaxen hair, which was tied back with a blue silk ribbon. Her skin was a pale honey gold, her grey eyes were fringed with thick, dark lashes, her lips were full and wide and sensual. She was wearing a dark blue velvet riding dress, a Christmas present from Lady Pandora.

Anna loved the dress. In her days of drab frocks and clumsy boots she had yearned for the kind of finery that she wore now. At times she had to pinch herself to make sure that she wasn't dreaming, because always, at the back of her mind, there was this feeling that it was all too good to be true and that she would waken from the dream at any minute.

But not now, she told herself quickly, I want to keep all of this for as long as I can.

The bubbles of joy rising in her breast, she lifted her face to the sky.

'A soul that flies too high will miss its way to heaven.' The words of her bedroom sampler popped into her mind. When Anna had confided her fears to Lady Pandora, she had laughed at the idea. 'Pay no heed, dear child,' she had advised. 'Heaven is a very long way from earth and I would think that any soul worth its salt would have to fly high to get there.'

Anna smiled at her thoughts and she urged Knight to go faster. Her pensive mood was gone and she felt the need of company now. When Lady Pandora was with her Anna could never be sure of the pace. Sometimes they rode demurely along, at others she gave her horse full rein so that his flying hooves threw up lumps of turf as he galloped.

Occasionally, she seemed to go wild altogether and would shout and whoop with abandon as she and her horse went thundering along.

'To hell with acting ladylike!' she had once told Anna merrily. 'It is an act, you know, Anna, all that bowing and scraping to convention and all the time we're not really impressing anyone but ourselves. Ever since I was a child I've had one great ambition in life. Can you guess what it is?'

Anna had looked at Lady Pandora's sparkling face and had said, 'No, but it's sure to be something outrageous.'

'Oh, it is! I'd simply adore to throw a party for all the stuffed shirts in the place and arrive downstairs for dinner absolutely stark naked. Oh, how I'd enjoy seeing the shock on their faces, but I'd never live it down. The wives would turn their backs on me forevermore, just in case I'd arrive at their parties in nothing but my birthday suit.'

Her words rang gaily in Anna's head as Knight galloped along the bridle path beside the river. Above them, the dour crags of Stor Mhor and Ben Corsa rose up, cradling the wild and lonely Pass of the Coffin into their sullen shoulders.

For generations, the people of the glen had made the arduous journey through the narrow gap in the mountains to bury their dead in the little lochside kirkyard of Glen Gorm, on the other side. Some stalwarts even went to church in Glen Gorm, either because their families had always done so or because they liked the minister there better than the one who preached in Corran Kirk.

Anna shivered as she passed the mist-swathed corries of the Pass of the Coffin and she was glad when the sluice-gates above the river came into view.

Some of the mill workers were sitting on the banks, enjoying the spring sunshine as they ate their lunchtime pieces.

'Hello there, Anna!' called one young man. 'Would you care to come and join us?'

'Another time, Danny,' she called back. 'I have to take Knight back to his stable.'

He watched as she galloped away. 'She grows more bonny every time I see her,' he said admiringly.

'She's getting too big for her boots,' sniffed a dark-haired girl sourly. 'She's only the daughter o' The Gatehouse after all. Maybe she thinks she's a lady, just because she works at the big house.'

'Anna Ban is a lady,' Danny said with a grin, giving the

girl a playful smack on the bottom. 'You're just jealous, Katie. If it was you riding about on a horse, your head would be twice the size it is now.'

'I still don't think she's a lady,' the girl persisted.

'Don't you be too sure, my girl.' Nellie Jean Anderson stood with her arms folded, gazing at Anna's receding figure. There was an odd little smile on Nellie Jean's lips, sort of secretive and smug.

'And what do you know about Anna that the rest o' us don't?' enquired Katie with a toss of her head.

'Now, that would be telling,' Nellie Jean said softly. 'All things come to she who waits – and that's all I'm saying on the subject.'

She walked away, her steps jaunty and light, leaving Danny and Katie to look at one another and wonder what the widow woman was talking about.

Anna rode briskly into the stableyard, anxious to get Knight settled so that she could return to the house to see if her ladyship was feeling better.

'I'll see to him now, Anna.' Jim, the stableboy, emerged from the hayshed to take Knight's reins.

'No – no, Jim, it's alright.' Anna's voice was hurried and breathless. 'I just remembered, I want to see Magnus about something.'

She mounted and rode away, her mind in a whirl. Through a gap in the beech hedge that surrounded the stableyard she had just glimpsed her father and Lady Pandora, sitting together in the little summerhouse in the orchard.

They had been deep in animated conversation and – Anna couldn't be sure – they might have been holding hands, the trees had made it difficult to see properly.

It wasn't unusual for Roderick to visit The House of Noble, after all, he was under-manager of the gunpowder mill and it was natural that he and Sir Malaroy Noble should meet to discuss working arrangements.

But there was no real reason for Roderick to rendezvous with Lady Pandora . . . except . . . Beth Jordan's words, spoken a long time ago in childish conviction, came back to Anna, 'Lady Pandora has power over men, she's a temptress and a flirt. She likes to see how many she can conquer.'

Anna shook her head, angry at herself for allowing such thoughts to enter her mind.

CHAPTER 2

Meetings

Anna had reached the bridge that led down to the lower fields. Ewes with their lambs were dotted over the meadows, their shrill bleating adding to the sense of new life filling the countryside.

Magnus was sitting under the hawthorn hedge at the edge of the freshly ploughed field, drinking a can of creamy milk. Beside him was Beth Jordan, daughter of William Jordan, manager of the powdermill, hugging her knees, her freckled face sparkling as she chatted to him.

Beth was a tall, elegant girl, almost sixteen, still as beautifully and expensively dressed as in her childhood. Her shining sandy hair was swept into an elaborate, too-mature, chignon, which emphasized her high forehead and long, white neck. She had thrown off her wide-brimmed hat, and it lay carelessly on the bank beside her. She looked cool, composed, and ladylike, but her eyes were restless and critical.

'Shifty-eyed,' Janet McCrae, proprietor of the Jenny All shop, had decided long ago.

'A ferret if ever there was one,' Tell Tale Todd declared.

'You watch that wee madam,' Maggie May of the Coach House Inn told Anna. 'She's a vixen and no mistake.'

'Ay,' agreed Moira O'Brady, the postmistress, 'she'd rob her own mother o' breath and give it to the de'il to blow up a storm.'

Beth had left the village school when she was twelve and for the last three years she had been taught at home by her tutor, Miss Pym, whom she simply loathed.

11

Beth had learned all the things that a young lady of her standing ought to know, including French, music, and etiquette. 'You must have etiquette, Beth,' Mrs Victoria Jordan had insisted. 'You will get nowhere in the world without it.'

'How can Miss Prim Pym teach etiquette?' Beth had objected. 'She's got the manners of a pig and she not only sounds like a horse, she looks like one.'

'Elizabeth, that's enough!' Mrs Jordan had scolded in outrage.

Privately, however, she had allowed herself a sneaky chuckle at her daughter's description of Miss Pym, whom Victoria Jordan had never really liked because she 'talked too much,' and was 'far too self-opinionated for a person in her position.'

Sometime in the future, at her grandmother's expense, Beth was going to go to a school for young ladies in England, an event that she was not looking forward to, as, despite all her airs and graces, she was very much a country girl at heart.

She had remained Anna's friend, not the best friend of far-off schooldays when big rosy apples and whispered secrets under the shady birches were the most important things in life, but someone who was always ready to lend an ear to little confidences.

Anna was aware of Beth's shortcomings, nevertheless she couldn't give her friend up that easily. No one made her laugh like Beth did and she needed someone of her own age to talk to now and again.

Magnus's hazel eyes lit up at Anna's approach. 'Just in time to share some o' the milk Beth brought. It was the very thing I needed to buck me up.'

Anna threw him a reproachful glance. 'I've offered a thousand times to bring you something to drink at lunchtime but you always refuse.'

'Ach well,' a flush spread over his tanned skin, 'you

know how I feel about that. You've had your years o' running after people, you're – above all that now.'

He helped her to dismount and when she stood before him he said quietly, 'You suit blue, Anna, it always was your colour.'

'It's nice but it's hot,' Anna spoke a trifle awkwardly. 'I was going back to change but thought I'd stop and see you first.'

'You'll see me at teatime.'

'I know, but . . . ' she paused, remembering Roderick with Lady Pandora. Magnus's hands were still holding onto hers, the heat of them seemed to surge through her. His crumpled collar was open, perspiration glistened on his broad chest, little rivers of it had soaked the front of his shirt. He looked hot and tired and her heart twisted with love for him. 'I saw you in the field as I was coming along the bridle path. I just wanted to talk to you for a minute, that's all.'

'Magnus is taking me to the May dance in Munkirk.' Beth, annoyed at Anna's intrusion, spoke rather sharply.

'More like her taking me,' Magnus grinned. 'She's just after asking me.'

'You should be honoured,' Beth said pointedly. 'James Heatherington asked if he could partner me but I wanted you, Magnus, you know I wanted you.' She stood up and moved closer to him, all the while appraising the startling beauty of Anna in her blue velvet riding frock. But she said nothing, instead she raised one white hand to her hair to pat the smooth coils in an affected gesture.

'Your hair's lovely, Beth,' Anna said warmly. 'I wish mine would stay up but it's too fine. Are you putting it up for the dance?'

'Of course!' Beth's sandy brows shot up. 'I'd never wear it down at a dance, it would be much too unsophisticated. What about you, are you going? If so, is William Walters taking you? I know for a fact he's mad on you.'

Anna giggled. 'William Walters? Why so prim all of a

sudden? You used to call him Snotty Watty and sometimes Snotters if you were in a really bad mood.'

Beth looked haughtily down her nose. 'Really, Anna, you can be very vulgar at times. I never called him Snotters . . . ' Her eyes sparkled, she grabbed Anna's arm. ' . . . Not for at least three years . . . And here you are bringing it all back, making me wish we never had to grow up.'

They both erupted into peals of laughter and Magnus smiled because they were a picture with the sun glinting in their hair and their faces aglow with mirth.

'Oh, Anna, you always did make me laugh,' Beth's voice was wistful for a moment. 'Our best-friend days were the finest in the world. I just know I'll never be that happy again. You said things that were funny and I tried to be as rude as possible. And now . . . ' She spread her fingers and examined her manicured nails. 'We both have to try and be mannerly and pretend to be ladylike all the time.'

'I'm not going to pretend,' Anna said with a frown. 'If I feel like speaking my mind, I'll do it – and to hell with what people think! Lady Pandora doesn't put on airs for anyone but that doesn't stop her being a lady.'

Beth's eyes glittered. 'Yes, but she really is a lady, isn't she? Gentry like her can behave how they will and it's alright, because they have a good pedigree. It's in the line – the breeding I mean. Other people – more ordinary people – have to work at it; they can't afford to get too complacent. One slip and it shows, simply because they haven't got the inbred poise to make it work properly.'

Magnus let out a shout of laughter. 'Hey, you two! This conversation's getting too serious for me to follow. In my opinion you're both still little girls who need an occasional spanking to keep you in hand!'

Beth pouted. 'I've never been spanked. Father has never laid a finger on me!'

'More's the pity.' Magnus looked her straight in the eye as he spoke. 'A bit o' discipline wouldn't have done you any harm, Beth, you're spoiled and you know it.'

Beth gazed at his tall, strong figure and there was a strange light in her eyes. She had always admired him and lately the feeling had grown into something stronger. The fact that he was only a farm labourer galled her but that didn't stop her from flirting with him.

Her mother wanted a good marriage for her and had been delighted when Lucas Noble, Lady Pandora's nephew, had shown an interest in her.

But Lucas was in England much of the time, at a military academy for young gentlemen, and knowing how easily her daughter was bored, and as an insurance for the future, Mrs Jordan invited 'suitable young men' to the house with the idea of keeping Beth amused.

Beth, however, was anything but amused at this arrangement. The young men in question were, according to Beth 'Too dreadful for words.' They either suffered from halitosis or dandruff or both. Some were awkward, others too self-assured. They neither looked right nor behaved properly and their conversation was usually limited to the subject of themselves.

As if reading Beth's mind, a thought struck Anna, 'Isn't Lucas coming home sometime in early May? And if so, won't he want to take you to the dance?'

Beth examined her nails once more and with an air of studied indifference she said airily, 'Oh, Lucas would never go to a village hop, besides he won't be home in time for the dance since he's spending a few days with friends in Surrey first.'

She omitted to say that she and Lucas had argued the last time he'd been home and had made no plans for the future. This had worried Beth a good deal. She wanted Lucas Noble and she wanted him badly. Her future would indeed be rosy if she could net such a desirable catch. Next time she saw him she had every intention of being very sweet and submissive to him.

Meantime, Magnus would help to fill the gap nicely. If Lucas got to hear about it she would wriggle out of it

15

somehow, she had always been good at that. Though Lucas was just as manipulative as she was, she had her ways of winning him round. She had learned early on that men, no matter what their station in life, were all the same where women were concerned – like little dogs sniffing out the juiciest bone . . .

Beth smiled to herself and, linking her arm through Magnus's, she gazed up at him. 'Sit with me awhile. In half an hour I must go home for a horrid piano lesson, so I'm relying on you to cheer me up.' She threw herself down on the bank once more, there to arrange herself decoratively on the daisy-strewn grass.

Magnus didn't rush to join her. Instead he took Anna's hand as she began to move away. A look passed between them; the moments seemed to stand still, laden with intimacy. Emotions that were sweet and warm and tender flowed between them, and neither of them wanted to break the spell.

'Magnus!' Beth's voice came petulantly, 'I'm waiting! Why are you looking at Anna like that? She's only your sister.'

The spell was broken. Magnus helped Anna mount and watched as she rode swiftly away.

'Come on, Magnus,' Beth demanded imperiously, 'I'm waiting.'

Magnus rounded on her. 'Well, you can just wait . . . ' he began angrily, only to soften at the sight of her sitting there watching him from under her lashes, a smile playing provocatively round the corners of her mouth.

She was a little madam was Beth, believing that every-one should come running to her at the snap of a finger. But there was something alluring about her, he had to admit that, something altogether tempting, and dangerous.

A girl like Beth was capable of anything if it meant getting her own way. Magnus knew that she was just using him while she needed him. She had bigger game to hunt. She had set her sights high: Lucas Noble was in her

16

firing range, but only just. Lucas was no fool, he wouldn't allow himself to be captured easily. Beth would have to employ all her skills as a huntress before she could bag that one . . .

Magnus went to sit by Beth, his smile giving no indication of the thoughts passing through his mind.

Anna induced Knight to a swift gallop. Her serene mood of the morning was gone, replaced by one so strange she couldn't understand it herself.

Seeing her father with Lady Pandora had upset her but that had nothing to do with this other thing, this forbidden emotion that gnawed at the very marrow of her being. She felt restless and uneasy. That look in Magnus's eyes when he had taken her hand in his, an intense look, filled with yearning, compelling her to be still and quiet, instilling in her a terrible longing for something that could never be . . . a feeling of wanting that was like a physical ache deep in her belly . . .

'Oh, God no!' The murmured protest seemed to fill her head. Knight cantered on, and in her turmoil she cared not where he was taking her, till his hooves slipped on wet grass. In fright he reared up, tossing her off his back. Down she slithered, into a deep and soggy ditch, the icy water seeping through her clothes and bringing her back to earth with a vengeance.

Knight kicked up his heels and rolled his eyes at her before ambling away to browse in a succulent patch of new grass, his reins trailing at his sides.

'Bugger it!' Anna struggled in the mud. 'Hell and Damn!' she cursed as she tried to sit up.

A shadow fell over her, she glanced up, and there looming above her was Sir Malaroy, sitting astride a sorrel-and-white roan gelding, an expression of amusement on his aristocratic face.

'Tut-tut,' he admonished dryly, 'such strong language from so sweet a mouth.'

17

Anna's face grew hot. She wasn't well acquainted with Sir Malaroy. He was a man who kept himself to himself and his path seldom crossed hers on her visits to Noble House.

Sometimes she had the feeling that he deliberately avoided her for he was always quick to take himself off whenever she appeared. But he had always been a reserved and private sort of man, seeking only the company of tried and trusted friends, so it perhaps wasn't so unusual that he didn't want to know a strange young girl who only came to his house to keep his wife amused.

So Anna tried not to allow herself to feel that he didn't like her very much.

She sat there in the ditch, extremely conscious of her dirty clothes. 'Please excuse me, Sir Malaroy.' She tried to choke down a bubble of mirth that arose suddenly in her throat. 'I thought I was alone, I didn't hear you coming or I would have held my tongue. But . . . ' she looked up at him, ' . . . you might have done the same in like circumstances.'

Sir Malaroy stared at her as if she was a ghost, dark and bitter thoughts pounding in his head. When he had set off on his horse to try to ride away some of his anger, he certainly hadn't expected to come across Anna McIntyre floundering in a ditch at his feet.

Anna of the fair and lovely face, who had haunted him and his house for the past year. His wife so adored her, there were times when Sir Malaroy couldn't stop the feelings of disquiet that crept over him. All because Pandora had been denied a child of her own; the child that he could never give her, because he was incapable of fathering children.

She had tried to gain happiness by filling her life with other children: her nephews Peter and Lucas, new protégés Ralph and Robert . . . and Anna, who seemed to fulfil her as none of the boys could.

He had been away for a month in England on business and had only returned last night. He didn't want to be reminded of Anna just yet.

Pandy had welcomed him home eagerly and they had wined and dined by candlelight, saying all they had to say with their eyes and their hands.

Later, in the bedroom, she had been seductive, passionate, and tender. The night had been perfect with their love for one another. He hadn't wanted it to end but morning had come, bringing with it Roderick McIntyre.

He had seen them together just a short while ago, Pandora and McIntyre, sitting close together in the summerhouse, deep in conversation – and – Sir Malaroy couldn't be sure – but it really had seemed to him that they had been holding hands.

Blind rage had possessed him, doubt and fear had choked him, surely – surely she couldn't see anything attractive in a boor like Roderick McIntyre! Men had always been in her life, young men who fell for her charms and hung about her like faithful puppies, but a game was all it was to Pandora . . . even with Andrew Mallard, the boys' tutor . . .

Now it seemed Roderick was filling the gap left by Mallard. A scoundrel like that! A being whose treachery and greed had brought misery to so many over the years . . . Sir Malaroy's mouth twisted . . . a lecher like that was never satisfied, he wanted it all, money, power, women . . .

Anna was watching him, her expression quizzical. It was then he noticed that her eyes were the colour of summer clouds, purple-grey, fringed by lashes that were incredibly thick and dark. A streak of dirt lay across the smooth bloom of her cheeks, her flaxen hair was blowing in the breeze. He held his breath. She wasn't so much beautiful as dazzling, no wonder Pandora was fascinated by her, he could hardly take his eyes off her.

Sir Malaroy dismounted from his horse and reached out to help Anna to her feet.

'I'm sorry about this, Sir Malaroy,' she apologised, 'I don't usually fall into ditches. It was just – well to tell the truth I was bewildered about something and didn't look where I was going. I'll have to learn to be my age.'

19

'You aren't much more than a child, surely,' he said dryly. 'Don't grow up before you have to.'

'I am grown up, Sir Malaroy, I was sixteen on my birthday last Hallowe'en.'

'I see, a little witch, with hair like sunshine and skin like roses, a witch of the day and not of the night.'

His words had awakened unpleasant childhood memories in Anna. As clearly as if it was yesterday she could remember her father taunting her, telling her she would one day become a witch, because her birthday fell on Hallowe'en.

Sir Malaroy smiled wryly at the expression on her face and, lifting her hand to his lips, he kissed it. 'Witch or no, you've helped me take my mind off myself. Will you ride back to the house with me, Anna? Even if only to tidy yourself. You can't face the world looking like a little gypsy.'

A surge of wonder rose in Anna's breast. For a few moments she forgot that she was just plain Anna McIntyre of The Gatehouse, so charmingly attentive was Sir Malaroy towards her.

'Come on,' he threw over his shoulder, 'I'll show you how not to fall off your horse! Race you to the stables – and this time don't forget to look where you're going!'

CHAPTER 3

Ralph and Robert

On arrival at the stableyard, Sir Malaroy's horse frisked and reared up, his foot caught in the stirrup and down he slithered in an undignified heap, head first, legs and feet in the air.

Anna stared at him half lying on the cobbles, unharmed but furious at himself. Her hand flew to her mouth. 'Sir Malaroy!' she cried breathlessly before erupting into peals of helpless laughter.

'Anna!' he protested stiffly. 'This isn't funny. Come over here at once and help me down properly.'

'I'm sorry,' she gasped. 'It's just – I've never been shown how not to fall off a horse like that before.'

She went into fresh gales of mirth while he glared at her and yelled at her to grab the horse before it 'dragged him to his death.'

Jim came running to see what all the noise was about and fast on his heels came Lady Pandora from the orchard. Her protégés, Ralph and Robert, together with their tutor, a studious-looking young man who went by the name of Michael Dick, appeared round the corner of the building and soon quite a crowd was gathered about the unfortunate Sir Malaroy.

'Oh dear, I hope you aren't hurt, your lordship,' Michael Dick muttered deferentially, taking off his glasses to rub them nervously on his sleeve, before popping them back onto his nose in a jerky, hurried fashion.

'My pride, man, only my pride,' growled Sir Malaroy as

21

everyone rushed to help him disengage his foot from the stirrup, no easy matter with them all getting in each other's way: the boys giggling, Lady Pandora purring soothingly in her husband's ear, Anna trying to stifle her laughter, Jim blowing down the horse's nose as he held its head, Michael Dick taking it all very seriously as he tried to organise the proceedings in his ineffectual manner.

Sir Malaroy himself, seeing the funny side of his predicament, began to laugh also, which didn't help matters but at last he was free to flex his limbs and give himself a thorough dusting down. The incident had lightened his heart. He seemed to have forgotten all about his earlier grievances. Lady Pandora was fussing over him, making him feel that he was the most important person in the world.

Anna began to make her way down the track from the stables. The portrait could wait. Lady Pandora was in a restless mood, Anna had seen it in her eyes – an almost feverish excitement brought on by – what? Certainly not the light-hearted incident with Sir Malaroy . . .

Anna remembered her father and Lady Pandora in the summerhouse. She took a deep breath and tried not to let her thoughts go further . . .

'Anna – will you be back tomorrow?'

A hand touched her arm and she spun round to see Robert Shamus O'Connor, a distant relative of Lady Pandora's whom she had rescued from an Irish orphanage. Robert was a tall, lanky boy of fifteen with curly, red-gold hair and eyes that were strikingly blue and oddly hypnotic in his smiling, open face. He was brimful of mischief and cheek but for all that, his natural charm and enthusiasm made it easy for people to like him.

Michael Dick was the exception. He did not find it easy dealing with 'the likes of Robert O'Connor', and always gave the impression that he only did so under sufferance and with the clear implication that his post at Noble House was only a temporary one.

'Of course I'll be back tomorrow, Robert,' Anna told him in bemusement. 'What makes you think I won't be?'

'I dunno, just something I feel – here . . . ' He placed his hand on his heart. 'And here . . . ' His other hand went to his head. 'It's the magic in me, Anna, I feel things that other folks don't.'

She smiled. 'Oh, ay, I know all about you, Robert, and the things you feel.'

'No you don't, not everything – not this.' Swiftly, he bent and kissed her, full and fair on the lips, his own mouth opening to enclose hers in a manner that was experienced for a seemingly innocent boy.

'It's alright,' he said before she could speak, a wide grin spreading over his face. 'I knew you'd enjoy it. Don't worry, I had plenty o' practice back home in Ireland. Used to hop out the window to a dance or two and there were always girls queuing up to visit me.'

Anna felt no anger towards him. Robert was always doing things that would have been outrageous in anybody else. His frank and friendly personality allowed him more freedom than most and it was difficult to take offence at his delight in life.

So different from Ralph Van Hueson, a much-removed cousin of Pandora's, who was a mixture of Welsh, Scottish, and Dutch blood through the twists and turns of ancestral marriages.

'Where do you dig them up, Pandy?' Sir Malaroy had wondered when she had proposed bringing the boys to live at Noble House.

'Oh, from all the airts,' she had replied airily. 'So far it's all been boys, but there will be girls too, all of them deserving a chance to prove themselves.'

Ralph was fourteen, as dark in colouring as in his nature: shy, sensitive and brooding, possessed of a temper that could simmer for days before it finally erupted, unlike Robert who might flare up like a torch half a dozen times in a day and just as quickly cool down.

Both boys had very different opinions on topical matters and occasionally came to blows during an argument, but normally they tolerated one another fairly well and were mutual in their dislike of 'Dicky Bird' as they called their tutor. This was mainly because, although they had known him only a few months, they had worshipped the athletic and unconventional Andrew Mallard, whom they had lovingly called 'Quack Quack', and would have resented anybody who took his place. That the 'anybody' should be Michael Dick, a 'Mr Nobody' in their view, was even more unfortunate for the gentleman in question, since he was averse to most sporting activities and complained of hay fever if he so much as put his nose outside the door.

Ralph, however, managed to disguise successfully his feelings for his tutor and was therefore that gentleman's favourite pupil, both for his attentive demeanour and his ability to absorb easily academic teaching.

Robert, on the other hand, seemed incapable of taking in anything, 'Save what he learns through the seat of his pants', to quote Molly the cook, who loved the boy and lavished food and lots of mothering on him whenever he visited her kitchens. Despite her flippant words Molly knew that Robert's learning came from his five senses and, 'Maybe a sixth wi' all that Irish in him,' she would say cryptically to her cronies. 'The lad can talk for hours about everything under the sun. He knows things that other lads o' his age don't and I love him like a son for all the pleasure he gives me wi' his blarney and his cheek.'

Ralph had followed Robert but stood some way off, taking in everything in his silent, watchful way.

'C'mon, Ralphie, come and say hallo to Anna!' Robert cried exuberantly.

But Ralph shook his head. 'It's alright, I'm going back anyway. Dicky Bird will wonder where we've got to. You'd better come along, too.'

'Suit yourself.' Robert wasn't really listening, so caught up was he in the sights and sounds of the countryside. Suddenly he leapt up in the air to catch expertly a butterfly that had come flitting along.

'Look, Anna.' Putting his curly red head next to her fair one he opened his cupped hand slightly to allow her to peep at his catch. 'It's beautiful, isn't it? The nicest flutterby you ever saw, all new and proud of itself.'

'Flutterby,' Anna repeated as she, too, stared fascinated at the delicate creature caught in the folds of his hand, 'That's a wonderful name for it . . . ' Whirling round she did a little dance and began to sing. 'Butterfly, flutterby, play with me, out in the sunshine for all to see, wings of bright colours flip-flapping along, flutterby, butterfly, let's all sing this song.'

A delighted Robert took up the ditty and holding out his free hand to her he whirled her round and waltzed her about till they were both giddy and out of breath.

'Are you watching, Anna?' he cried. Lifting up his hand he opened it and the butterfly went fluttering away to join another of its kind amongst the wildflowers in the verge.

'You're like a butterfly, Anna,' Robert told her, 'all fair and gossamer looking.'

'Thanks, Robert, you're a flatterer.'

'No, I just say what I think, no ulterior motive. I said you were like a butterfly because that's how I see you now. Tomorrow you might look like a dragonfly or sound like a frog with a sore throat – if you get my meaning.'

She giggled and took his hand. 'I get it, Robert. Now, I must go, I'll see you tomorrow.'

'Ay, tomorrow, Anna, take care,' he called as she went off down the track.

As soon as she was out of sight Robert ran to where Ralph was waiting and immediately rounded on him. 'What's wrong with you?' he demanded fiercely. 'Why couldn't you come over to say hallo to Anna? Are you afraid o' her or something? Every time you see her you look as if you're shitting a brick!'

Ralph's dark eyes flashed in annoyance. 'Of course I'm not afraid! Why should I be? I just don't know what to say to her, that's all.'

'Is it? You never used to be like that. When Peter was here, you used to talk to her whenever you got the chance. She's easy enough to get on with, I never have any bother.'

He scrutinised the other boy more closely. There was a haunted look about Ralph these days – but no – it went further back than that! To the time of the deaths of Andrew Mallard and Peter Noble. Ralph had taken that dreadful affair very badly. He had liked Peter and had hero-worshipped Andrew Mallard. Since then, his nights had been torn apart by bad dreams which had become worse as the days and weeks passed.

In desperation Lady Pandora had put the two boys into the same room, hoping that Robert's cheerful presence would help to alleviate matters. For a time, it had worked. Ralph had calmed down, his nights had been more restful. Robert had then broached the subject of returning to his own room because he claimed that Ralph snored and talked in his sleep and Ralph had agreed to this readily enough.

But the dreams had come back again, worse than before, and Robert had good-naturedly moved all his stuff back into Ralph's room, 'Even though,' he had said with exaggerated resignation, 'I myself will get no sleep at all with all the moaning and groaning and the dreadful snorting that's worse than all of O'Flaherty's pigs put together.'

Despite his teasing, he felt sorry for Ralph. The only things that disturbed Robert's sleep were physical and were perfectly normal in a healthy, fifteen-year-old boy: sometimes he was awakened by an empty stomach or a full bladder, at others by the sexual desires of his maturing body. Otherwise, he was at peace with the world and enjoyed himself as only a boy of his eager spirit could.

Throwing his arm round Ralph's shoulder he spoke to him soothingly as they walked along. 'Can't you tell me what ails you, Ralphie me lad? I know you miss Quack Quack, I miss him too. It was a terrible thing that happened to him and Peter. I myself was in the doldrums for days afterwards. I couldn't take in the fact that they were both dead and I was all for hiding myself away to have a bit of a think about everything. So I did just that and got myself nowhere at all. My head was going round in circles. I would look at Anna and see the sadness in her face; I would watch Lucas and wonder what was going on behind that mask he wears to hide his thoughts.

'Aunt Dora was the very opposite, she was all for weeping and wailing and wringing her hands but in the end it all came to the same thing. Grief is grief, whichever way you look at it, and I was doing no good at all mooning around with my thoughts. So after a while I told myself "Robert, me lad, this is no use, no use at all, life goes on and you'll wear yourself into a shadow if you don't watch out." And that was that. I gave myself a bit o' a shake up and went to the kitchen to see Molly who gave me a whole apple pie to myself, so worried was she by the state of my health and how thin I'd become.'

By the end of this discourse Ralph simply couldn't keep a straight face. Throwing back his head he gave a shout of laughter and said resignedly, 'Don't you ever stop talking? Where do you get it all from, Robert O'Connor?'

Robert's grin was disarming. 'Sure from the wee folk themselves. I always passed the time o' day with them back home in Wicklow. I used to wonder, mind you, why they sometimes fell asleep when I was yarning with them but there, it goes to show, even the fairy folk have their limits and need their sleep like the rest of us.'

He became serious, no easy thing for him to do with the sap rising within him in keeping with the spring day, but not for long. So ebullient did he feel he simply couldn't

27

resist taking a leap across the ditch to grab at a branch of hazel catkin.

'For Aunt Dora,' he declared, waving aloft his trophy, 'she loves putting things in vases. Now then, Ralphie, don't think you're getting away with it. You've got something on your mind, something pretty big. It's been there since Quack Quack died and it isn't going away, in fact I'm thinking it's getting worse as time goes on. Last night you near frightened the shit out o' me with your ravings. You were scared of something, really scared and kept saying "No, no, no, don't do it, please don't do it." On and on you went and I got so scared myself I felt the hairs rising at the back o' my very own neck.'

'It's nothing,' Ralph said brusquely. 'Leave me alone! Just leave me alone! You're like an old woman the way you go on. Dicky Bird's got nothing on you! Go and talk to the fairies! That's if they can stay awake long enough to listen to your rubbish!'

Shaking off Robert's hand he began to run but Robert's long legs soon covered the distance. 'Take that back! Or – or I'll make you choke on it!'

'Try it! Just try it!' taunted Ralph.

Robert's temper flared, his ready fist shot out. Both boys were rolling in the dust when Michael Dick came striding along to see what was keeping them.

'Boys!' he cried grimly. 'That's enough! Quite enough for one day! Robert, no doubt you started it. Get along up to the house and wash yourself at once. You too, Ralph. And don't let her ladyship or his lordship see you in such a disgraceful state. I've never had to deal with the likes of this in all my days of teaching. Thank goodness I won't have to put up with it for very long! His lordship wouldn't be pleased if he knew how much all this upsets me, not pleased at all!'

Michael Dick had a habit of repeating himself when he spoke, he also seldom referred to his employers as anything else but 'her ladyship' and 'his lordship'. Whenever he was

28

upset he rarely failed to remove his specs and wipe them on his sleeve. Today was no exception, off came the glasses, jerkily and speedily they received a polish on his sleeve in order to remove the steam from the lens.

The tutor's fussy manner and mode of speech were manna to his pupils. Sheepishly they regarded one another. 'You first, my Lordship,' murmured Robert with a straight face.

'No, I insist that you go first – your Grace,' Ralph whispered. 'Age before beauty and all that.'

Choking with laughter they went hastily on their way, taking a short cut through the orchard to get to the house, Michael Dick trailing along in their wake, muttering under his breath.

Anna felt uplifted by her little encounter with Robert and her steps were light as she walked through the Clachan of Corran. The children were coming out of school, tongues wagging busily now that they were out of Miss Priscilla's rule.

Anna never passed the little school without thinking of her own schooldays spent there. At the time she had thought they were the happiest in her life, and that leaving school would be the end of the world, but that had been before Miss Priscilla had taken her under her wing; before those brief but magical months of love she had shared with Peter.

Everything had changed in just a few short years and sometimes she thought how wonderful it would be to go back in time to those days of simple joys and innocent pastimes.

Several of the children called out greetings to her as she approached and one or two tagged along with her, their bare feet padding on the stony road.

Anna loved talking to them and enjoyed doing pencil sketches of them as they played, preferring their natural-ness to the arranged poses of the children of the gentry in their too-clean clothes.

Daft Donal was coming along, his unruly hair ruffling in the wind. Although he was twenty-four, not a single whisker sprouted on a face that was (according to the villagers) 'as smooth as a baby's bum'; he was like an eternal child, bemused and baffled by the things that went on around him.

Because he had no parents the villagers tried to help him in every way they could: Maggie May regularly plied him with food; old Grace made it her business to make him soak in her big wooden washtub once every month. She also mended his clothes, darned his socks and knitted him woollen scarves and gloves to keep him warm during his wanderings.

It was easy to do these things for Donal because he was as amiable as a trusting puppy. The other two McDonalds were altogether different. Davie, the eldest brother, was dour and ungrateful and spurned all offers of help, while their sister Sally's unmanageable bouts of wild behaviour made all attempts to keep her clean an utter impossibility.

The Reverend Alastair Simpson, vicar of the parish, was concerned about both Sally and Donal's welfare and had tried to reason with Davie, but had only ever met with black surly looks and an aggrieved air of silence.

Donal's odd little habits had multiplied over the years making him a target for much teasing from the village youngsters. But his infectious good nature also ensured his popularity with them so that they allowed him to share in their games.

'Twelve o'clock! Time to stop!' At the sight of the children his high voice soared forth while he waved his watch back and forth like a pendulum. Stopping dead in his tracks he cocked his hand to his ear with an exaggerated show of concentration, as if expecting a reply to come echoing down from the hills.

'Come on, daftie!' yelled the boys in delight. 'Let's hear your silly old watch then!'

Donal hastened to oblige and solemnly held the watch

30

to the ears of the giggling throng. It was a useless timepiece however, Davie having crushed it under his heel years ago. Just the same, Donal cherished it and lived in the hope that it would start ticking again, even though telling the time was an instinct with him now.

'I'll let you hear my da's watch,' offered one wily youngster, who saw an easy means in Donal, of help with the afternoon chores. 'Just you come home with me and Ma will give you a bowl of soup. Would you like that?'

'Ay, I'd like that fine, Donal hungry.'

He went off, clutching the boy's hand trustingly and Laura McCrae said to Anna, 'What makes people go daft like Donal?'

'I suppose he was born like that, Laura, and he seems happy enough in his own wee world.'

'I know, but it's still a shame. Donal's nice, not like Sally or Davie. Mam says they've got the devil in them. I think Donal should have been made normal, he's too nice to be a daftie.' Laura was silent for a time then she said slowly, 'Your mother wasn't born daft, was she? Mam says she was a kind, good lady before she went into the loony bin. It isn't fair, I'd hate it if my mother went off her head because people would laugh and say nasty things.'

They had reached the door of The Gatehouse. Anna looked down at Laura's small, anxious face. 'Only unkind people would laugh, Laura, and only because they don't understand and are afraid.'

Laura nodded, reluctantly disengaging her hand. 'I've to help Mam in the shop. She's always busy with the mill folk at dinnertime and now that Nora does for your father I have to do her share as well.' She gave a mischievous smile. 'At least when you're daft you don't have to work or go to school. No wonder Donal's so happy.'

Anna smiled too, but in her heart she wondered if she would ever be allowed to forget that her mother had 'gone away to the madhouse' all these long years ago. Anna had been only six years old at the time, yet still she remembered

31

the warmth of those arms that had once enclosed her with protective love.

Why couldn't people just remember the 'good kind woman' instead of harping on about the dreadful mental illness that had taken her out of Anna's life so completely?

A woman labelled forevermore as a 'daftie' when all the time Anna believed that she couldn't be mad and that one day she would come back to the children she had loved and who had never forgotten her.

CHAPTER 4

Confrontations

The minute Anna stepped over the threshold she sensed the blackness of her father's mood. He was sitting alone by the hearth in the kitchen, moodily smoking his pipe, deep in a gloomy reverie.

His mood had enveloped him since his meeting that morning with Lady Pandora in the summerhouse.

It had been desperation that had made him seek her out in such a blatant fashion, that and a dark desire to show her that he meant business, no matter how much it inconvenienced and embarrassed her.

To hell with her feelings! It was his own he was concerned with. He had been patient with her for long enough. She had manipulated him as if he was an idiotic puppet, pulling him this way and that according to her whims.

How he had suffered it for so long he didn't know. The years of waiting! Hoping! Making do with Nellie Jean when all the time he wanted Pandora. She had become an obsession with him, and when Sir Malaroy had gone off on his business trip to England it had seemed to Roderick a perfect opportunity to carry out some of his little plans.

It was a dangerous game, flirting with the wife of his employer. Sir Malaroy was a placid man but his patience had already been stretched to the limits and there was no telling how much he could take before he finally snapped. So, Roderick had been careful about Pandora, too careful perhaps. It was high time she began to sweat a bit, she had had her own way for too long.

33

During the weeks of her husband's absence, when Roderick's hopes and desires for her were at their highest, she had filled The House of Noble with guests, people who rode and hunted and talked too loudly, and so effectively had she infiltrated every corner of the house, there were no chances for the kind of intimacies Roderick had dreamed of sharing with Pandora.

'The pretence is finished with, my lady,' he had brusquely told her that morning. 'I want to know what happened to all the bonny promises you made me these past years. You said things! Hinted at what you would give me in return for the companionship o' my daughter.'

She had raised her brows at him and the expression in her eyes had been both amused and quizzical. 'Promises? My dear Roderick, I have no recollection of anything of that nature. It is true I wanted Anna as my companion. The moment I saw the child I longed to have her near me so that I could nurture the sensitivities I knew were in her. I wanted to give her affection and caring, all the things I could feel were lacking in her life.'

'Ah, yes, all very flowery and dramatic, but what about my needs? You flaunt yourself before men, Pandora, and God knows how many poor bastards have lain awake at night dreaming, about you. But here is one for whom the dreaming is over; the time has come for action. You made it plain that certain conditions would be fulfilled in return for Anna and I won't be fobbed off any longer.'

'Conditions! Really, Roderick, you have more imagination than I credited you with! As far as I'm concerned, you wanted only one thing in return for Anna, as you put it. Money, Roderick! Always with you it's money. I remember you saying that Anna was worth her weight in gold. To me she is worth more than anything that money can buy, to you she is just a commodity to be bargained over. You have profited handsomely from the child, as well you know.'

'I should think so too,' he had growled. 'I sacrificed a

34

lot for the little madam and it's high time I got something for all the years o' hardship.'

'Hardship indeed! Life was never hard for you, Roderick. You'll never be deprived of your little comforts, you'll always manage to feather your nest, somehow, anyhow.'

At that point Roderick had begun to sweat. 'Be careful, my lady. Just because you are who you are doesn't give you the right to demean an honest working man like myself.'

Lady Pandora had laughed at that. 'Really, and I always got the impression that you considered yourself a step above such a description. But we're getting away from the point here. We were talking about your favourite subject. Money! And how much of it you can get from me. Don't forget, as well as Anna's salary, I also pay you to let her come here, with more than enough left over to allow Nora McCrae to keep house for you.

'I'm a wealthy woman, Roderick, but no amount of riches can buy the sort of things that really matter. It can't buy me the right to have children, but in Anna I have found fulfilment. She has compensated me beyond measure and is like a daughter to me. I have come to regard her as such. It grieves me that my hold on her is through such a fickle thing as money, but if that's the only way I can have her, then so be it.'

She had looked at him then with pleading eyes. 'Please, never take Anna away from me, it would break both our hearts. And don't ever tell her that her very own father only allowed her her freedom because he was paid to do so. Knowledge of that sort would crush the spirit of any child.'

At that Roderick's face had grown red with chagrin. 'How dare you speak like that to me, woman! If I have taken your money it's only to keep my girl clothed and shod! Anna always had a lot o' fancy notions and your interference in her life has only served to feed her vanity. You have stuffed her head with pretty ideas about herself and led her to believe that it's alright for her to waste her

35

time in useless pursuits like horse riding and painting – the sort o' things that satisfy the whims o' the idle rich.'

Lady Pandora's face went white at his words. 'I will ignore that last remark as one of little worth but I will not sit here and listen to you sneering at Anna's talents, when it's a well-known fact that you profit very nicely from them. As for keeping her clothed and shod – it is I who have provided her with the only decent clothes she has! Oh yes! You make quite a fuss over your dealings with old Grace for Anna's dresses but I am not entirely isolated from the community, sir! I know full well that it is Mrs McCrae who supplies you in all faith with her good, thick, cheap material!'

Roderick had risen then, standing up to tower above her, his thick legs straddled, his fists clenching at his sides. 'I need take no more o' this talk from you, my good lady! I've been very patient with you. I've sacrificed my girl to you, a girl who is more than needed in her own home – wi' her own kind! Anna doesn't belong in your world and I will see to it that she never does. Good day to you – your ladyship!'

'Roderick.' She had said his name softly but with just the right note of authority to arrest his departure. 'You are in a good position as under-manager of the mill – but you are not indispensable.'

His eyes glittered coldly. 'So, you have a mind to try a wee bit o' blackmail on me, eh, my dear? I wonder what Sir Malaroy would think o' that. As a matter o' fact . . . ' He came back to loom above her once more. 'I dare you to try and persuade your husband to get rid o' me. It would be very interesting to see the results. He already suspects that there's something going on between us and would just see your girlish tales as a manoeuvre to try and rid yourself o' me because the going's become too hot.'

Lady Pandora's shoulders drooped suddenly in a defeated fashion. 'Don't take Anna away from me, Roderick. Tell me what you want from me. Money? Is that it? More money?'

'Not money – not for now anyway.'

'Then what – what must I give you?'

Dropping down beside her, his eyes raked her face. 'You – give me you! Give me what I've dreamed of for four long years!'

She shrank away from him in horror. 'No, not that! I can't! I couldn't do that to my dearest Malaroy.'

'Malaroy!' He spat out the name disdainfully. 'Don't tell me you've started to consider the poor bugger's feelings now! Do you think he's forgotten how you carried on with Mallard? Not to mention giving the eye to every hot little runt who passes your way. They fall at your feet, Pandora, they see the invitation in those bonny eyes o' yours, the lure o' your lips, the promise o' paradise in the way you parade yourself in front o' the poor sods. You dazzle them with your light and if the notion takes you, you might take one o' them to your bed because it amuses you to see their reaction to such a breathtaking favour . . . '

'No! Stop it! I've never . . . '

'Never what? Lain with a boy lover? Come now, you sweet innocent, I have it on good authority that you like them young – hot! Take it from me, my lady, experience is what counts – and maturity.'

So saying he took her icy hands in his sweating palms, excitement surging through him. 'Pandora, I can show you how to really love, to make it last all night long – once – twice – thrice . . . ' Licking his lips he pressed himself against her till his coarse-featured face was barely an inch from hers.

She could see the hairs in his nostrils, could smell the sickly, heavy odour of his perspiring body. He was fast losing his control and was roughly guiding her hand to the taut pillar between his legs.

'Now,' he grunted hoarsely. 'I can't wait any longer! I'll bolt the door and put cushions on the floor. No one will see us, have no fear o' that. And I promise, you'll want more o' the same when I'm finished wi' you. Christ, woman! Can't you see I'm crazy about you! Touch me, play wi' me . . . '

His buttons popped as he exposed himself and then his hand was on her thigh, he was pulling at her dress, roughly kneading her flesh.

Jamming her fist into her mouth to stop herself from screaming she panted, 'Get out of here, you filthy devil! I won't liken you to an animal for they behave within the laws of decency. You – you are nothing more than a lecherous madman!'

Roderick stumbled to his feet, frustrated and enraged. 'And you, madam, are no better than a high-class whore – and an unpaid one at that! Even the back-street sluts are worth a few coppers for a quick peep and a poke! Unlike you, they know what their fannies are for and make use o' them accordingly!'

Grabbing his hat and his cane from the bench he snarled, 'Good day to you – *Lady* Pandora! You won't see Anna in your house again for I cannot spare her to you longer!'

She hadn't cried or pleaded or done any of the things that he had hoped she would at the last moment. Instead, she got very regally to her feet, her whole bearing one of dignity. Looking him straight in the eye she said evenly, 'You are a man of little worth, Mr McIntyre, a charlatan and a boor. Please take yourself from my sight at once. I'm sure you must have duties to attend. The company doesn't pay you good wages for doing nothing. Get about your business and stand aside to let me past.'

As he sat by the fire, furiously puffing at his pipe, the memory of that parting shot lay in his mind like a lump of lead. When the door opened to admit Anna, he turned his head very slowly to glare at her with hatred. Here was the cause of all the trouble! Right from the beginning it had been Anna, a thorn in his side, a disturbing influence on all whose paths she crossed.

She stood there in the kitchen, a flaxen-haired nymph, a creature at one with the earth and the sun and who embraced life with a passion that was almost tangible.

She was a blythe spirit, one who belonged to a world of light and air – but she didn't belong here, in the home he had provided. He had imposed restrictions on her that ought to have crushed her but which had only served to make her stronger.

Nothing he had done had held her down and he had never been able to take it. There had always been her silent defiance, her pride, her sparkling delight in life, shining out of her eyes. No matter how much he had tried to thrash these things out of her, they had remained, a testimony to the kind of inner breeding he wasn't able to understand.

'Don't stand there gaping, girl,' he snarled. 'It's bad manners to gape! Shut the door and get me my dinner.'

Slowly and warily she came forward, knowing even before he spoke that her brief wonderful months of freedom were already over.

'Didn't Nora leave your dinner, Father?' she asked, feeling strange and breathless as she spoke. 'She usually leaves something in the oven.'

'Damn Nora!' he roared. 'I sent the nosy bitch packing and she won't be coming back. There's no need for her to be prying about my home when I have a daughter who's perfectly capable of looking after things.'

Reaching for an apron he threw it at her. 'Here! Put this on and get about your duties. Everything's back to normal for you, girl! God knows what possessed me, allowing you to gallivant around the countryside, growing too big for your boots. Well, there will be no more o' it. You won't be going back to Noble House. I spoke to Lady Pandora this morning and told her she won't be seeing you again.'

'And . . . what did she say?' Anna whispered, through pale lips.

'Say? Say? Who the hell is she to make decisions for you. What I say is law, never forget that, and while you're at it, you might show a bit o' gratitude for everything I've done for you. Who do you think pays for all those silly fal-de-rals you wear on your back? The tooth fairy? The wee red elf at the bottom of the garden!'

Anna looked at his leering face and shivered, but her chin went up in defiance and when she spoke her voice was firm and clear. 'No, Father, I'm too old to believe in fairy stories – even if you aren't – and if you think it's you who pays for my clothes then you must certainly be living in cloud-cuckoo-land.'

With a growl of rage Roderick jumped to his feet, throwing back his chair with such force it clattered noisily to the floor. 'Say that again!' he taunted, advancing towards her menacingly.

Anna's chin trembled, the swiftness of her heartbeat made her feel faint, fear was turning her insides to jelly. She knew she had to make a stand, now or never. She was a child no more, and she had to show him that, as far as she was concerned, his days of dominion were over.

'Lady Pandora buys me my clothes,' she said steadily. 'After years of wearing the ugly things you dressed me in I was only too ready to take advantage of her kindness, and in case you've forgotten –' her head went up higher, '– the money you get from my paintings more than pays for my bed and board.'

'You little slut!' Her father's fist rose and fell; blood spurted from her lip; she felt her legs giving way. He then straddled her, deliberately grinding his heel into her ankle.

She let out a cry. It was all coming back, the horror, the sickening uncertainties of her early childhood.

The last time he had beaten her had been about the time of her thirteenth birthday. Magnus had been very angry when he had found out about the beating and had declared his intention of facing up to Roderick. Anna, however, had stayed him, telling him they were too young to fight such a tyrant.

But she wasn't too young now. She was sixteen. She was a woman.

Getting to her feet she faced her father. 'I'm old enough now to make my own decisions, Father,' she cried passionately. 'You can't stop me going to Noble House – unless you're planning to put me in chains and lock me in the cellar!'

Roderick's fingers dug into the soft flesh of her arm. 'If I have to, madam, I will! You won't go to that house again – if you know what's good for you.'

'And what about my visits to Knock Farm? Are you going to put an end to those, too? Miss Priscilla taught me well but I still have a lot to learn. Sir Hugh Cameron has asked me over to Moor House to paint his family. He's a man of great influence. Just think o' the triumph for you, Father? Your very own daughter, painting portraits of the titled gentry.'

His sweating face leered into hers. 'Don't use that insolent tone with me, madam. I have no intention of thwarting your ambitions,' his voice had grown oily, his words more affable, 'you ought to know by now that I have your interests at heart and would never stand in your way. Why d'you think I let you go to Knock Farm in the first place? By all means continue your studies, go to the homes o' these fine people who honour you wi' their patronage. I'm a fair man, Anna, I've protected you and your brothers from burdens that I and I alone must carry. Whatever you think o' me now you will one day look back and be thankful to the Lord that you had a father like me.'

He was rocking on his heels as he spoke, hands folded behind his back in a typically arrogant pose. Anna looked at him with contempt. 'Ay, my cup runneth over indeed. How could I be anything else but grateful to a father who lines his pockets with ill-gotten gains? Oh, ay, I know all about you and the terrible things you've done for sillar. You practically sold me to Lady Pandora, didn't you? Just like a slave in the marketplace! I knew it, but I was too happy to do anything about it. And now you preach to me

41

about my welfare when all the time you have your sights set on the little goose that lays the golden eggs . . . '

He advanced towards her once more, snarling like a raving dog. She backed away from him, terrified, yet unable to stop talking about the things that had festered inside of her for so long.

'As well as all that I haven't forgotten about Peter and how he died,' she half-sobbed. 'I loved him and he was taken away from me – just as Mother was taken away. In a different way from Peter, but she might as well be dead too. I'll find out what happened to her though, and I'll find out about Peter – and Mr Mallard. The police think it was an accident – folks around here think differently – some say he was murdered . . . '

Roderick had stopped dead in his tracks to stare at her, something in his expression so strange she could do nothing but stare back at him, as if hypnotised. Moments passed, laden with sickening anxiety, then the wild beast returned to him, his eyes blazed, his fist smashed into her jaw and she fell again to the floor. This time she couldn't get up.

Head spinning, stomach churning, she was only barely aware that Magnus had arrived on the scene in a tornado of flying fists. Flesh smacked into flesh and she knew that her father had met his match – at long last.

CHAPTER 5

Burdens

Anna struggled to sit up, in time to see her father staggering backwards across the room. There was a tremendous clatter as he landed in the hearth, sending the companion set flying, scattering the fuel in the hod, his elbow catching on the handle of the soup pan in such a way that its contents came splattering down over him.

Fortunately for him the soup hadn't yet reached a temperature high enough to cause any degree of burning. As it was, he made a sorry sight, sprawled on the floor with his head in the hearth, covered in thick yellow liquid that oozed from his face to his neck and into the collar of his clothing.

Magnus had dealt him a sledgehammer blow but he was already hauling himself into a sitting position, dragging his hand over his face, staring in disbelief at the blood he drew away from his mouth. Blood also bubbled from his nose, clogging it, dripping down to stain the iron-grey hairs of his neatly clipped moustache. Gasping for breath he coughed and spluttered and all the while Magnus stood over him, fists bunched, ready to strike again if need be.

Cautiously, Roderick moved his limbs. Getting to his knees he crawled across the room on all fours to haul himself onto a chair where he sprawled his length, chest heaving, one trembling hand raised time and again to wipe the gore from his face.

'Bastard!' he muttered viciously. 'You'll be sorry for this, I promise you!'

White faced and strained looking, Magnus was also breathing heavily, but his voice was steady enough when he said, 'You'll never touch Anna again. As long as I'm here to protect her, you won't harm a hair o' her head. And by God! I mean what I say!'

Roderick was recovering rapidly. He glared at his son with loathing. 'As long as you're here, eh? If I were you I wouldn't put too much sillar on that cosy little notion.'

'Try putting me out! Just try it! This is our home as well as yours. Your days o' lording it are over with. From now on you'll behave yourself – or else.'

Gently he helped Anna to her feet and led her to the sofa where he made her lie down, talking soothingly to her as he placed a cushion under her head and a rug over her knees.

'Very touching,' sneered Roderick. 'A devoted brother and sister, all lovey-dovey and caring for one another. Well, I tell you this, look to each other while you can, for you mistook my meaning just now, boy. One day, maybe not so far off, you will have to leave this house – and that goes for the pair o' you.'

There was something so insidious in his tone it made brother and sister look at one another in trepidation. Their father was capable of anything and after what had happened today they knew they would have to be on their guard with him – day and night.

Roderick was sitting boldly up in his chair now, ominously calm, his breathing, his demeanour, back to normal, only his bloody nose and stained clothing bearing evidence of what had occurred.

Anna and Magnus had expected fury, tantrums, certainly not this: a pensive-looking Roderick, one who seemed to be mulling something over in his mind with great deliberation and whose silence intensified the atmosphere of tension that had settled over the room.

Then, quite suddenly and abruptly, he leaned forward to gaze at them intently and when he spoke it was in a soft, apologetic voice. 'There's something you should both know. Something so terrible I never wanted it to come out. I tried to keep it from you in order to protect you and it's been a sore burden for me to bear all these years. Now, the truth has to be known, Magnus's behaviour today has set the seal on that.'

'You're talking in riddles,' Magnus spoke shakily. There was a strong feeling of malevolence in the air , as if the forces of evil slithering out of Roderick's mouth had insinuated themselves into every dark and secret corner of the house.

Roderick laughed mirthlessly. 'Let me make myself plainer, boy. For a long time now I've known that one day – you – all of you – would lose your reason. Do you remember years ago, when your mother was ill with pneumonia and I had to bide in Kilkenzie to be near the asylum?'

'Ay, you were away for a week,' Anna whispered. 'We wanted to go as well but you wouldn't let us.'

Sorrowfully Roderick shook his head. 'I couldn't let you visit your mother because to see her in her madness would have been a hellish nightmare. She wasn't the woman I married. God no! A wild-eyed stranger, laughing, screaming, uttering the foulest filth you ever heard.'

He shook his head again and looked sad. 'Oh, no, I couldn't let my children see that – hear that . . . ' He paused to gaze at Anna. 'I didn't want you to see the kind o' creature you would one day become, lassie.'

'Stop that!' cried Magnus harshly. 'It's lies! Don't believe a word he says, Anna, he's only trying to torment us!'

Roderick looked at his son with pity. 'Hold your tongue, lad, till you hear me out. The doctors had a long talk wi' me that time I stayed at Kilkenzie.

'They told me that they had discovered some more about your mother's condition, that it's hereditary, able to be passed on to her children . . . ' He passed a hand over his eyes. 'There's no escape and there have been times when I thought I would go mad too, having to bear the brunt o' such knowledge. She allowed me to marry her and have children before telling me about her family's history o' mental illness. Her grandmother had died in an asylum, so too had her sister but even then I was stupid enough to let myself believe it was just something that could happen in any family. Only after the doctors had spoken to me did I realise that she had been too selfish to let such ugly lunacy die out . . . ' Shaking his head vehemently he cried, 'That's the gift your precious mother has given you and God help me! I hate her for it!'

Burying his head in his hands he rocked himself back and forth, back and forth, real tears running under his fingers.

Magnus swayed on his feet and sat down suddenly while Anna stared in shocked disbelief at her father. 'It's not true,' she whispered. 'It can't be true. Mother was too good, too considerate, to ever let a thing like that happen.'

Roderick was trembling. Taking his hands from his red-rimmed eyes he fumbled for a handkerchief and blew his nose. He was a chaste and saddened figure and for the first time brother and sister saw genuine sorrow on his face.

'I'm sorry, lass,' he mumbled brokenly. 'You had to know, it's true, all o' it. I've tried to forget – and in so doing I've sinned before God. Compensations – they help for a wee while but in the end . . . '

He spread his hands in appeal. 'I only ask one thing o' you both. Adam. He isn't as strong as either of you. I've always known that and I ask you never to let him know any o' this. What happened here today was none o' his doing. A man can only take so much and I have to say that I was goaded into speaking my mind by your behaviour, Magnus, and by the way your sister spoke to me. Any minute now, Adam will come through that door, and I ask each o' you to try and behave as normal.' He glanced from one white face to the other. 'Can you promise me that? It won't be easy, but we must try and put a face on it – it's the only thing left now.'

Anna felt herself drown in terror. Wordlessly, she nodded while Magnus, a look in his hazel eyes of one already demented, went to mop up the hearth.

Roderick got up to make his way to his room. He was still shaking, and a muscle in his jaw was twitching violently, but a wash in cold water soon restored his ruddy complexion and when he appeared once more in the kitchen wearing a freshly laundered shirt, he was the Roderick that Anna and Magnus knew so well.

A few minutes later Adam came bounding in, a broad-shouldered, crudely handsome fifteen year old, sniffing the air, throwing his cap onto a peg on the wall with an expert flick of his wrist.

Anna had laid the table and the kitchen was warm and peaceful. Shafts of sunlight lay over the polished wooden floor; Tibby the cat was snapping at flies on the window ledge; the drone of machinery from the boiler house infiltrated the quietness without unduly disturbing it.

Briskly Adam rubbed his hands together. 'What's for dinner? I'm starving. One o' the wagons ran off the rails this morning and I all but lifted it back myself. Some o' the lads have muscles like water and just stood by watching in amazement. Boxer Sam had great muscles. Some say he could lift the rear end o' a Clydesdale and make it walk on its front legs. It's a pity he doesn't work at the mill anymore, I could have had a bit o' fun wi' him.'

'A great pity.' Roderick spoke heavily, one eyelid flicking slightly at the memory of how he had engineered Boxer Sam's dismissal by planting matches, strictly forbidden in a gunpowder mill, in his clothing and making sure that William Jordan discovered them.

Roderick had wanted rid of Boxer Sam for years, mainly because of his swaggering ways and monopolisation of Nellie Jean, but the big Munkirk man hadn't been easy to get rid of. For a start he knew rather too much about some of Roderick's unsavoury dealings and made good use of

47

his knowledge accordingly. For another he was well liked by everyone, including William Jordan, who hadn't seemed at all convinced that a man of Sam's experience with gunpowder would have been stupid enough to carry matches on his person.

'Sam's worked here for years. He's a responsible sort and his record of safety is second to none,' Jordan had argued. 'I find it hard to believe that he would start to get careless after all this time.'

Nevertheless the charge was a serious one, no inflammables in the mill buildings was a strict ruling and here was Sam, caught red-handed with matches in his pocket, in the potentially dangerous confines of the testing shed. The evidence was stacked against him and William Jordan had no other option but to fire him.

Boxer Sam had created quite a scene about what he considered to be an unfair dismissal and had vowed that one day he would return to avenge Roderick. He had been gone from the mill for nearly a year now and it had been reported that he was working somewhere in England. Nevertheless, Roderick felt uneasy every time he thought about the incident and Nellie Jean didn't help matters by continually bemoaning Sam's departure from the area.

Adam's mention of Boxer Sam had been calculatingly innocent. He was well aware that his father had been instrumental in getting rid of Sam and Adam liked nothing better than to see Roderick squirm.

He couldn't remember a time of fatherly warmth and caring; his life had been a test of endurance against mental and emotional brutality, and it gave him great satisfaction to know that he could somehow pay his father back, albeit only in words.

Adam saw the nervous tic of his father's eye and he was well pleased at such a reaction. Peering closer he said, with exaggerated concern, 'What happened to your lip, Father, it's all bruised and bloody, have you been in a fight? Who . . . ?'

'Oh, sit down, Adam, and stop blethering on like an old woman!' Roderick snapped irritably.

Adam, sensing that something was greatly amiss, lowered himself onto a chair at the table to survey his family. Noting his brother's sullen expression and red knuckles he came to the conclusion that there had been a show down between Magnus and Roderick and he was sorry that he had missed it.

Anna was serving dinner, her face turned away from the light. All the colour had gone from it, leaving it so pale that Adam paused to stare at her with his spoon half-way to his mouth. She was like the Anna of the old days, docile and silent. The light had gone from her eyes and her shoulders were hunched despairingly. There was an aura of defeat about her that made him want to cry out to her that he loved her . . .

Adam swallowed hard. It was more than love, it was enchantment. These past months she had filled the house with a warmth that flowed into every drab corner. He had felt secure and satisfied with his world. It was the happiest time he had known since his mother had gone away to some nameless madhouse. She had never loved him as much as she had loved Magnus and Anna, but at least she had held him in her arms and she had been warm, warm and safe . . .

Anna had been like that lately, carefree, spreading her happiness, now here she was, shrouded in a misery that seemed to billow out and suck away the sunshine.

'Anna!' he cried sharply. 'What's wrong? What's wrong, Anna?'

She raised her face to look at him and he saw the purple bruises on her jaw, the swollen flesh of her lip.

'Who hit you like that?' he yelled, panic rising in him because he knew only too well the answer to his question. 'And where's Nora? Why isn't she here to serve dinner? Why is everybody so quiet?!'

Scraping back his chair he made to get up but Roderick

stayed him with a heavy hand. 'Stop worrying, son, and calm yourself at once. Nora won't be coming back, I never liked having the nosy bitch here in my house anyway. From now on your sister will be looking after everything, just as she did before she got a lot o' fancy notions in her head. She didn't like the idea, so she had to be punished. You know you all have to be punished if you don't obey the rules o' the house – don't you, Adam?'

Adam's heartbeat boomed in his ears. 'Ay, Father,' he said stiffly and picked up his spoon.

CHAPTER 6

Nightmares

Robert tossed and turned, trying to find a comfortable position in his bed, which seemed to be all lumps and bumps. It was cold as well, penetrating the chinks in his blankets whenever he moved a muscle, and there was a distinctly freezing patch at the bottom, as if the sheets had been dipped in ice.

Above everything, his mind just wouldn't be still; how could anyone sleep with Ralph moaning and groaning in the next bed – like a demented spook wandering the night, making sure it kept everyone awake.

Robert turned on his back and gave a mighty sigh. He was getting pretty fed up with Ralph and these bad dreams of his. They were becoming an almost nightly occurrence and, in a burst of frustration, Robert half thought of getting up and giving his companion a good shaking.

But that wouldn't help matters. Ralph would only sit up in bed like a bolt from a cannon, all bleary-eyed and hair standing on end, while he demanded to know what was happening.

Robert hunched up his knees and lay still for a few moments, listening to Ralph's ramblings.

'No, don't do it,' Ralph was muttering. 'Please don't do it. Don't hurt Mr Mallard. I can't bear it. Don't, please don't. The rope. You can't use the rope. Afraid. So afraid . . .'

His words became blurred and indistinct but Robert wasn't concentrating anymore. His mouth was bone dry; he felt himself growing hot; sweat bathed his body. Mallard!

It was the first time in his ravings that Ralph had mentioned any names. And why Mallard? What had their previous tutor to do with a young boy's secret fears? And a rope! 'You can't use the rope!'

Robert sat bolt upright in bed, staring into the darkness, feeling the hairs rising at the nape of his neck. Quack Quack had met his death at the end of a rope! An accident the police had said. The people of Glen Tarsa had other opinions.

'Murder!' Tell Tale Todd, who had discovered the body, had declared darkly. 'I'll never forget the sight o' that poor cratur', swaying there amongst the trees, as dead as a doornail. He didn't do that himself. He was too experienced in such matters to go and hang himself wi' his very own rope.'

'Maybe it was suicide,' Moira O'Brady had hazarded. 'We all know what was going on between him and her ladyship. It could be that she spurned him in the end and he wasn't able to take it. You know the old saying, "Give a man enough rope and he'll hang himself."'

'Ach no! That's daft, as fine you know!' Maggie May had objected forcibly, her double chins quivering with indignation. 'The man was young and fit wi' everything to live for! Her ladyship would never have been cruel enough to drive him to kill himself.'

'And Master Peter,' Ben McLeod said sadly, 'killed by his fall on the rocks o' the riverbank. Only a lad, only sixteen.'

'Ay, a tragic way to end a young life,' Janet McCrae had agreed. 'Anna will never get over it. Such bonny sweethearts they were, happy and innocent.'

'A double murder,' Tell Tale Todd's friend, old Shoris, decided with a shake of his grizzled grey head. 'And the bugger who did it is getting away wi' it. He must be feeling right pleased wi' himself. The police in these parts are as soft as cow dung.'

'Ay, but he'll pay for it,' old Grace uttered grimly, her

52

blue eyes glittering with anger. 'In the end, he'll pay for it – though what good it will do Anna is another matter. Ignorance is sometimes the best medicine.'

'She'll have the satisfaction o' knowing that her lad's death will be avenged,' Tell Tale Todd said soothingly.

'Ay,' Grace nodded, a strange look on her face as she collected her groceries and departed the shop.

Robert thought about these things as he lay in the darkness, a strange feeling of loneliness creeping over him . . . And something else – fear – Ralph's fear – transferring itself to him, growing stronger as the minutes passed till it seemed as if a hostile presence had come slinking into the room to spread a black cloak of unease over everything.

Ralph had stopped his ravings and was now breathing evenly, though every so often he would shift in his bed and give vent to a tormented moan that sent icy shivers along Robert's spine.

'Mother o' God,' he whispered, 'would you be so good as to bring a bit o' peace into this room this night. I'm scared out me wits, so I am, and could fair be doing wi' a bit o' comfort to myself. Grant this, oh, Sacred Mary, and I promise I'll try and be nicer to everybody – including old Dicky Bird himself. Amen.'

He felt better, so much so that an old familiar ache began to gnaw at his belly. Hunger. These days he was always hungry for something. His maturing body was forever demanding sustenance of some sort. He had always liked girls and had played not-so-innocent games with them from an early age. When he was older the games had grown into something more serious and his sexual needs had been met on a regular enough basis to satisfy even him.

A man with a boy's face. That was how someone had once described him. Lusty and fiery, direct in his approach to even the shyest of girls, he had been well attended by the maidens who had chanced his way.

Since coming to Noble House, however, his dealings with the fair sex had been few and far between with the result that more than just Ralph disturbed his dreamings.

Luckily, Dicky Bird with his teachings, Aunt Dora with her capacity to keep youngsters amused, the never-ending interests of the surrounding countryside, the joys of horse riding and hill climbing more than made up for the things that were lacking in his life and saw to it that he tumbled into bed exhausted most nights.

Tonight he wasn't thinking about girls, he was thinking about one lovely, rather roly-poly woman, namely Molly the Cook, whose dimpled arms were never slow to enclose him in a motherly sort of way and who took a great pleasure in plying him with her delicious pies and pastries whenever he appeared in her kitchen.

Molly spoiled him, as susceptible to his charms as any of the young girls he had known in his life. And Molly wouldn't like it at all if she thought he was suffering the kind of discomfort that came within her range of curing. So surely she wouldn't mind if he were to sneak down to the kitchen and help himself to a pie or two?

She would understand and might even pat him on the head if she were to find out just how much her pastries had helped him to get through this night.

So he convinced himself as he lay there with his stomach rumbling until, spurred on by his increasing emptiness, he threw back the bedclothes, donned his dressing gown and slippers, and went gliding silently out of the room.

The house was dark and deserted looking, and the stairs creaked as he descended them. He wasn't light of foot and fell down the last two steps, his heart galloping into his throat as he stood still, listening.

But all was quiet, the house slept on undisturbed. His courage restored, he made his way along the draughty corridors to the back of the house where a flight of stone steps led down to the pantries and the kitchen.

Baird, the butler, held the keys to one of the pantries but

the other, the one in which Molly stored all the goodies and which was situated just off the kitchen, was bound to be unlocked and ready to yield up its bounties.

Soundlessly he opened the kitchen door, all his thoughts centred on the feast that awaited him.

The room was warm and smelled deliciously of new-baked bread and oven scones. Like an eager hound he quested the air, his mouth watering, his eyes adjusting to the dark as he made his way forward, his slippered feet making little or no sound on the stone tiles of the floor.

It was only then that he became aware of faint moaning from behind the door of the scullery. His scalp crawled, his heartbeat accelerated once more, all the superstitions that were inherent in him came leaping to the fore.

Ghosts! An old house like this must be crawling with them! Didn't the old Spey-wife, who had come begging for scraps at the orphanage, warn him against the sort of wrongdoing that would bring all the spooks of hell leaping out to punish him?

And he was wrong doing. Sneaking about the house like this, intent on raiding Molly's pantry after she had laboured and sweated all day to fill it.

Deciding that he preferred the more human sounds of Ralph's tormented utterings to the noises he was now hearing, he made to depart the scene, but something, some instinct, made him stay where he was . . .

The groanings from the scullery were growing in volume. Surely he recognised those animal-like expressions of human enjoyment? Curiosity getting the better of him, he crept closer to the door to put his ear against it.

The moanings and sighings were clearer now, and with a resolute movement Robert twisted the knob and threw open the door, a smile of devilment touching his mouth as he visualised the surprise his intrusion would cause.

Even so, he was totally unprepared for the sight that met his eyes, for there was Mary the kitchenmaid, sprawled on her back on the hard wooden table, legs in the air, bare breasts bouncing, Adam McIntyre riding her for all he was worth, the pair of them grunting and groaning like all of O'Flaherty's pigs put together and a little bit more besides.

'Holy Mother o' God!' Robert exclaimed. 'And here was me thinking that all the banshees o' Ireland were after me for my sins!'

A candle on the sink boards was sending its fluttering light around the small enclosure, alighting uncertainly on Mary's skirt and knickers lying in a heap on the floor, together with Adam's hastily discarded trousers.

The sight kindled Robert's sense of humour even more and it was only by clapping his hand to his mouth that he managed to stop himself from laughing out loud. Mary, eyes round, mouth agape, could only stare dumbfounded at the figure framed in the doorway, while Adam, his ardour somewhat dampened, jumped away from her, cursing as he bent down to the floor to grovel for his trousers.

It was a scene that Robert himself was familiar with, for hadn't he had similar escapades back home in Ireland? Things were different now, however. The woman he affectionately called Aunt Dora had taken him away from all that. She had given him a home, a wonderful home it was too, never in all his wildest imaginings had he expected anything like it.

She had given him the chance to make something of his life and over and above all that, and most importantly, she had been instrumental in making him feel he belonged to a real family at last. He adored and respected her and never, never would he dream of doing anything that might upset her. He didn't take kindly to people who did, especially those whose place it was to be trustworthy and loyal.

With all that in mind he felt his sympathies waning for the hapless pair in front of him.

He looked at Mary. He neither liked nor trusted her very much. Her face was foxy and thin, her eyes close-set, her movements shifty. She had a habit of looking furtively over her shoulder, giving the impression that she was up to no good. Once he had surprised her in an upstairs corridor, her ear clamped against a door, her expression at being disturbed one of annoyance rather than guilt, as if to imply that he was the one at fault for being there at that particular moment.

And here she was, caught once more off her guard, only on this occasion she was concerned by the fact. 'Oh, please, Master Robert,' she pleaded tearfully, 'don't tell the mistress. I'll lose my job if she hears o' this and my father would kill me if such a thing got to his ears!'

Robert fixed her with his blue, hypnotic stare, effective even in candlelight. 'I won't be saying anything this time but don't be letting it happen again – that's all!'

So saying, he turned to Adam whom he didn't know very well but had heard plenty about. 'As for you, Adam McIntyre, take yourself out o' this house and don't be coming near it again – or you'll have me to reckon with.'

'Is that so, big boy . . . ' Adam began belligerently only to check himself when he saw the determined gleam in Robert's eyes and the fists raised, ready for action.

'That's so,' Robert said coolly and turning on his heel he vacated the scullery, leaving Adam and Mary to look at one another.

'Well, now he's gone we can get on wi' it,' Adam said without remorse. 'Come on, get them off, I was just about there when that bastard came barging in. Just feel me, Mary lass, good and big, eh? The way you like it.'

But she pushed him away. 'Are you daft altogether, Adam McIntyre? He could come back again and I'm no' losing my job, for you or anybody.'

'Is that so? Have you thought that you might lose me if you start to grow all coy wi' me now. There's plenty more fish in the sea besides you. I can get anybody I like,' he finished boastfully.

Mary liked Adam, she liked him very much indeed –

even though he seemed besotted by that snobbish madam, Beth Jordan. At times he was rough and boorish, at others he was thoughtful and generous, showering her with small gifts, making her feel loved and wanted, things that Mary had known little of till meeting him.

The very idea of him deserting her made her feel sick and at his words she hastened to say, 'Tomorrow night, Adam, in the hayshed behind the bothy. I'll let you have anything you like then.'

Gripping her cheek roughly between his thumb and forefinger, he said harshly, 'You had better – or else – and another thing, it's a while since you found out more o' the secrets o' this house. Dark-horse Ralph, for instance. He's hiding something and I want to know what it is. You must hear him and that Irish fairy talking together. Dreams you said it was, bothering him, keeping him awake at night. Something's bound to slip out sooner or later and you be there to hear what it is. Promise me.'

'Ay, Adam, I promise.' Mary felt exhausted suddenly. She had never understood Adam's keenness to know what went on behind the closed doors of Noble House, for he never told her what he did, or intended to do, with the scraps of information she passed onto him. She knew, of course, that he was up to no good and the idea that he was just using her for his own ends often crossed her mind.

Then she would shrug off her unease and close her mind to such thoughts. He was just being curious, that was all, and what harm could there be in trading a few snippets of idle gossip for his attentions. Just as long as she was careful she could keep her job and go on seeing him and no one would be any the wiser.

With that in mind she took his hand and led him to the little entrance door at the back of the scullery where she kissed him and huskily told him to, 'Bide your time till the following night and I'll make it worth your while.'

*   *   *

58

Robert shut the scullery door and stood in the kitchen, puffing up his chest. Well done, me lad, he told himself, to be sure you showed those two who was boss just now.

For the first time he realised that to be 'Master Robert' gave him some position in the household and so taken was he with the idea he almost forgot his reasons for coming down to the kitchen in the first place. But a rumble from his stomach soon reminded him and flitting over to the pantry, he heaped a plate with an assortment of pies and scones, filled a glass with creamy milk, and made his way out of the kitchen, carefully balancing the plate in his hand.

The silence of the house enclosed him again and draughts penetrated his clothing. Discarding the idea of demolishing his feast in his cold bedroom he instead made his way to the sitting room where he knew the fire would still be burning.

The door creaked softly as he opened it; the cosy glow from the fire attracted him like a magnet and to this goal he made his way – only to pull up in surprise, for there was Lady Pandora sitting alone on the sofa, her slender figure outlined in the firelight.

'Aunt Dora!' he gasped. 'I didn't expect to see you here.'

'Nor I you,' she said in a startled voice.

'I couldn't sleep, Ralph was dreaming again. He fair gives me the creeps with all that jabbering he does in his sleep. I just lay there listening, me very marrow turning to ice, till I knew I had to get away from him for a while.'

'So you went straight to the kitchen?'

'Och to be sure, Auntie, I was that hungry I could have eaten a scabby horse – but I had to make do instead with some o' Molly's cakes.'

'So I see.' Throwing back her head Lady Pandora let out a cry of laughter. 'And the sight of all that lovely food has set me off, too. A scabby horse I couldn't eat but perhaps one of those pastries . . . '

He threw her one of his cheeky grins. 'Sure, you can

share the lot with me, Auntie, if you wouldn't mind telling Molly in the morning how her pantry came to be half empty and her milk luggy half full.'

Lady Pandora giggled. 'You're a rogue, Robert Shamus O'Connor. God knows where your Noble blood is hiding, but it's there somewhere, lurking in all the Irish that's in you. Sit beside me and talk to me, you're just the tonic I need to cheer me up.'

Robert needed no second bidding. Companionably they sat together by the fire, eating scones and drinking milk, too busy to talk till Robert said curiously, 'I know why you couldn't sleep, Auntie, you're worried about Anna, aren't you?'

She stared at him. 'However did you know that?'

'Ah well, it's the magic in me to be sure. I told that to Anna only a few days ago because I knew she wouldn't laugh at me. I feel things in people, their troubles an' all. I had a feeling something was coming to Anna, something that would take away her happiness.'

'Oh, Robert.' Lady Pandora put her hand over his and squeezed it. 'How right you are. You see, three days ago I had words with her father and since then I haven't set eyes on the child. I'm worried about her – I feel – that some harm has come to her.'

'You like her a lot, don't you, Aunt Dora?'

'Indeed I do. She's like a daughter to me. Ever since she came into my life I can't imagine it without her.'

'Why couldn't you have children o' your own, Auntie? You like them more than Mrs Murphy liked hers – though mind – she had nine and five o' them girls. Trouble they were, every one o' them.'

'You do ask a lot of questions, Robert, and who on earth is Mrs Murphy?'

'Ah, well now, wasn't she the mother o' the colleens who used to torment me for me favours.'

'All of them?'

'Ah, well, I'm thinking there must have been four at

least, the fifth had no taste, no taste at all for she went and fell in love with Danny O'Brien who had nothing but religion in him.'

'But, Robert, you're only fifteen. These girls must surely have been of assorted ages.'

Robert's eyes gleamed. 'Some younger, some older. I could never make up me mind which I liked best since one lot I could teach while the rest thought they could teach me. I'm not complaining, mind, it was all very satisfying while it lasted.'

Lady Pandora's eyes flashed in amusement. 'And here was me thinking you were just an innocent boy who had to be protected from life's realities.'

'Some realities are nicer than others, Auntie, and at heart I'm still just an innocent Irish lad at the mercy o' me betters. But if I'm minding right, we were talking about you before you managed to wangle the questions round to me. I was asking why you never had children o' your own? A fine lady like yourself with a heart full o' love for waifs and strays like myself.'

'You do get to the point, Robert.'

'I know, it's just in me nature,' he answered, with such disarming frankness she shook her head and said simply, 'By the laws of nature some people can't have children, Robert. Sadly, Sir Malaroy and myself come within that category.'

Robert put a sympathetic hand on her shoulder. 'In all me born days I've never come across the likes o' such loyalty, for I'm thinking it isn't yourself that you speak of. If you say otherwise then I am, after all, nothing but an ignorant Irish lad who knows nothing o' the ways o' the world.'

'Perhaps, for your age, you know too much,' Lady Pandora said softly, getting up to push him in the direction of the door. 'Off to bed with you or you'll never get up in the morning, and think what Mr Dick will have to say about that.'

At the door he turned. 'Don't be worrying your head about Anna. She'll come back to you, one day she'll come back.'

'I hope so, Robert. I do very much hope so,' she answered, a catch in her voice as she turned away quickly to hide the gleam of tears in her eyes.

CHAPTER 7

Questions

Miss Priscilla McLeod stood staring at the sturdy wooden door of The Gatehouse, her lips pursed into grim lines. The last time she had been here was more than three years ago. Then she had come to enquire of Roderick McIntyre why he was making his daughter leave school. His answers to her questions had been brusque and non-committal but, just the same, she had come away triumphant, having secured his grudging permission to allow Anna to continue her studies on a home-tuition basis at Knock Farm.

Miss Priscilla had thought never to come back to this house, now here she was once more, on a quest to discover why the girl hadn't been seen in the glen for nearly a week, never mind missing her twice-weekly visits to the farm.

True, Adam had turned up with a note, one which said that his sister was ill in bed with 'flu but would resume her normal activities as soon as she was better.

This was all very unsatisfactory to Miss Priscilla. Anna had been in the best of health and spirits the last time they had met and on no account was Roderick McIntyre getting away with a curt note delivered rather guiltily by his youngest son.

Miss Priscilla wasn't at all looking forward to another confrontation with a man whom she had never liked nor trusted. However, she had never been one to allow herself to be intimidated by anyone and with that in mind, she straightened her back, pushed out her scrawny bosom, settled her specs more firmly on the end of her nose and raised her hand to the door knocker.

It was Roderick himself who answered, wrenching the door open in some annoyance to glare outside. At the sight of the schoolteacher standing on his doorstep he composed himself quickly, albeit with an effort, since he had scant time or patience with the woman who had so thoroughly put him in his place over his daughter's welfare.

'Ah, 'tis yourself, my good lady,' he managed to say affably. 'And what brings you here at this time o' day – just as I was sitting into my dinner?'

'Good day to you, Mr McIntyre,' Miss Priscilla returned stiffly. 'I have come to inquire about Anna.'

'Yes, yes, of course, Anna. Well, I must say, it's very kind o' you to be concerned about the lass, Miss – er . . . '

The schoolteacher looked down her nose at him. He had always affected memory loss over the question of her name – as if to get home to her that he regarded her as a person of little consequence.

'The name, Mr McIntyre, is Miss McLeod – as fine you know. And yes, I am concerned about Anna. No one has seen her for several days. The note you sent with your son explained little and I am wondering if I may be able to see Anna, just to reassure myself that all is well with her.'

At that, Roderick's face darkened. Stepping outside, he closed the door behind him and said flatly, 'Indeed I cannot allow that, my good lady. The 'flu, you know, is highly contagious and very weakening. Anna is where she ought to be, tucked up cosily in bed with myself attending every one o' her wee whims.'

'If she is that ill, I take it you have called the doctor?'

'Doctor? Come now, Miss – er – McLeod, the girl is ill, I didn't say she was dying. A few days rest in bed will see her up and about in no time. I can assure you that she is in no danger of any sort.'

A sense of frustration seized Miss Priscilla. It was obvious that she wasn't to be allowed to see Anna, her father was making sure of that. 'I do hope so, Mr McIntyre,' she said sharply. 'Sir Hugh Cameron called in to see me. He wants

Anna to begin a portrait painting of his young son and daughter and I was unable to tell him when it could be started.'

'Of course – Sir Hugh,' Roderick looked thoughtful, 'mustn't keep his sort waiting, must we? I'll tell Anna about it and I'm sure she'll be along to see you as soon as she's able.'

Miss Priscilla rummaged in her bag and withdrew a book. 'Give this to Anna along with my love – it will help to while away the hours for her. Tell her I shall expect to see her in a few days – if not before.'

Roderick took the book. 'Quite, quite. And now – if you'll excuse me – I must get back to my dinner before it becomes fit only for the hens.'

The door closed. Miss Priscilla stood looking at it for some time, then suddenly and uncharacteristically she made a face at it and went on her way – feeling much, much better.

On his way down from the Leanachorran home farm Magnus spied Miss Priscilla's unmistakable figure in the distance and he wondered if he ought to cut along to the bridle path by the river in order to avoid her. He knew she was certain to ask questions about Anna. Everyone was asking questions about his sister and he had reached the stage when he could take no more of them.

Ever since that terrible scene in the kitchen, when their father had revealed those dreadful things about their mother, Magnus's brain had whirled in agonising circles till he had felt he was going mad already.

He couldn't sleep, he couldn't rest, and he had come to the conclusion that the only way to get any peace of mind was to try and uncover some of the mysteries that surrounded his mother's illness.

But who, who, could possibly help him, he had asked himself, till he thought about Mr Simpson, the minister, a man more qualified than any other to know what went on in the parish.

After days of indecision Magnus had, that morning, gone to ask Jacky the foreman if he could take a couple of hours off.

'Take the rest o' the day if you like, son,' Jacky had said, gazing keenly into Magnus's drawn face. 'You look done in, feeling ill, eh? Maybe that 'flu your sister has.'

'No, an hour or two's fine, Jacky.' From the corner of his eye Magnus had seen Lady Pandora making her way down to the stableyard and he wanted to get away before she, too, began quizzing him about Anna.

But he had been too late. 'Wait for me down by the bridge, Magnus,' she had called. 'I've been wanting to speak to you.'

Arms folded on the mossy parapet he had stood on the bridge, staring down at the fast-flowing waters, churning, churning, like the nerves that tightened his belly whenever he thought about his mother.

Lady Pandora had been her usual bright and charming self as she stood talking to him in the unaffected and easy way that so endeared her to everyone.

But she was trying too hard to be normal and her barriers quickly crumbled when Magnus said quietly, 'I know what it is, my lady, you want to ask me about Anna, don't you?'

The colour had drained from her face, leaving it very pale. 'Yes, oh yes, my dear Magnus. No doubt you are aware that your father and I had a row about her. I haven't been able to sleep since then. What's happened to her? Oh how is my dearest, darling girl?'

'She's – she won't be coming back to you, my lady. Father is against it. You must know the reasons for that better than I do. I'm sorry. Anna was very happy with you but it might be better if . . . if you don't try and make contact with her again. I'd hate to see her hurt any more than she is already.'

He omitted to mention the plans that had been forming in his head since the showdown with his father. To get Anna away from The Gatehouse, to find another job – one that had a house to go with it – anywhere – just as long as he could get his sister as far away from Roderick as possible. Ever since he had started work he had somehow managed to save a few coppers from his weekly pay packet and though it didn't amount to very much it would hopefully be enough to get him started.

At his words, Lady Pandora's hand went quickly to her eyes then hastily she composed herself. 'Forgive me, I weep only for selfish reasons. The house is so empty and quiet without her. I do understand what you're saying, Magnus. Even so, if it's at all within my powers, I mean to have Anna back with me. Meantime, tell her I send my love and that I miss her so very, very much. Also, if she ever needs or wants anything – anything at all – she must tell me and I'll get it for her.'

Her hand had closed briefly over his and then she had walked slowly away, her steps heavy, her whole attitude one of unhappiness.

The interlude had done nothing to improve Magnus's state of mind. He was in no mood for further interrogation and was most relieved to note that Miss Priscilla had disappeared into tiny Moss Cottage wherein lived old Grace Anderson.

Even though there was no-one else on the road Magnus didn't relax till he was well clear of the village, The Gatehouse, and the powdermill.

Munkirk village was two miles distant but Magnus was used to walking and, indeed, welcomed the chance to be alone with his thoughts for awhile.

His pace quickened and he shivered a little as he neared the foot of Mill Brae and the spot where Andrew Mallard and Peter Noble had met their deaths.

Once past The Rumbling Brig the road meandered along by the river where wild daffodils danced in the breeze and clumps of primroses starred the mossy earth beneath the trees. Fluffy white clouds sailed serenely along in the blue sky; the river gurgled smoothly over the stones;

a buck rabbit scuttled off into the trees as Magnus's feet crunched on the road.

It was a glorious spring day, filled with the promise of new life, but Magnus saw none of it, absorbed as he was with his troubled thoughts.

The Manse lay on the shores of Loch Longart, a finger of sea running in from the Firth of Clyde, surrounded by the rugged hills of Cowal.

The Manse itself was a sturdy big sandstone house sitting rather self-consciously in an acre of partially over-grown garden, where crocus and hyacinth were struggling gamely to raise their heads heavenwards.

Mrs Rachael Simpson opened the door to Magnus, her strong, mobile face filled with enquiry that quickly turned to a welcoming smile at the sight of the visitor.

Mrs Simpson was a person who displayed a rather frivo-lous façade to the world but underneath it all was an intelligent woman with a keen sense of perception.

'You must have smelled the tea, dear boy,' she beamed. 'Jean has just brought it in this minute. Mr Simpson is down by the shore, plootering around with that dreadful boat. He does nothing with it but scrape it and paint it and I do believe he's forgotten that it ought to go into the water sometimes. On you go down. I'll get Jean to bring you tea and some of my special home-made scones – straight off the girdle.'

The back garden of The Manse ran down to the dappled shallows of the loch. It was here that Magnus found the Reverend Alastair Simpson, dressed in a pair of paint-spattered trousers and a baggy tweed jacket. He looked so different from his neat Sunday image that Magnus paused for a moment to look further along the shore, as if expecting to see a sedate clerical figure strolling along with bowed head and clasped hands.

But the man in the baggy jacket was advancing towards him, wiping grubby hands on an equally grubby rag.

'Magnus! Magnus McIntyre! I won't shake hands but do come along down to the water's edge. It's my favourite place in my spare time and so much better than the house on a day like this. I normally receive visitors indoors, of course, but I know you're a man of the open air like myself. Jean will be bringing tea down shortly – I can smell the scones from here – you don't mind having tea out here?'

Without waiting for an answer he took Magnus by the shoulder and propelled him towards a large rock that was being gently splashed by the receding tide.

A clinker dinghy, varnished to a shiny conker red, was bobbing in the seaweedy shallows and the minister gazed at it proudly. 'Just trying it out for seaworthiness. I don't know why I bother, because I never have the time to go out in her but I enjoy working with boats, though Rachael – Mrs Simpson that is – is forever on at me to do something other than paint and de-barnacle her – the boat that is,' he ended with a roguish grin.

He turned. 'Ah, here's Jean with the tea. Sit down on this rock, Magnus, sorry I can't offer you something more comfortable, but it can't be any worse than the pews in kirk.'

His eyes twinkled in his fresh-complexioned face, the sun gleamed on his mop of silvery white hair, and Magnus found himself relaxing as he realized this visit wasn't going to be the stiff affair that he had imagined.

Jean, the little maidservant, neat in her grey alpaca dress and white cotton apron, came down the garden steps, bearing a tray laden with tea and hot buttered scones.

At the sight of Magnus, with his tanned good looks and firmly muscled body, she fluttered her eyelashes and peeped at him coyly from the frilled rim of her mobcap.

'That will be all, Jean,' the minister said with a smile.

'Sir.' She turned away, throwing a dimpled look at Magnus over her shoulder as she daintily ascended the steps.

Magnus waited till she was out of sight then, leaning forward, he said in a low voice, 'Mr Simpson, I've come to ask you about my mother. You were the only person I could think of who might be able to help me. I know you've been to see her once or twice in the – hospital – and I wondered – could you tell me – what she was like?'

As he was speaking his fingers were working nervously on the handle of his cup, his voice was shaking a little and he bit his lip as he went on, 'Does she rant and rave – and say terrible things? Is she really – incurably insane?'

'My dear boy.' The minister saw that his young visitor was in a distressed state of mind and putting a firm hand on the boy's shoulder, he said gently, 'It's true, I have paid your mother the occasional visit and, over the years – yes – her condition appears to have deteriorated, but no, Magnus, she doesn't rave and shout, except perhaps when someone or something upsets the peace of her mind.'

Mr Simpson took a large bite of his buttered scone and gazed thoughtfully over the water. 'She has locked the doors, Magnus, and all but thrown away the keys and is a lost, lonely soul, living in a quiet little world of her own. But she is gentle – oh, what a gentle woman she is. She wouldn't hurt a fly if she could help it . . . '

He paused for a few moments, during which he took several gulps of his tea and rather noisily swallowed a mouthful of scone. Thus satisfied he turned to Magnus to look him straight in the eye and say slowly, 'You know, my boy, it wouldn't do her any harm if you were to go and see her. You're a man, now and perhaps it's time you saw her for yourself. Oh, it might upset you to see her as she is but she is your mother and you really ought to pay her a visit. Your father is against your going, I believe?'

'He told us she shouts like a maniac and said he didn't want any o' us to see her like that.' Magnus's tone was bitter at the recollection of that scene in the kitchen – the things Roderick had revealed . . .

'Of course he must want to safeguard you.' The minister spoke carefully, a frown creasing his brow. He had never taken to Roderick McIntyre: he was too plausible, too eager to impress everyone with his devout attention to church affairs.

The Reverend Simpson had heard things about Roderick McIntyre, disquieting rumours about the man's treatment of his family. There had also been unsavoury hints about his drinking and womanizing. Once or twice the minister had seen Roderick emerging from The Munkirk Inn but hadn't given it a second thought. Many respectable people took refreshment now and then – nothing in it at all. Still, there were things – other things – that were entirely unconnected with drink . . .

He remembered Lillian McIntyre's hand in his on one of his visits, her eyes pleading with him as she begged, 'Don't let *him* come near me. Every night I pray to God to keep him away. He's mad . . . mad . . . '

The minister looked kindly at Magnus. 'Listen to me, I'm going round to Kilkenzie next week. Why don't you and the others come with me? It can't do any harm and it might do all of you some good. I know a nice little inn where we can spend the night. I'll ask your father about it on Sunday.'

Magnus's eyes lit up. To see his mother. To talk to her. Even if she didn't know him as her son how wonderful to see again the sweet face of his memories . . . to hear her voice . . .

'Mr Simpson, I'd like that. Oh, God . . . ' He lifted his face to the sky as if to keep his tears from spilling. 'Ay, I'd like that,' he repeated huskily, 'and so would Anna – and Adam.'

At that moment his father's voice seemed to boom inside his head, telling him that his mother's madness was hereditary and that one day he – Anna – and Adam – would go the same way. His happiness left him. His body drooped, his hands hung limply over his knees, and he stared unseeingly at his feet, feeling as if he was gazing inwards at a world of deepest despair – one from which there was no escape . . .

'Is – there something else, Magnus?' The minister's voice came as if from a distant plain.

Magnus shook his head and stood up. 'No, nothing. You've been a grand help, I'm glad I came. Good day to you and thank you.'

'My boy.' Mr Simpson took Magnus's hands and squeezed them reassuringly. 'I'll always be here if you need me, don't ever forget that, and try not to worry anymore about your mother. I'm sure everything will be alright in the end. Come on, I'll walk with you up to the gate.'

'Ach no, don't bother,' Magnus said with a smile. 'You get back to your boat, I've taken up enough o' your spare time. I'll see myself out.'

But the minister didn't go back to his boat, he watched Magnus making his way up the steps and then he stood, lost in thought, shaking his head every so often as he went over in his mind the strangeness of Magnus's visit, the haunted look in the boy's eyes.

'Something odd here, very odd indeed,' the Reverend Alastair Simpson murmured to himself, distractedly running his grubby fingers through his silvery mop.

After a few minutes he, too, left the shore to make his way into The Manse by the back door where he removed his boots before Rachael could nag him for leaving dirty marks on the floor.

CHAPTER 8

Disappointments

Magnus made his way to the front of The Manse, his mind filled with the conversation he had just had with the minister. He wasn't to be alone with his thoughts for very long, however. Beth Jordan and her mother had just alighted from a rumble and were coming up the path, their skirts held a sedate inch above their ankles to allow them better balance on the rough paving stones.

'Why, Magnus.' Mrs Victoria Jordan, a tall, angular woman with a large mouth and a discontented face, uttered a rather reserved greeting, for she did not approve of her daughter's friendship with Roderick McIntyre's eldest son.

Of course she knew that Beth was only amusing herself with the boy, Beth had always enjoyed playing with someone, a fact that had caused her mother many disquieting moments as she had wondered where it would all lead in the end.

'How are you? Still working hard, I hope?' Mrs Jordan went on absently, at a loss for something meaningful to say. It was always the same when one came up against the working classes. Their experience of life and its finer aspects was so limited and she couldn't very well be expected to rattle on about cows and horses when she'd never had any reason to deal with the dreadful creatures. They did smell so and always seemed to be doing nasty things in the fields whenever one had to pass them by.

Of course, if one was inclined to it, sitting on top of a horse was a different matter entirely. The gentry went in for it in a big way. A horse came into its own then and appeared to be a very noble creature indeed as it cantered through the countryside, proudly bearing a lady or gentleman on its back.

In these respects it didn't seem to matter what emerged from the horse's hind end – one would be facing front and too high up to notice . . . Mrs Jordan went into a muse. What a pity Beth had never been keen on horseriding. She could just picture her daughter, riding straight-backed and sophisticated through the fields, a young man beside her, both of them laughing and talking as they went along . . .

It might not be too late though. If the friendship between Beth and Lucas Noble were to develop favourably then all things pertaining to the Nobles' way of life would also become Beth's . . .

The pictures flitting through Victoria Jordan's head were most pleasant, so much so she was able to smile quite charmingly at Magnus. 'A pity about the smell though,' she said vaguely. 'No matter how high one is sitting, if the wind was from the wrong direction it could be quite off-putting. Never mind, the compensations must be worth it, otherwise they wouldn't do it, would they?'

With that she swept majestically up to the front door of The Manse and was soon swallowed inside, though her loud, high voice, uttering a string of frivolous comments, came floating back to the two young people outside.

'What was all that about?' Magnus asked in bewilderment.

'Oh, nothing,' Beth replied with a laugh, 'Just Mother cooking things up in her head again. She's always done it but seems to be getting worse as she gets older. Perhaps it's something to do with the change.'

'The change?'

'Och, the change of life, silly.' Beth tried to sound knowledgeable, despite the fact that she wasn't entirely sure of what she was talking about. 'I heard Mother discussing it with that old frump, Fanny McWhirter, who wears the dreadful frocks – as if she would know anything about anything to do with the human body. It was all about hot flushes and itches and things like that, the two of them speaking in hushed voices, as if they had uncovered some horrible secret about the universe. It all sounded so awful I just had to peep through the keyhole and there was Fanny McWhirter, her face as scarlet as her rouge and Mother looking as if she would like to disappear up the chimney. It must have been dreadfully important to her because she's always so full of confidence in the normal way of things.

'After that they began to talk about how embarrassed they would be having to talk to a doctor about their symptoms and then Fat Jane came with tea and I had to stop listening just as it was getting to the interesting bits.'

Magnus looked unenlightened and Beth, feeling out of her depth, brushed the subject aside and linked her arm through his in a possessive manner. 'This is a lovely surprise, Magnus, meeting you here at fusty old Simpson's place. I've been shopping with Mother and managed to get the most exquisite length of material from McKenzie's. The seamstress at Larchwood has taken all my measurements . . . ' Here she pushed out her curvaceous bosom, ' . . . and is going to make it into a dress for the Easter dance. She's an absolute professional, does everything properly and really listens to what you want. Old Grace is alright but she's becoming a bit dottery. After all, she is getting on and her seams are beginning to wobble all over the place. Mother only ever asked her to make cushions and things out of a sense of neighbourliness . . . '

She paused to study Magnus's face. 'You are listening, I hope? You seem a million miles away. People have been saying things about your father; that he and Lady Pandora had some sort of row which he took out on Anna. That wouldn't surprise me in the least. Old Iron Rod always was a beast to her. I do hope she'll manage to come to tea on Saturday, I couldn't bear it if Anna wasn't there. Those simpering ladies of Mother's do nothing but gossip and stuff their faces with Fat Jane's cakes and they smell of mothballs – amongst other things.' Pausing for breath she looked at Magnus questioningly. 'What exactly is wrong with Anna anyway? No one has seen her for ages and I want to tell her about my dress. Och, never mind, I can see you don't want to talk about it. Oh, I am looking forward to this dance, Magnus. Things have been so dull lately with Miss Prim Pym being at her boring best, Mother going all funny with this change business, and Father locking himself in his study to get a bit of peace. I know it's just the village hall here in Munkirk, not a real ballroom like they have in Torquay, but these little dances can quite often be such fun . . . '

'I'm sorry, Beth, I'm not going. I never really wanted to and now my mind's made up.' As he spoke, Magnus pulled his arm away to look steadily into Beth's eyes which had grown round with shock.

'Not going! Whatever do you mean, Magnus McIntyre? Not going? After Mother taking all the trouble to have a new dress made . . . '

'Och, c'mon, Beth! Your mother buys dresses for you every other week, new clothes are no novelty for a girl like you. You dress like a princess just to go shopping. Just look at you now. Anyone would think you'd just stepped out o' a fashion magazine.'

He was right. She made an attractive picture in a coat of bronze velvet edged with honey-coloured fur. She was wearing a hat of the same colour, decorated with brownish-pink curled plumes. It sat very prettily on her elegant coiffure and he thought to himself that she had the makings of a beauty.

But her mouth was too down-turned, the tiny lines at the corners were set for life; her large, pale-blue eyes were restless and critical; her expression a combination of petulance and haughtiness. She fully believed that she could and should get anything she wanted, no matter whom she hurt in the process. The selfishness had been born in her,

76

though her mother's indulgence of her had undoubtedly contributed to such notions of superiority.

Magnus felt strangely sorry for Beth as she stood there, mouth quivering, eyes swimming with tears of frustrated rage.

'I'm sorry, Beth,' he told her quietly, reaching out to touch her arm.

But she shook him off and angrily stamped one expensively shod foot on a patch of the Reverend Simpson's best hyacinth. 'Sorry! Sorry!' she cried, her voice rising to a pitch of hysteria. 'How dare you make fickle remarks to me, Magnus McIntyre! You promised you'd take me to that silly little dance and I hope you have a very good reason for refusing to do so.'

Magnus did have a good reason, several in fact, but none that Beth would understand. How could he tell her about Anna? Forbidden to go outside till the purple bruises on her face had disappeared. The least he could do was stay by her side till she was strong enough to face the world again. The other reason, perhaps the greatest of all, was his decision not to become attached to any girl till he found out more about his future.

'You'll find someone else, Beth,' he said soothingly. 'You're a very attractive girl and should have no bother. You said yourself that Jim Heatherington was keen to take you.'

Beth struggled to control herself. Furiously she chewed her lip and took a deep breath. But it was no use. Disappointment swamped her. She had wanted Magnus to take her to the Munkirk dance. It had been a triumph for her when he had succumbed to her persuasions. Now this. It was too much! Much too much!

'Elizabeth!' her mother's voice floated imperiously. 'Come inside this minute. It is not seemly for a young lady to talk to men in public!'

Beth gazed at Magnus standing tall and straight before her. He wasn't strikingly handsome yet there was something about him, a strength of character, a depth of spirit in his hazel eyes that was like a lamp shining in the darkness. Long ago, when she had still been a child, he had been an Adonis to her, a feeling that had grown stronger with the passing years.

He looked tired, she thought; there was a loneliness about him that made her want to reach out to embrace him . . . but he could never be hers . . . she had always known that. She was destined for better things while he . . . he would always be just Magnus McIntyre, a farm labourer, no ambitions, no wealth. And he had hurt her, he had hurt her very badly indeed . . .

'Oh, I'll get someone else alright, Magnus,' she said bitterly. 'I can have my pick of young men, sons of the gentry – but they bore me, Magnus, they are dull and they bore me very much. I'll make use of them while I may, however, though in the end I'll come back to the McIntyres. Even if it's years from now, and I'm married to someone like Lucas Noble, I'll come back to the McIntyres, you can be sure of that.'

She paused, a strange expression in her eyes. 'I know why you won't come, it's Anna isn't it?' She went on softly, 'You've always preferred her to me. You know, you behave as if you are more than brother and sister . . . '

Turning abruptly, she walked very tall to the door of The Manse, leaving a trail of crushed hyacinths in her wake. Magnus stood watching her go, a deep unease in him as he thought about that parting shot of hers. 'You know, you behave as if you are more than brother and sister.'

In some strange way he knew she was right. He had always had strong feelings for his sister, sometimes so strong they threatened to overwhelm him. Beth was a clever lass, no doubt about that, but surely she was making too much of it?

These thoughts pursued Magnus as he went to the gate. Shaking his head angrily, he tried to focus his thoughts on Beth, not dear Anna . . .

He had always sensed the ruthlessness in her, her ability to hurt whom she pleased if it meant getting her own way. Beth passed her time to suit her own whims. She would have liked to pass it with him, despite the fact that she had set her cap at Lucas Noble.

Lucas Noble. Anything but deadly dull, with his arrogant good looks and his passionate desires. Beth would have her work cut out ensnaring that one. But she was wily, and she was determined, and she knew how to use her feminine wiles to their full advantage – and if gossip was anything to go by she had already used them on Lucas in an effort to gain a foothold in The House of Noble.

Magnus opened the gate.

Before it had clicked shut behind him he knew that Beth would one day get her way with Lucas. He might fight tooth and claw to resist her but somehow, sometime, he would be caught, like an animal in a trap . . .

Magnus looked at the blue sky and took a deep breath, feeling very, very glad that he had escaped Beth's clutches. He had enough to occupy him without his emotions being further involved and he went on his way without a backward glance.

'Elizabeth, come away from that window at once,' Mrs Jordan sharply told her daughter. 'Isn't it enough that you've just frittered away your time with that young man without staring after him in that unashamed manner?'

Beth took a last, lingering look through the window. Magnus had stopped at the gate. Surely, oh surely he would turn and look back, so that she could at least have the satisfaction of knowing that he was thinking about her. But no, he went on, through the gate and along the street, never pausing once, doing nothing at all to indicate that she occupied any of his thoughts.

Flouncing over to the couch she dumped herself down beside her mother to put her chin into her hands and glare belligerently into space.

'Really, Elizabeth, you mustn't scowl like that,' scolded Mrs Jordan. 'You'll get lines on your forehead if you go on in such a manner. You're a young lady now and must stop behaving so childishly where young men are concerned, especially with those who don't merit your attentions.'

'You will take tea?' Rachael Simpson boomed as she entered the room to receive the visitors. She always spoke in a loud voice whenever she had to have dealings with the Jordan women, perhaps as a defence mechanism against two people who could not only talk the hind legs off a donkey, but the eldest could bray like one as well!

When something struck Mrs Jordan as funny, notably her own critical remarks, she would throw back her head and give full throttle to her magnificent lungs. Beth had not yet achieved this feat but she would, one day she would, Mrs Simpson was quite convinced of that.

'Forgive me for taking so long to make an appearance,' she went on. 'I was just supervising Jean with this evening's dinner. Mr Simpson likes his meat medium to rare and Jean will overcook it if I forget to instruct her to the contrary.'

Jean came in with the tea, not quite so smilingly as she had done with Magnus, mainly because she was busy now with other duties and didn't consider a visit from the Jordan women ample enough cause for interruption in her work schedule.

Clattering the tray down on the table she made a cursory bob, threw Beth a look that said, 'It's alright for the likes of you,' and haughtily departed the room.

'Really!' trumpeted Mrs Jordan, 'girls these days! Next thing they'll be aping their betters, if we're not careful to keep them in their place!'

Mr Simpson appeared, somewhat red about the ears after a brisk verbal exchange with his wife who would, on no account, allow him to enter the parlour without first changing his trousers and combing his hair.

'Mrs Jordan,' he extended his hand in greeting. 'How

nice to see you. Do carry on with your tea, I'm afraid I was – er – otherwise engaged when you stopped by.'

Mrs Jordan took a dainty sip of tea, her pinkie finger held stiffly erect. 'I know, the McIntyre boy,' she said with a conspiratorial nod. 'Nothing wrong there, I hope? Though, mind you, is there ever anything else but trouble in that household? Mr McIntyre now, really a very strange man when all is said and done. Outwardly a stalwart and trustworthy person but one hears things you know, whispers of cruelty and degradation. And his wife, insane beyond help. One wonders if all the family are similarly inclined.'

'No, it wasn't Magnus who kept me back,' Mr Simpson said hastily, wanting at that moment to throttle Victoria Jordan with his own bare hands. 'It was other matters, other matters entirely . . .'

His wife saw that he was having a job fighting down his anger, an emotion that was unusual for him as he was a placid man as a rule. 'Do try one of my scones,' she said quickly, thrusting the plate at her visitors, 'I made them myself, not more than an hour ago.'

'Really?' Tentatively Mrs Jordan accepted a scone, pausing with it in her hand to turn it this way and that, as if she was examining it under a microscope. Her large lips enclosed it, she nibbled off a minute portion.

'Mm, yes, quite good, Mrs Simpson. Of course, Mrs Higgins never overdoes it with the baking powder, and her glaze is never quite so sweet, while this is just a weeny bit on the sickly side, if you understand my meaning. Otherwise, fine, yes, I think it passes muster, my dear.'

It was the turn of the minister's wife to grow red in the face, a fact that did not go unnoticed by her husband who, recognising the danger of criticizing her culinary abilities, hastily intervened.

'Yes, well, I don't want to rush you, Mrs Jordan, but I am naturally wondering what brings you here today. No doubt it must be important, otherwise I know you would have waited till Sunday to speak to me.'

Mrs Jordan shifted in her seat, grimacing pointedly as an errant spring penetrated the padding of her corsets. 'Indeed it is important, Mr Simpson. It's about the arrangement of the church flowers. Mrs Patterson is all very well but I would be lying if I said she approached her duties in any sort of artistic fashion. A farmer's wife and all that, hardly the sort to know anything much about the finer things. As you know, I regularly give flowers to the church and it pains me to see them stuck higgledy-piggledy any-old-how into a vase. So I was wondering, could you have a word with her about it?'

'Ah, yes, of course, the kirk flowers.' Mr Simpson's tone was distinctly lacking in enthusiasm, while Beth, who had until that point been enjoying the exchanges over the scones, gave vent to an audible yawn, wishing that she could make her escape from the minister's stuffy parlour. 'Elizabeth!' rebuked Mrs Jordan acidly. 'How often have I told you! It is rude to yawn in company. You know, I'll really have to talk to Miss Pym about this. What on earth is she doing with you these days? Your father doesn't pay her a good salary for her to just sit back on her laurels. Etiquette, Elizabeth, I instructed her to teach you etiquette and here you are, gaping at young men in the street and yawning your head off like any common urchin!'

'Och, Mother!' Beth had had enough scoldings for one day and manners or no, she was going to have her say. 'Haven't I told you already? Miss Prim Pym couldn't teach etiquette to a pig! I doubt if she would even know how to spell the word. Besides all that, she didn't even know which spoon to use when she first came to us. I saw her, watching me to see which one I would pick up first, so when all's said and done, it was *me* who taught her the little niceties of life!'

'Elizabeth!' Mrs Jordan was so shocked by her daughter's rudeness she choked on a crumb of Rachael Simpson's scone, an action that she abhorred so much in anyone else that the disciples of her 'Saturday Ladies Social Club', as Beth called them, had to force themselves to peck at Fat

Jane's delicious cakes, since to gobble and subsequently choke would bring untold shame upon them.

Beth rushed to pummel her mother's back, saying as she did so, 'Really, Mother, you shouldn't bolt your food like that, especially after telling me to mind my manners.'

At this, Mrs Jordan became so red in the face that Mr Simpson opened the door to yell down the passage for Jean to bring some water. A few minutes later Jean came puffing in, greatly put about by this further intrusion into her routine.

'Where would you like the water, sir?' she asked, ignoring Mrs Jordan and addressing herself to the minister. 'I was sure I brought plenty wi' the tea.'

'Not *hot* water, Jean,' said Mrs Simpson, eyeing the steaming jug in Jean's hands. 'Cold water – in a glass – for Mrs Jordan. Oh, never mind, I'll get it myself before the poor woman chokes herself to death.'

Some time later, when peace was restored and Mrs Victoria Jordan was sitting back on the sofa, a bit watery-eyed but otherwise recovered, Mr Simpson said in a somewhat troubled manner, 'Forgive me for once more bringing up the subject, Beth, but this teacher of yours, Miss Pym . . . unsure of which spoon to use? But surely – isn't she a minister's daughter?'

Mrs Simpson let out a snort of laughter, and looked at her husband, his eyes were twinkling. She gazed at Beth, whose hand went to her mouth to stifle a fit of the giggles. All three looked at one another and erupted into uproarious mirth.

Mrs Jordan stared at them all. Really! What was the world coming to? For Beth there was an excuse, she was young and had much to learn. But a man of the cloth, conducting himself in such a manner! And his wife not much better! Wait till she told her Sunday ladies about this. They wouldn't like it. They wouldn't like it one bit!

* * *

At the door, Mrs Simpson took Beth's hand. She had often felt a sympathy for the girl, being told not to do this, to learn how to do that. No wonder she was rebellious and had to defend herself somehow against a mother like Mrs Victoria Jordan.

'I truly enjoyed your visit, Beth,' Mrs Simpson said warmly. 'Like myself you have a sense of humour, even though it's occasionally misplaced. Don't hesitate to come and see me whenever you feel the need. Our door is always open.'

Beth's view of Mrs Simpson had changed during the course of that afternoon. Hitherto, she had regarded the minister's wife as a person of little significance. Now, she saw that the lady in question had other facets to her nature and Beth felt as if she had made a friend, someone who would be there to give advice and help if ever the need arose.

'And another thing,' Mrs Simpson went on. 'I've heard that Lucas Noble will be home sometime soon. Why don't you both come to visit, you'd be most welcome.'

The idea of bringing Lucas to The Manse had never occurred to Beth, nor did it particularly appeal to her. She had other plans for Lucas but she was grateful to Mrs Simpson for mentioning his name in connection with hers. It took away the sting of Magnus's refusal to take her to the dance and made her feel another step closer to Lucas Noble of Noble House.

'Elizabeth, are you coming?' Mrs Jordan's voice rent the air.

Beth held out her hand to the minister's wife. 'Thank you, Mrs Simpson, I'll keep that in mind. I enjoyed myself today, too, especially when Mother choked.'

With a mischievous grin she went to join her mother at the gate, a spring in her step, a sprite in her eye as she turned to wave to a smiling Mrs Simpson standing within the sturdy portals of The Manse.

* * *

84

'You should have gone to the dance with her, Magnus,' Anna told him, when he returned from The Manse. 'I hate the idea o' you staying here because o' me.'

Tenderly, he stroked the vicious purple marks on her face. 'Wheesht, Anna, I never really wanted to go in the first place. I won't leave you, now or ever, *he* won't hurt you again, not as long as I'm here to look after you.'

His hazel eyes were dark with feeling, his nearness made her feel breathless and strange. It was the sort of emotion that one might experience with a lover and for the umpteenth time she asked herself why she should be affected this way by her own brother. She didn't know, she wondered if she ever would.

Magnus had said the answers to everything lay in the past. Perhaps one day they would find out what it all meant, meantime they would both have to try and be content with what they had together.

But it was becoming harder, every moment, every day, brought new challenges for them both. Anna wanted to be near him – yet she knew she had to distance herself from him . . .

Gently she took his hand away from her face. 'I know you'll look after me, Magnus, but I still have to fight my own battles. There are so many, all o' them pulling me this way and that. Despite his tyranny, Father is sometimes the least o' my problems.'

Magnus knew what she meant. He moved away from her and went quickly outside.

CHAPTER 9

Manoeuvres

The Saturday Ladies Social Club, as Beth had titled it, was in full swing. The hum of voices vibrated through the sitting room of Corran House, the Jordan residence, the air fairly rang with the clatter of teacups not to mention the tinkle of glasses as the ladies partook of their favourite afternoon tipple of Mrs Victoria Jordan's second-best sherry.

Not that the ladies had any inkling that it was second best, each one being of the firm belief that she was among the favoured few of Victoria Jordan's circle.

But the real élite, in that lady's book, were the more exclusive friends she reserved for Sabbath afternoons: middle-class social climbers who ostensibly presented themselves as pillars of the church and of the community, even though they would have stabbed one another in the back if it meant gaining an extra foothold on the rung to the top.

The Saturday ladies knew, of course, about the Sunday gatherings but were naive enough to think that their hostess was merely doing her utmost to fit everybody into her schedule and had, perforce, to spread the numbers over two consecutive days.

Mrs Jordan was a creature much taken to whims. Occasionally she took it into her head to demote a Sunday lady to her Saturday coterie or to promote a Saturday lady to her Sabbath meetings. Either way, the new arrangement came as something of a shock to the people concerned: a hitherto pampered middle class snob, insulted beyond measure by demotion, soon deserted the scene to seek more favourable company elsewhere.

Not so the jumped-up Saturday lady. She had arrived, she had joined *the* club, the Victoria Jordan Sunday Club, as Beth had, again, aptly named it. Here the genuine crystal glasses chinked, filled with the very best sherry served from cut-glass decanters that sat decorously on polished silver trays.

Here the ladies didn't gossip, they talked, intelligently and meaningfully, or discussed important issues; they never gulped whilst drinking liquid of any sort, sipping was the order of the day, especially when partaking of tea – during this procedure the pinkie had to be held stiffly erect and the upper lip suspended well over the rim of the cup to ensure that the contents passed quietly down the throat; passing wind from the nether region was unheard of, as was slurping, burping, and gobbling, even if Fat Jane's delicious cakes and dainty sandwiches made one want to bolt them down as speedily as possible.

The Sunday ladies never truly relaxed in their seats, rather they sat on the edge, very upright, very dignified. The conversation was prim to the point of it being prudish, the topics ranging from those of a hallowed nature to what Mrs So-and-So had said to Lady Such-and-Such and how thrilling it was that dear little Prudence had been invited to the Hunt Ball at Something-Something House.

The initiation of a Saturday lady into this austere scene was often intimidating to say the least and proved that Mrs Victoria Jordan had become an expert in cultivating those who would prove to be of most use to her.

She was not a wealthy woman, although she would, one day, benefit from the demise of her modestly affluent parents. Until then she simply gave the impression that she was a woman of prosperity in her own right. So success-fully had she pulled the wool over everyone's eyes she had even convinced herself that she was everything she made herself out to be and it always came as something of a shock to her when her husband confronted her with yet another pile of bills waiting to be paid.

From an early age Beth had been expected to attend both the Saturday and the Sunday gatherings, each of which bored her excessively and would have been intolerable if it hadn't been for the presence of Anna.

Anna had always been Beth's saving grace, right from the time they had been children together.

Anna had been open and generous with just about everything she had to offer; she had fed Beth's vanity with her compliments; she had never stinted her affection and admiration; she had given freely of her time whenever and wherever she could. Though Beth had taken care never to let her friend see how valuable she was, she knew in her heart that life in Glen Tarsa without Anna would be very dull indeed.

Just as it was today! Anna incarcerated indoors because of the things her father had done to her. Only rumours of course but Beth knew well enough by now that gossip about Roderick usually turned out to be true.

She had tried to see Anna, not by going directly to The Gatehouse, that would have been unthinkable with old Iron Rod about, but she had sent a note via Adam, making an arrangement for herself and Anna to meet at the Overhanging Rocks above The Cauldron.

Anna hadn't appeared at the appointed time. Magnus had come in her place, saying that his sister wasn't yet well enough to be outdoors but that she sent her love and would see her friend as soon as she was able.

Beth had been cool with Magnus, letting him see that she wasn't at all pleased at the way he had treated her over the dance.

He had stood beside her, tall and straight, and for a moment her heart had melted. She had wanted to touch him, to tell him how much she admired and wanted him,

88

but she hadn't done any of those things. She had flounced away instead, all the while wishing that she wasn't such a victim of her own stubborn nature, telling herself that all she needed to do to make him change his mind about the dance was to run back and throw her arms about him

She hadn't of course, she was Beth Jordan after all and it was up to him to make amends with her. He wouldn't, though. It was Anna he wanted to be with. Strange for a brother and sister to behave as they did towards one another – one never happy without the other . . . Beth had gone on her way, a frown of puzzlement on her brow.

Now it was Saturday, the dance was taking place in Munkirk village hall that night, and she had no one to take her, no one that she wanted anyway. Her mother had rhymed off the names of a dozen 'suitable young men' but Beth had discounted them all as being 'too dull for words'.

She sat on the window seat, gazing across at The Gatehouse, trying not to listen to the buzz and chatter in the room. A sigh escaped her. She wished that Magnus would appear from his house and see her and perhaps change his mind at the last minute, she wished that Anna were here . . .

'Elizabeth!' her mother's loud voice broke rudely into her musings. 'Stop dreaming and pass round the cakes.'

The supreme moment had arrived, the one that everyone had been waiting for. The ladies stopped talking, all eyes were on the cake stand containing the delicacies that Fat Jane had laboured all of yesterday to produce.

With another gusty sigh Beth rose to her feet. Grabbing two laden plates she pushed them under the twitching nostrils of Miss Fanny McWhirter who was looking resplendent in her summer frock of blue silk, decorated with sprigs of red and yellow rosebuds.

Fanny McWhirter's fingers hovered. 'Now, which shall

I have?' she pondered, as if her decision was of earth-shattering importance. 'Should it be just a teeny-weeny fairy cake? Or an empire biscuit? Or . . . '

Moments passed, laden with suspense, as her fingers fluttered indecisively above the plate. 'I wonder, those cream éclairs look delicious but one has to be careful of one's figure . . . '

'Why not have all three?' Beth suggested acidly. 'It won't make all that much difference.'

Fanny McWhirter looked up at Beth with reproachful eyes. 'Really, my dear child, you do say the oddest things sometimes . . . ' Her gaze was drawn back to the plate, her thickly painted lips parted. 'Och, why not? It's only once a week after all . . . '

She had made her choice, she homed in on the éclair, bit into it with gusto, and cream oozed profusely from her lips. Miss McWhirter threw etiquette to the wind, her tongue came out to mop up the delicious mess, far better than a hanky any day, she daringly decided, glancing quickly round the room to see if anybody had noticed her lapse from grace.

But everyone was too taken with watching the progress of the plates around the room to pay much attention to Fanny McWhirter.

Only Miss Primrose Pym, Beth's home tuition teacher, seemed disinterested in Fat Jane's baking. From the start, Beth had called her Miss Prim Pym because of her habit of talking obsessively about her dead father, 'God rest him,' who had been a Church of Scotland minister.

Miss Pym was braying away in a loud voice. When Mrs Jordan was present Miss Pym was inclined to talk louder and faster than usual and Beth often wondered if this was because she was trying to out-talk and out-smart the other woman.

Today Miss Pym wasn't talking about her father. She was discussing Michael Dick, the man who taught Lady Pandora's protégés.

And Miss Pym's eyes were shining as she went on about Michael Dick: how upstanding and decent he was, how good was his character, how exemplary his teaching, such a fine example to the boys even, though they didn't always seem to appreciate the fact.

Beth stared at her teacher. Miss Pym had buck teeth, wiry hair tied back in a bun, blotched skin, and a stubby figure. It had always infuriated Beth that she had never managed to discover Miss Pym's age but to amuse herself she had put her down as anything between thirty-five and fifty.

Beth was possessed of an active imagination but never, never, in her wildest fancies, had she associated her teacher with a man – of any sort – except, perhaps, her late, lamented father.

Now, here she was, blabbing on about Michael Dick, someone who, in Beth's opinion, was so busily engaged in thinking about himself, he couldn't possibly be interested in anyone outside his own domain, especially a woman as lacking in physical attractions as was Miss Pym.

For a moment Beth could think of nothing to say, but when she found her tongue it was to utter in a voice filled with astonishment, 'I didn't know you knew Mr Dick, Miss Pym.'

'Really, Beth,' Miss Pym blushed to the roots of her mousy hair, 'it never ceases to amaze me that you think you should know everything about everyone. For your information, my acquaintance with Mr Dick is purely on the grounds of our mutual interest in teaching.'

'Really?' Beth placed a heavy intonation on the word, she grinned, Miss Pym squirmed, and hastily left the room on a flimsy pretext.

Beth moved onto the next would-be recipient of Fat Jane's cakes, namely Mrs Euphemia Smythe, who had married a rich man and who was now a rich widow. She had changed her name from Smith to Smythe because a knowing friend had told it not only sounded better but also looked more dignified when written down.

Beth knew that her mother was only using Mrs Smythe as never, never, in the normal way of things, would she have considered entertaining a woman possessed of such an obviously robust and frank character.

To Beth, Mrs Smythe was like a breath of fresh air, she was warm and friendly, charming and disarming, all of which qualities appealed to Beth and made her hope that such a woman wouldn't end up being hurt and disillusioned by the falseness and snobbery she would undoubtedly encounter when she eventually landed up in The Victoria Jordan Sunday Club.

'Have an éclair, Mrs Smythe,' Beth invited, holding the plate temptingly close to that lady's nose. Not that Mrs Smythe needed either coaxing or tempting. Without any hesitation whatsoever, her plump fingers, encircled with precious gems of all sorts, pounced on the juiciest morsel on the plate.

'Don't go away just yet, Beth,' she instructed, through a mouthful of scone and blackcurrant jam all mixed up with feather fluff. 'I've been wanting to ask you if you would like to come along to Deerfield House to try out the horses.' Her eyelid came down in an unmistakable wink. 'You don't have to, of course, could never stand all that riding nonsense myself, or rather . . . ' Her stomach began gently to wobble, ' . . . the poor brutes could never stand me – my weight, I mean . . . '

At this, she went off into shrieks of merriment while Beth stood there with the plates, chuckling at the sight of Mrs Smythe rolling about in her seat like a jelly while the other ladies squinted disapprovingly down their noses at such rude enjoyment.

It took Mrs Smythe several moments to regain her breath, but when she did she beamed at Beth and went on in a quiet voice, 'About the horses, dear, I know that's why I'm here, why your mother asked me, I'm hardly the type for this sort of thing . . . ' She glanced round at all the prim faces, ' . . . am I now?'

The import of her conversation struck Beth like a thunderbolt. Mrs Euphemia Smythe *KNEW*, she had seen through her hostess's motives! And, if her attitude was anything to judge by, she was enjoying the whole thing enormously.

There and then Beth realised that there was undoubtedly more to the lady than met the eye. Underneath all the jollity there lurked a very shrewd and discerning woman and Beth positively glowed at the idea of her mother being beaten at her own little game.

'Don't worry about it, Beth,' Mrs Smythe went on with a smile. 'I'm not here for the good of my health . . . only for Mrs Higgins's baking. Good cooks are hard to come by and she's got a reputation as being one of the best. If I can bag her for myself then all of this will have been worthwhile.'

Beth stared. 'You're not thinking of taking Fat Jane away, I hope? She's like one of the family.'

'Fat Jane!' Mrs Smythe went off into fresh gales of laughter. Wiping her eyes she looked at Beth and shook her head. 'A lass after my own heart. Fat Jane indeed! We'd get on well, you and me, and I mean it when I say you can come and try out the horses. If that doesn't suit you can come and keep me company instead. The house could be doing with some young blood.'

In her enthusiasm her voice was rising, and in the next breath she said loudly, 'Bring that young rogue, Lucas, with you. I believe he came home last night. In fact, I saw him passing by in a carriage this morning . . . ' She gazed keenly at Beth, ' . . . I was surprised you weren't in it with him till I saw he was accompanied by somebody else. Couldn't make her out all that well but she looked a real little lady.'

The room had gone suddenly silent; the chatter, the clatter, had ceased, and Beth found herself growing cold. Lucas home! Without a word to her! And he had someone else with him. Another girl! A real little lady, according to Mrs Smythe.

'Of course Elizabeth knew!' Mrs Jordan's loud voice rent the air but for once Beth was glad of her intervention. 'In fact, she's going along to Noble House to see Lucas right now . . . isn't that so, Beth?'

'That's so, Mother.' Beth picked up on the pretence and, glancing at the clock, she cried, 'Oh, is that the time? I'll have to rush, please excuse me everyone.'

At that William Jordan, who had been hiding in the corner, sprung to his feet with alacrity. 'And I said I'd go with you, Beth, I have to see Sir Malaroy on a business matter and what better than to kill two birds with one stone.'

His wife glowered at him, long and hard. She was well aware that he only tolerated these weekend affairs of hers for the sake of peace and quiet and was always ready to make his escape at the least possible excuse. He was a patient man but there was only so much that he could take and this afternoon, with the sun splitting the trees outside, he'd had just about enough.

Mrs Jordan could say nothing, not in front of her ladies, but the look she threw at him spoke volumes as he hurriedly left the room.

Beth was looking cool and attractive in her summer dress of pale green linen with a hat of the same colour shading her face. She felt good. Lucas was home, soon she would see him. They would have a wonderful time together, walking, talking . . . making love! Oh yes, definitely making love! From the start he hadn't been able to resist her.

They were two of a kind, he and she, fiery, insatiable . . . They would do all the things they both enjoyed so much . . . Her imagination ran away with her . . . Perhaps it wasn't too late to get him to take her to the dance tonight . . .

In his own way he was as impulsive as she was and hated to be tied down to convention. It didn't matter about the 'real little lady', as Mrs Smythe had called her. Beth knew that she could manipulate Lucas to her ways of thinking – she would soon sort out his lady friend!

Seizing her father's arm she gave a little skip of happiness as they walked along the sun-dappled road. He smiled at her. Despite her sulks and tantrums they had always got along well together and, in recent years, they had enjoyed a levity with one another that might have surprised Mrs Jordan if she had heard the sort of confidences they shared.

'God bless Mrs Smythe,' he said gleefully. 'She saved my bacon back there. I don't think I could have stood another moment cooped up in that stuffy room with the smells of camphor and lavender making my head reel.'

Beth laughed. 'Among other things! As for Mrs Smythe, she's not as artless as she seems. I think she's found Mother out! From the way she spoke I gathered she's got her eye on Fat Jane and is only playing Mother along for her own ends.'

William Jordan turned a tragic face on his daughter. '*Eh!* Not our Mrs Higgins! She can't possibly take Mrs Higgins away from us!'

'She could if she really wanted, loyal as Fat Jane is. I don't suppose she would say no if she were offered a handsome rise in pay.'

Her father groaned. 'And I certainly can't up it at the moment! Your mother spends money as fast as I make it. But can you imagine life without Mrs Higgins? No more of that wonderful baking; no more pot roasts and pork joints dripping with mouth-watering juices; no more of those secret recipes that she got from her mother who got it from her mother before her. Some silly unimaginative girl or some dour stodgy woman in her place! What's more, your mother would drive us all crazy, interfering in the kitchen, whereas she doesn't dare poke her nose in on what Mrs Higgins considers to be her domain. It doesn't bear thinking about!'

'Och, don't worry, Father,' Beth said comfortably. 'I'll try and see that it doesn't happen. I think I can manage Mrs Effie Smythe all right – she's fat, she's friendly, and she's fun, and I like her a lot. She's asked me to visit her at Deerfield so I'll just pop along there every so often to keep her amused and make her see the error of her ways regarding Fat Jane.'

They had passed the village and were now approaching the foot of Noble House driveway. A rumble of cartwheels at their back made them step smartly onto the verge and Tell Tale Todd gave them a cheery wave and a nod before turning his horse's nose towards the big house.

Todd was late with his Saturday deliveries, having stopped for 'a breather' at Shoris Ferguson's house by the Rumbling Brig. The warm day had lured them outside to sit on kitchen chairs in the sun while they enjoyed their drams and now Todd was in a hurry to finish his rounds so that he could enjoy more 'breathers' in The Munkirk Inn that night.

'That man!' Beth said crossly, dusting down her dress. 'He'd be late for his own funeral if he thought he could stop for a gossip and a dram first!'

When they got to the house father and daughter went their separate ways, he going indoors to seek out Sir Malaroy, she making her way to the lawns at the back of the house, because she knew Lucas and was certain that he wouldn't want to be inside on a day like this.

She heard the voices and the laughter before she saw anyone, then they were there, playing croquet on the lawn: a small, fair nymph of a girl wearing a pale blue dress with a broad sash that emphasised her tiny waist, with Lucas bending over her, his hands clasping hers as he helped her guide the mallet.

Their heads were very close, their mouths almost touching as she turned and gazed into his face.

He glanced up suddenly and saw Beth, standing some way off, and raising his hand in greeting, he cried out her name and came running towards her. 'Beth!' he said again, his dark eyes filling with that mocking laughter she knew so well, his full, sensual mouth quirking into a smile.

He eyed her up and down, obviously enjoying the sight of her curvaceous young figure, the glint of her sandy fair hair in the sun, the tremble of her wide, shapely mouth. A hungry mouth! That was how he saw it. Hungry for his kisses, drowning him in her passion, swallowing him up with fire and lust and desire! A tremor of longing shot through him. He wanted to feel that mouth on his, there and then he wanted to grab her and throw her down on the grass and just take her.

She wanted it too, she was trying very hard to be cool but he knew differently, she was excited at seeing him. It was all there, in the flush of her face, in the spark of her pale blue eyes.

'You look – good, Beth,' he said casually, 'I was wondering when you would appear. I thought you weren't speaking to me after that row we had the last time. Are you here to apologise?'

Beth's eyes glittered. He knew how to rile her all right. She was immediately on the defensive with him and wasn't slow to answer him back. 'No, Lucas Noble, I am not here to apologise. I'm here to give you the chance to do that!'

He grinned. 'For what? You taking a tantrum and smacking me on the face! By golly, you haven't changed one bit, have you? Still a little madam who expects everyone to come running at the snap of a finger. Well, you've picked the wrong one this time. I'm Lucas Noble – remember – and I don't kowtow to anyone, be they big or small or just plain nobodies.'

Her nostrils flared. 'You're a snob, Lucas Noble! Always were and always will be!'

'Me? A snob?' he released a spurt of laughter. 'What if I am? At least I admit it and don't go around pretending to be something I'm not.'

Beth, infuriated beyond measure, stamped her foot. 'Damn you, Lucas Noble! You're just trying to upset me! Is it because of her? Your little lady friend? Is this your way of trying to get rid of me?'

At that moment the 'little lady' came tripping daintily over to Lucas to wrap her arm possessively round his and say in a breathless, tinkly sort of voice, 'What's the matter, Lucas? You aren't having a row with this . . . ' Her deep blue eyes regarded Beth with amusement, ' . . . *visitor*, are you?'

The girl's hair shone like threads of gold in the sun, arranged round her head in tiny curls, tendrils of it hanging down in front of her small, white ears. Her mouth was rosy and round and petulant, her face was cameo-shaped, her features fine and delicate, her figure petite and child-like.

She was exquisite and Beth immediately hated her.

Lucas grinned, and introduced the girls to each other. 'Beth Jordan – Lady Yvonne Marchmont from Hampshire. I thought it would be a good idea to bring her up to Scotland to meet Aunt Dora and Uncle Malaroy. We're only here for a day or two and are planning to make the most of every minute.'

Beth positively bristled with rage, but somehow she managed to keep her composure, especially in front of the 'real little lady' who was watching her with barely concealed triumph. 'I see, how nice.' Beth's voice was brittle and cold. 'Don't let me keep you then, I must be off anyway, Father will be waiting.'

She turned and walked stiffly away, every fibre in her making her long to run from the scene as fast as she could. But she wouldn't. Not in front of that little upstart with her simpering voice and ridiculous clothes!

'Beth!' Lucas came running after her. Catching her by the arm, he spun her round to face him. 'No need to take off like that! It's – I've been looking forward to seeing you – really I have. Come and have a glass of lemonade. Yvonne won't bite, for all you know you might even get to like her. You might find you have things in common . . . '

'Me! Have anything in common with that – that horrible little prude!' Beth hissed. 'Oh, you can laugh, but I know just by looking at her she's got ice in her veins! She – she

98

probably wears a chastity belt and has thrown away the key! Enjoy yourself with that, Lucas Noble – if you can. I might be a snob but at least – I'm – I'm a human snob!'

With that she threw him off and walked away, her head held high while he watched her go, not knowing whether to laugh or run after her. But he decided against the latter. Let her go! She was too hot for him to handle! That temper! Her rudeness! Her assumption that he should be there for her whenever she wanted him . . . His eyes darkened . . . he remembered things about her, that sparkle, the way her eyes lit up when they met, her passion and eagerness for life! Pursing his lips in regret he turned and walked back slowly to his 'real little lady'.

Tell Tale Todd had taken his delivery van round to the tradesman's entrance at the back of the big house. Despite his anxiety to be on his way he had time to pause for a while to observe the activities of the three young people on the croquet lawn.

It looked as if Master Lucas was having some sort of a row with Beth Jordan while the girl with the golden hair stood by, watching.

'A proper little lady that one,' Mary came out to join Todd, sniffing disdainfully as she spoke. 'Lady Yvonne Marchmont from England, a real madam if ever there was one. She's got the whole household running to her bidding. Do this, do that, come here, go there, fetch this, bring that. Much as I've never liked Beth Jordan I prefer her to little Miss Bossy Boots any day o' the week.'

She and Todd stood side by side, watching everything avidly. When Beth stamped her foot and shouted at Lucas, Todd's eyes gleamed. When she stomped away in a rage Todd smirked to himself. Beth was in the huff about something and the lass with the golden hair was clinging to Master Lucas as if she owned him.

Beth wouldn't like that, she wouldn't like it one bit . . . Todd rubbed his chin thoughtfully. On his way home he might just stop at Janet McCrae's for a cup of tea and a blether . . .

Beth stormed past at that moment, looking neither to the right nor to the left of her. Her face was scarlet, and she was in a state of high dudgeon.

Mary and Todd looked at one another. There was always something going on at Noble House to make life interesting, and when Mary said, 'Beth's mother won't like it when she hears about this and serve her right too. She's always tried to make that daughter o' hers something she isn't,' Todd couldn't have agreed more.

A madness had seized Beth. Her mind was in turmoil. Damn Lucas Noble! She would show him that she didn't need him! Magnus too! She would show them all! By hook or by crook she was going to this dance tonight and she had decided who was going to take her!

Making an excuse to her father she left him to make his own way home while she flounced along the road to The Gatehouse. Boldly she rattled the knocker. To hell with old Iron Rod, she didn't care if he was in or not. It was Adam she had come to see and it was Adam who answered the door.

'Beth . . . ' he began but she didn't give him time to speak. Brushing past him she strode into the living room leaving him to follow behind.

Roderick was out, Magnus and Anna were in, both of them startled by the unexpected intrusion.

'Anna!' Beth went forward to take her friend in her arms. 'It's been ages! Oh, your poor face . . . ' She stared at the bruises on her friend's mouth and cheeks. 'I knew, of course, that dreadful old Iron Rod had been up to his old tricks but I never realised it would be this bad.'

Completely ignoring Magnus she turned her attention to Adam. Stretching out her hands to him in an exaggerated gesture she cried, 'Adam! The very person I wanted to see.'

Quickly she explained her reason for being there. When she had finished speaking an astonished Adam gaped at her for several moments before he stuttered, 'Ay, Beth, of course I'll take you to the dance. It's short notice, but I don't mind.'

Beth's eyes gleamed and she threw Magnus a sly, side-long glance. 'I knew I could rely on you, Adam. We'll have a wonderful time, you can be sure of that. I must rush, there's so much to do. Father will take us, we'll meet you at the foot of the drive at half past eight.'

She swept out, as breezily as she had entered. With a whoop of excitement a jubilant Adam rushed through to his room to look out the clothes he would be needing that evening.

CHAPTER 10

A Lesson

On Sunday, Lady Pandora was seated on one of the hard wooden pews at the back of tiny Corran Kirk, her eyes eagerly raking the congregation for a sign of Anna.

In the normal way of things, Lady Pandora and her family attended the High Kirk in the coastal resort of Dunmor, several miles distant, but today she had opted for the little Church of Scotland with its one-and-only stained-glass window and its air of timeless reverence.

With her she had brought Ralph and Robert though the former had objected strongly to this, saying that he preferred to go with Sir Malaroy and Lucas to the High Kirk in Dunmor.

'Don't be silly, Ralph,' she had chided. 'You've always said you didn't like the High Kirk so this is your chance to see what a real country church looks like.'

'I don't like any churches, Aunt Dora,' he had growled sullenly. 'They smell dusty and the people look like cardboard cut-outs on a stage, all stiff and serious, as if they weren't real but were acting out a part. They don't look like that on other days of the week. Besides all that, they smell of camphor and mint and some of them have sweaty feet – or sweaty somethings.'

'Sure, and I'll say Amen to all o' that, Ralphie, me lad,' Robert had put in with a devilish grin. 'But you forgot to mention the black clothes and the look o' mourning they have about them, not forgetting the ladies in their hats with pins and feathers in them that either stab or tickle you to death, depending on how close you get. Then, of course, there's the question o' wind. Last week I heard old Mr Thomson letting go, right there in his seat, as loud and as potent as any one of O'Flaherty's pigs. He was fly, mind you, waiting till Mrs Campbell struck up the organ before having his say.'

'And what about the snoring and grunting during the service itself?' Ralph had gone on, his eyes beginning to sparkle. 'Folk making up for having to rise at the crack of dawn; the little puffs and snorts, the gentle nudges which make them pay rigid attention till the eyelids start dropping again . . .'

'Boys, that's quite enough,' Lady Pandora had scolded, though her own eyes had been twinkling at their youthful observations.

And really, how right they were, she thought as she sat in Corran Kirk, scanning the rows of heads in front: heads that were held rigidly to attention; black-clad shoulders that were stiff with righteousness; the smells of camphor and mint mingling together; the plumes in the women's hats waving about; the large, showy feather in Mrs Victoria Jordan's hat slicing through the air as she turned her head this way and that, observing everything in her critical fashion, craning her neck to peer sourly at the flowers that were displayed on either side of the pulpit.

Lady Pandora caught Robert's eye, he winked at her, and she hid a smile, but it was a smile that didn't touch her heart. She had seen that Anna wasn't in her usual place between her brothers at the front of the kirk, and the concern that Lady Pandora had previously experienced was nothing to the feeling of alarm that seized her now, a feeling that swelled within her till she felt her heart would burst with it.

Old Grace leaned towards her, her sweet, old face troubled under its mop of silvery hair which not even her best Sunday bonnet could constrain. 'You can look till your blind, my lady,' she murmured, 'but you'll no' see Anna Ban in kirk today.'

'Why, Grace, what's happened to her?'

'Ach, well, a body hears tell. They're saying that her father has hit her that sore, the poor lass is too marked to be allowed out the door. I'm thinking it must be the case, too. Anna is a regular visitor to my house and she's no' been near me for nigh on a week. Also . . . ' She leaned closer, ' . . . word was sent by one o' her brothers to Miss Priscilla at Knock Farm, a note that said she was ill and wouldn't be along for a whilie.'

'Oh, dear God, no,' Lady Pandora protested, her hand clenching so tightly on her Bible, the fingers turned white. She sat back in her seat to gaze at the pew occupied by Roderick McIntyre, her heart twisting with loathing at the sight of him sitting there, his shoulders hunched, his iron-grey head humbly bowed as the strains of the organ vibrated through the kirk, his whole attitude suggesting a total dedication to all things pertaining to Holy worship.

Lady Pandora's mind whirled as she tried to sort out her thoughts. A feeling of panic seized her, a tide of dizziness swept over her, she felt as if the walls of the church were closing in on her.

'Are you alright, my lady?' Old Grace asked, her voice sharp with concern. 'Your poor face is whiter than the snow. Would you no like to step outside for a breath o' air?'

'Grace.' Lady Pandora seized the old lady's hand. 'I wonder, do you think it would be unfitting if I were to go along to see Anna? Now. While everyone else is out of the house? Just for a few moments – just for a word or two . . . '

Grace's kind old eyes grew misty. 'Ach, my poor, poor lass, your heart is troubled, I know, but Anna has her pride and if she's marked like they say she is then a visit from you might only serve to embarrass her. Besides, that de'il o' a father o' hers would be bound to find out and it would just get her into more trouble.'

Lady Pandora searched hurriedly inside her muff for a hanky which she held to her eyes. 'You're right of course. Magnus told me the same thing but I chose not to listen to him. You and I have one thing in common, Grace, we both love Anna, though yours is a wiser heart than mine. Oh dear, I mustn't cry in church. I think I'll have to go outside for that breath of air after all. If I don't come back in, give my apologies to Mr Simpson, will you?'

Turning to the boys she instructed them to remain where they were till the end of the service then, rising, she made her way out of the church as quietly as she could. Even so, quite a few heads turned to watch her go. It wasn't every Sunday that the Corran Kirk was honoured by the presence of her ladyship and several faces registered disappointment at her departure.

'Maybe this wee place is no' good enough for her,' old Shoris whispered to Moira O'Brady, bathing her in whisky fumes in the process.

'It's certainly too good for the likes o' you,' Moira hissed back. 'Pickling yourself in alcohol before entering the house o' the Lord. You should be ashamed o' yourself, Shoris Ferguson.'

'Indeed, you are right there, Moira,' whispered Tell Tale Todd piously. 'A time and a place, that's what I say, a time and a place for everything.'

At that, Moira turned on him with a vengeance. 'Ay, well, it's time you practised what you preached, Todd Hunter. You smell no better than Shoris, despite what you say. Knowing you, you will no doubt have had whisky for your breakfast and a bit more besides. I'll make certain I don't sit next to either o' you in future.'

Her voice had risen, and there came a few 'tutting' and 'shushing' sounds from her immediate neighbours, but Mr Simpson ascended the pulpit stairs to begin his sermon, and the fidgeting and rustlings died away as his voice soared forth.

Roderick was well aware that Lady Pandora had slipped into the back of the church before the start of the service and had just as quietly made her exit a few minutes ago.

He smiled to himself with satisfaction. No need to guess who she was looking for! She was suffering alright, no doubt of that.

Give it time, that was all, just a little more time and she would come crawling . . .

Beside him, Adam gave a wide, unsuppressed yawn and Roderick poked him in the ribs. 'Enough o' that, my lad,' he warned, sotto voce. 'You must not yawn in the house o' the Lord. Your excesses o' last night mustn't interfere wi' God's worship.'

Adam hid a smile. Sanctimonious old sod! He had the cheek to speak to him about excesses when only last night he had surpassed himself by getting so drunk he had been unable to satisfy Nellie Jean's sexual appetites.

Adam had met her at midnight, flouncing out of The Gatehouse just as he was getting home from the dance at Munkirk.

She had been wild and dishevelled-looking, with her black hair mussed about her face and her clothes in disarray. At thirty-nine she was still a handsome woman, with her rounded curves and nipped-in waist, but her self-indulgences were gradually taking their toll – no amount of powder and rouge could conceal the haggard lines on her face.

'Well now, if it isn't young Adam,' she had greeted him with sarcasm. 'Spreading your little wings, I see. Well, I hope you can fly higher than your old man in there. He's past it already. A couple o' drams and he's wilting like a dying dandelion these days.'

Adam had smelt the drink on her breath and in the darkness his lip had curled contemptuously. He'd teach the silly bitch a lesson, show her that he was no longer the frightened boy who had once listened to her and his father lusting together in his mother's bed.

The fires of his own lust were burning within him that night. He had just left Beth after escorting her to the dance, an action that had caused quite a furore a couple of hours before the event.

106

Beth's mother, hardly able to believe that her daughter had passed over one McIntyre boy for another, had waxed eloquent on the subject. 'Really, Elizabeth,' she had stormed. 'I'm sure I don't know what's gotten into you these days! Adam McIntyre of all people! The boy has been a blight to this community ever since he and his family came here. What's wrong with James Heatherington, I'd like to know? And these other young men of decent standing? As well as all that, what happened between you and Lucas this afternoon? He mightn't like the idea of you gadding about enjoying yourself without him?'

'He's got somebody else, Mother,' Beth had said diffidently. 'And, no doubt, he's enjoying himself without me. Anyway, there's no firm understanding between us – not yet – so this silly little dance at Munkirk won't do either of us any harm. My time with Lucas will come or my name isn't Elizabeth Ellen Jordan – meantime, I'm going to let Adam McIntyre take me to this dance in spite of what you say – and that's all there is to it.'

It hadn't, however, been the end of the matter for Victoria Jordan. Seeing that argument was of little use where her daughter was concerned, she had resorted instead to a tight-lipped silence, one that did not dismay Beth in the least and worried her father even less.

Peace was a hard commodity to come by in a household ruled by women and he set out to make the most of it while it lasted, which wouldn't be very long – knowing his wife's capacity for letting her tongue wag non stop.

Adam, the subject of all the controversy, had also, at first, been puzzled by Beth's change of heart. She had asked him outright to escort her to the dance, being very sweet and charming about it, noticeably in front of Magnus, whom she had pointedly ignored.

Adam had quickly realised that she was just making use of him but he hadn't cared. He had always been drawn to Beth and here was his chance to get to know her better. Mary would be mad at him when she found out but he would soon wheedle her round to his way of thinking. She was soft on him, was Mary, and he could do practically anything and get away with it.

It had all been worth it. The evening had been a success, from beginning to end, even though Mrs Jordan had seen fit to chaperone her daughter personally, much to the amusement of everyone there.

Beth had had the devil in her that night. She had tormented both her mother and Adam by flirting with as many men as she could, infuriating their girlfriends in the process, teasing Adam to the limits. But Adam was able for her. Pretending not to notice he had danced with other girls, even buck-toothed Violet Patterson and tubby little Bunty Walters.

Beth hadn't liked that. During the break she had escaped her mother's eagle eye to confront him outside the hall.

He hadn't given her a chance to talk. Instead he had pulled her roughly into his arms to kiss her fiercely and fondle her breasts. At first she had struggled, but it had been a half-hearted attempt. Soon, she was responding to him passionately while the cool night air washed over them and the sea gurgled amongst the rocks on the shore.

She had been unusually quiet on the way home. Her father had collected them in his gig and they had sat together in the back, saying nothing, then her hand had crept into his and though the night was cold her flesh had been burning.

In those moments they both knew that, even if nothing else existed between them, their desire for one another was so overwhelming they wouldn't rest till it had been fulfilled.

When they parted Adam had been aching with frustration. The appearance of Nellie Jean had added fuel to his fires and she hadn't been prepared for him when he had lunged at her, pinning her against a wall, savagely crushing his mouth to hers.

108

The smell of her whisky-laden breath had revolted him yet still he had kept kissing her till she pushed him violently away and gasped, 'What the hell do you think you're playing at! You randy little runt!'

'*He* left you high and dry, didn't he, Mrs Anderson?' Adam taunted sneeringly. 'What's wrong? Aren't you up to some younger blood? Getting dried-up in your old age?'

He had picked the wrong person to laugh at. Nellie Jean was more than a match for him, as her next words proved. 'You know,' she had said softly, 'I think *all* of you McIntyres are just a wee bit mad. Be that as it may, I'm quite well able to deal with little boys with hot trousers. I am, however, past having a bit in the bushes with a little creepie-crawlie like you, trying to get into my bloomers. It's time you had your beauty sleep, laddie, your cradle will be getting cold.'

'Not as cold as your well-worn arse, Mrs Anderson,' he had hissed jeeringly. 'Ay, indeed, Father isn't the only one who is past it.'

Her burst of smothered laughter had surprised him, but not as much as her hand on his arm, steering him up the dark road to her house, he putting up a show of resistance because after all his swaggering, he couldn't let her see it had all been a bluff.

His experiences with Mary had led him to believe that he knew it all, but after that night with Nellie Jean he soon realised how wrong he'd been. She had thrown him on the bed and had all but undressed him, after which she had cavorted on top of him, teasing and tormenting him, bringing him to such an unbearable pitch of longing he had cried out for her to release him.

When she did it had been over for him in a few explosive moments, leaving him utterly drained, Nellie Jean kneeling above him, her big breasts flopping against his face, her delighted laughter ringing in his ears.

'There you are, my bonny wee boy,' she had hurled at him. 'Quite a change from wetting nappies, eh? Now . . .'

Disdainfully she had thrown his clothes at him, ' . . . Get dressed and go home to Daddy, and you'd better not be telling anyone that Nellie Jean made a wee man o' you or you'll be the laughing stock o' the nursery.'

At the door she had smiled at him mischievously. 'Next time – if you're lucky enough to have a next time wi' me – you'll maybe be able to do something to satisfy *me*. Meantime, go home, little boy, and dry your ears!'

CHAPTER 11

A Proposition

The recollection of that parting shot made Adam now squirm with embarrassment, even while a warmth invaded his belly. Now he knew why his father pursued Nellie Jean so persistently. She was a fiery bitch and no mistake!

He had imagined himself to be experienced for his age, thinking he'd had it all with Mary, now he knew what he was missing. He'd had a taste of the real thing and he'd certainly want more . . . He went into a muse as he wondered if he could teach Mary how to please him better – but she was so tame compared to Nellie Jean. Still, there was always Beth . . .

The minister's voice was droning on, but Adam didn't hear a word of what he was saying. He was too busy squinting across the aisle at Beth who was sitting beside her parents.

She was very upright and attentive looking, haughty, too, with her strong profile and curving eyebrows.

Adam knew that it was all just a façade. Underneath that cool exterior Beth's blood coursed hotly. Although she wasn't quite sixteen she had the desires of a grown woman – the same sort of desires that had flowed in him for years.

He even felt them with his sister Anna when he watched her undressing in the grey-dark of their room. She was always just a shadow, an enticing female shadow whose breasts he occasionally glimpsed when she was slipping into her nightdress.

He was sorry she wasn't in kirk. It wasn't the same without her. He liked walking home with her afterwards. She was so enthusiastic about everything; the things the minister had said; the people they had spoken to; the merits of the countryside; the wayside flowers.

He knew she wasn't a devoutly religious person. Ever since their mother had been 'taken away' her faith in God had diminished but she went to church anyway because she enjoyed meeting the folk of the glen and catching up on all the news.

This past week she hadn't left the house because of the bruises on her face. Their father had been careless. He used to leave them where they wouldn't show. No-one could point the finger then – at him! The bastard who ruled them all with a rod of iron and who kept on getting away with everything – maybe even murder!

Adam felt himself growing hot as that one terrible word beat inside his head. Murder! There had been whisperings in the glen about the deaths of Andrew Mallard and Peter Noble. Very few, it seemed, had been satisfied by the official verdict of accidental death. Andrew Mallard had been young and he had been tough, a man who was perfectly capable of looking after himself.

Furthermore, as the people hereabouts hadn't known him all that well, there had been no reason for anyone to dislike him – all except Roderick, who had hated the man for throwing him out of Noble House.

Mary had told Adam all about that. Roderick had been pestering Lady Pandora, Mallard had intervened, had sent Roderick packing with his tail between his legs. No-one did that to Roderick McIntyre and got away with it – no-one . . .

Adam felt himself sweating, supposing, just supposing he and his brother and sister were all living under the same roof as a murderer . . . !

He gulped and hastily tried to divert his thoughts into other channels and found himself thinking again of Anna, trapped in the house, like an animal, afraid to show her face because of *him* . . .

The service was at an end, the congregation drifting out into the sun-bathed glen. Mr Simpson was at the door, shaking each hand as it was proffered.

Mrs Jordan awaited her turn with barely concealed impatience. 'Mr Simpson,' she began, eventually jostling her way forcibly forward. 'About the flowers. I really don't see any improvement whatsoever in the altar arrangements. Perhaps you haven't had a word with Mrs Patterson yet? I was wondering . . . '

Behind her Mr Jordan raised his eyes heavenwards and prayed for patience, while his daughter smiled politely and pressed herself against Adam, who had managed to squeeze himself between her and fat old 'Gabby' McTavish of Broom Farm.

Adam responded to Beth's encouragement by daringly placing his hand on her buttock and rubbing hard.

'Really, Adam McIntyre,' Beth murmured softly, 'I'll have to pay you back for that, won't I? Tomorrow evening, the woodshed behind the quarry. Around nine. There's no one about at that time.'

Adam was so surprised by this that he didn't immediately grasp her meaning. When it sunk in, he gasped hoarsely, 'Right, Beth, I'll be there, you can bet on it.'

'Victoria.' Mr Jordan had come to the end of his patience. 'Mrs Higgins will have dinner ready. I'm sure you can speak to Mr Simpson about the flowers another time.'

The look of gratitude on the minister's face was intense, especially as he had spied Mrs Patterson's round, pleasant face hovering in the background. 'Yes indeed, I'll be glad to do that, Mrs Jordan, meantime, good day to you, so pleased you enjoyed the service.'

'Oh, but . . . ' Mrs Jordan opened her mouth to protest

but her husband ushered both her and his daughter firmly along the path and out of the gate.

Roderick, his duties as a church elder over with, was emerging from the dim interior of the building and almost collided with Ralph and Robert at the door.

The incident had a startling effect on Ralph: his face went deathly white and he backed away from the large, stocky figure of Roderick as if he was the devil personified.

'What is it, lad?' Roderick said affably. 'Got a bit o' a fright, eh? Well, run along now, mustn't keep her ladyship waiting.'

Ralph gladly scuttled away to where Lady Pandora was waiting in the gig but Robert held back to stare questioningly at Roderick, his blue, hypnotic stare unblinking, his whole attitude one of silent accusation.

Roderick felt uncomfortable under such intense scrutiny. For some reason, he didn't know why, he imagined that the boy could read the secrets of his mind and Roderick didn't like that, he didn't at all like it.

'Get along, lad,' he grunted brusquely. 'In case you don't know, it's rude to stare – has no-one ever seen fit to teach you some manners?'

Robert shifted his gaze – only to let it alight on Adam who had joined his father at the door.

Adam stared back in his cheeky way, then he remembered that scene with Mary in the kitchen in Noble House when Robert had caught him literally with his trousers down. Adam licked his lips, he squirmed like a two-year-old, caught in some naughty act. Irish fairy! he thought scornfully, I'll show him who's boss! He'd better learn not to glower at me if he knows what's good for him!

Adam said nothing, however, but backed off ever so slightly while Robert stood his ground, his unwavering glance going from Father to son for quite a few moments before he ran to join the other members of Noble House waiting for him in the gig.

The whip cracked, Neil Black, anxious to get home for his dinner, coaxed the horses to a brisk trot, and the gig was soon just a dot in the distance.

Roderick, oddly unnerved by his encounter with Robert, turned to his son and said, 'What was all that about, I'd like to know?'

Adam averted his eyes. 'Don't ask me, it was you he was looking at . . .'

'Mr McIntyre, a moment please.' The minister had shaken his last hand and was most anxious that Roderick shouldn't slip away before he got the chance to speak to him.

'Ay, Mr Simpson.'

'Perhaps we should go inside, we'll have more privacy there.'

A few minutes later, the minister was conferring earnestly with the under-manager of the powdermill. Roderick listened with apparent attentiveness, though every so often he raised his eyes to glare resentfully at Magnus who was watching proceedings from the door.

All through the minister's dialogue Roderick had nodded and smiled. Inwardly he was in turmoil. Questions poured into his head. How could he reject the minister's proposal? It would look bad, very bad indeed if he were to refuse the children a visit to their mother.

But personal matters were at stake here not to mention the dangers attached to such a concession. For years he had managed to keep his family away from the asylum. Why should he give in now? Just because Magnus had dared to seek outside help?

And Lillian. What of her? On his last visit she had raved at him and had seemed beyond caring about anything. Her memories of her family were as little children. She wouldn't know them as they were now, and when she didn't know people she became suspicious – and that was when she started her demented ramblings . . .

A satisfied smile touched Roderick's mouth, his

confidence returned . . . They wouldn't get any sense out of her. She wouldn't be able to tell them anything . . .

'Well, how kind o' you to make such an offer, minister,' he intoned heartily. 'Ay, Magnus must be feeling very anxious to have sought your advice the way he has. I have tried to protect him and the others from the realities attached to their mother's illness, but children grow up, they want to find out things for themselves.

'She won't remember any o' them, you know. That was one o' the reasons I never wanted them to visit – especially wee Anna. It's a big responsibility for you, Mr Simpson, but if you're prepared to take it on, far be it for me to try and stop you. Of course, you do understand there will be the devil to pay afterwards. When they see their mother as she is now it could have far-reaching effects on them. Who knows where it all might lead, but as you're a man o' God, I'm sure He will give you the strength to deal wi' each crisis which might come along. 'Tis just a pity I can't go with you, but duties – one has duties to attend to, Mr Simpson.'

The minister's keen eyes pierced Roderick's black gaze. 'Ay, we all have our duties, Mr McIntyre, though sometimes we don't get them into their proper order.'

'Quite, quite, but . . . ' Roderick spread his hands, ' . . . the daily bread, minister, someone has to earn that. As it is, Adam will be gone from the mill for two days and Magnus will have to take time off from the farm. Then there's Anna – a wonderful lass – she quite spoils me you know. With her away I'll have her tasks to see to – over and above my own very busy schedule as mill under-manager . . . '

'Will Thursday suit?' The minister's voice was rather cold.

'Thursday – ah – let me see.' Roderick thought of Anna's bruises. A bit more subdued than they had been. By Thursday they should have disappeared completely. He shouldn't have hit her so hard. It was damned inconvenient having to make excuses for her all the time. Everybody, it seemed, wanted to know what had happened to her. Why she hadn't been seen outside for so long. No-one seemed to accept it when he told them she was ill. Nosy buggers! As if it was any of their business! Especially that old bat from Knock Farm, Miss Frumpy McLeod. Sniffing around, looking at him as if he was dirt!

Still, some good had come out of it all. Lady Pandora for instance. All red-eyed and heartbroken because her little darling wasn't around to amuse her. Well, she could stew in her own juice for a while, it would do her good to be kept hanging. She would come round to his way of thinking in the end and then . . .

Unconsciously, he rubbed his big hands together in an anticipatory gesture and beamed at the minister. 'Thursday will suit perfectly, Mr Simpson. I'll pay for everything, of course, no question o' that. It's a fair journey to Kilkenzie and wi' prices these days . . . Last time I visited my wife I paid five shillings for the coach and steamer over to Inverdrum and another bob or two for the coach to Kilkenzie. On top of all that was the cost o' getting my head down for the night – robbers – all o' them.'

'You will not be out of pocket, Mr McIntyre. Magnus has already settled that matter with me. He is a young man of great character and enterprise,' Mr Simpson responded frostily.

'Ay, indeed, he and Adam are good boys.'

The minister glanced at Adam, who was idly scratching the polished wood of the pew he was sitting on, using a sixpence he had daringly filched from the collection plate. He nodded politely. 'Hmm, yes, I see, well, I will bid you good day, Mr McIntyre. Tell the children I will pick them up at the road end on Thursday morning around eight.'

The Reverend ushered them to the door, where he smiled at Magnus and placed a reassuring hand on his shoulder, then he strode off down the path, his silvery head shining in the sun. To Magnus, in those moments, it appeared as a saintly halo and silently he blessed Reverend Alastair Simpson for his light and his goodness.

CHAPTER 12

Nocturnal Affairs

As promised, Beth was waiting for Adam in the woodshed behind the quarry, pacing up and down impatiently because Adam was late and Beth did not like to be kept waiting – by anybody – far less Adam McIntyre of The Gatehouse who was, when all was said and done, just one of the mill workers and a rather lowly one to boot.

For fully fifteen minutes she fumed and fretted and was on the point of leaving when Adam finally made an appearance, all hot and bothered and breathing heavily.

'Sorry, Beth,' he apologised before she could speak. 'I had some chores to do before I could get away and – and then I ran all the way here without stopping . . . '

He couldn't tell Beth the real reason for his lateness – not now – not after what he had done to that stupid bitch, Silly Sally . . .

His pupils dilated as he remembered the scene with Sally, the eldest of the McDonald family. Sally was always frightening the village children by jumping out at them when they least expected it, the most realistic impressions of cows and cockerels issuing from her frothing lips.

Over the years Adam had certainly had his share of her attentions which hadn't lessened as he had grown older. In fact, Sally seemed to take a delight in singling him out, as if, somewhere in the mists of her simple mind, she knew that both he and his father had never been kind to her and her two brothers, Davie and Donal, and this was her unsophisticated way of getting her own back.

Adam had vowed one day to get even with her for all the heart-stopping moments she had caused him, though his better senses warned him against an actual physical confrontation with someone of such obvious mental frailty.

So Sally continued her little vendetta against him, choosing her times well, knowing the places where her unexpected appearances would have the most dramatic effect, favouring dusk and dawn, since she had discovered that human defences were at their lowest at those points in the day.

In her saner moments, despite her perpetual state of filth, Sally was an extremely beautiful young woman, with her olive skin, fine features, and huge black eyes. During spells of mental tranquillity she was a dreamy, sensitive creature, content to wander the countryside, smoking her clay pipe as she gathered nuts and berries which she stuffed into her roomy pockets as an automatic safeguard against the times of hunger that Davie so frequently enforced on her.

Adam, however, failed to see any good points in her make-up. To him she was a totally unbalanced creature who should have been locked away years ago, along with the rest of her family.

That night Sally had been abroad since teatime, hungry, thirsty, and miserable, Davie having been drinking and taking his temper out on both her and Donal, hitting them and finally throwing them out of the house without letting them have so much as a crust of bread.

She had been, therefore, in a very excitable frame of mind when she spied Adam emerging from The Gatehouse, hands in his pockets, head bent, all his attention focused on his rendezvous with Beth.

As stealthy as a cat stalking its prey, Sally had crept along behind the wall to lie in wait at a gap in the stones.

Adam's thoughts had been a million miles away when a cacophony of bovine bellows had suddenly erupted at his elbow, and there was Sally, dancing about in front of him, her tattered dress covered in dried mud, twigs and leaves matted into her mop of gypsy black hair, her mouth twisted and slobbering.

He was certainly in no mood to put up with this latest attack on his defences and, grabbing her roughly by the throat, he had shaken her like a rat, his face red and contorted as he uttered a string of obscenities directly into her ear.

Sally's head had wobbled like a rag doll on her shoulders; the slavers had run from her mouth; her eyes had been glazed and terrified.

Her apparent fear of him had given Adam great satisfaction; the feel of her windpipe under his fingers had made him laugh.

Something had risen in him, an injection of power, a feeling so overwhelming it was as if he had been taken over by another being outside his control. He had started striking Sally then, so hard that every blow sent her head spinning on the fragile stalk of her neck.

'Bitch!' he'd ground out. 'Bastard bitch! I warned you I'd pay you back! I warned you!'

He was beyond all control now: the slaps had turned into punches; blood from her eyes, nose, and mouth had run under his fingers. Only when she had let out a strangled cry and collapsed in a bloody heap on the ground did he finally let go, though, even then, he dealt her inert body a vicious kick with his steel-capped boots.

His breath had come in great gasps, the sweat had poured from his face. Leaving Sally on the verge where she had dropped he had stumbled away to wash his face and hands in one of the many little streams that tumbled down from the hills.

The blood on his shirt hadn't been easy to get rid of. He had rubbed and scrubbed but only succeeded in reducing the stains to brownish marks and impatiently abandoned the task in his hurry to get to Beth.

*   *   *

120

'Just look at the state of you, Adam McIntyre!' Beth cried when his limp excuses were over with. 'You're soaked through! What on earth have you been doing?'

'Giving myself a good wash before meeting you, Beth,' he said glibly. 'I was filthy after cleaning out the henhouse.'

She put out one tentative finger to touch him and her mouth twisted in disgust. 'Really, Adam, what do you take me for? I certainly can't let you come near me now.'

'We can soon solve that problem.' He began to peel off his shirt, a confident smile lifting the corners of his full, sensual mouth.

His body was firm and well built, his skin tanned from his days of outdoor work. Beth looked at his muscles rippling under his smooth skin; at his ruggedly handsome face, his snapping, dark eyes, his cap of curly brown hair. He was crude, braggish, unruly. There was something almost primitive in the cut of his features – something animal-like in the way he walked and carried himself.

Beth knew that was why she was so attracted to him and a shiver of pure excitement touched her spine.

Now he was removing his boots, his trousers. He hadn't laid a finger on her but already he was in a high state of sexual arousal. Without being able to help herself she stared and stared at him. He was big! She hadn't realised that any man could be so big – and he was barely sixteen – just a boy . . .

'Adam – I don't think . . . ' she began, but that was as far as she got.

'It's what you wanted, Beth,' he said hoarsely. 'Why you asked me to come here tonight . . . ' Seizing her by the shoulders he smothered her with hard, demanding kisses, while his hands tore at her clothing, practically ripping her dress from her body.

In minutes she was as naked as he was and she wasn't protesting any more. Breathlessly, she pressed her breasts against the hard wall of his chest, eagerly she met his kisses with hers. When his hand slid between her legs she forgot

121

everything and everyone – even Lucas Noble of Noble House . . .

Adam was remembering his time with Nellie Jean, the things she had taught him, the things she had done to him . . .

'You'll have to please me too, Beth,' he gasped, 'I'll tell you, I'll tell you what to do.'

They went wild, kissing, touching, playing till neither could wait any longer. Together they fell into a pile of wood shavings, their bodies writhing in total abandonment, their cries of pleasure mingling together.

When finally he drove himself into her, she gasped as pain shot through her, but it was a sensation that ran parallel with wave upon wave of exquisite, burning pleasure. She moulded herself to him, her whole being thrilling to every violent thrust of his pelvis, her legs enfolding him, forcing him in, ever deeper . . .

The wind rattled the roof, the night grew darker, an owl hooted from the trees. But for Adam and Beth there was no night or day in their moments of passion.

At last Beth got to her feet to dust herself down and examine her abandoned clothing anxiously. 'You shouldn't have been so rough, Adam,' she scolded as she regained her senses. 'What will Mother say if she sees my dress in shreds? I'll have to get back before I'm missed. I sneaked out of the house after telling everyone I was going to my room and I only hope I can get back in again without anyone seeing me.'

'Ach, you can throw the dress away. You've got so many o' them no-one will miss it.' Pulling her to him again Adam cupped her breasts in his hands. 'It was worth it, eh, Beth? And don't tell me you didn't enjoy getting your clothes torn off because I know you'd be lying if you did.'

She ignored his question. 'Adam, you do know that this is just between you and me, don't you? We've always had little secrets that no-one must know of except us.'

'Ay, you don't have to worry. I know fine you wouldn't want anybody knowing you let the likes o' me get inside your knickers.'

'No need to be so crude, Adam. Oh, never mind . . . ' She was getting dressed as she spoke, hurriedly pulling on her clothes, tidying her hair. ' . . . I simply must get home. How do I look?'

He gave a wicked snigger. 'As if you've just been well and truly laid! It's nothing to be ashamed of.'

'Adam McIntyre!'

'Och, c'mon, it was good, wasn't it, Beth?'

'Y – es, it was good, Adam, but it's over, so don't talk about it anymore.'

'When will I see you again?'

'When I'm ready – so don't go making a nuisance of yourself. I really must get home . . . ' Going to the door she opened it a peep to look this way and that before hurrying away downhill towards the lights of Corran House shining through the trees.

Adam, too, made his way downhill, his mind filled with the things he had done with Beth. It had been wonderful. She was a hot piece and no mistake! He hadn't needed to show her all that much and it was easy to tell she'd been with a man before – or maybe several for all he knew. And to think old Ma Jordan was so uppity and had almost burst her stays trying to make a lady out of her daughter all these years . . .

'Adam.'

The voice came at Adam out of the darkness and for the second time that night he just about jumped out of his skin with fright.

'It's only me, Mary.' The voice was nearer now and a few seconds later, Mary, the Noble House kitchenmaid, hove into view.

'Mary!' he cried, anger lending an edge to his voice. 'You near scared the shit out o' me creeping up on me like that.'

'I didn't creep, I was just walking along the road and saw you.'

Adam took a deep breath as he tried to steady his thumping heart. 'What are you doing out here at this time o' night?' he demanded. 'Sneaking about all by yourself?'

Mary tossed her head. 'I told you, I wasn't sneaking – and I could ask you the same question.' She moved closer to him to peer into his face and her nose twitched. 'You smell funny and you've got a guilty look on your face. Just where have you been, Adam McIntyre? And who have you been with? Were you meeting that Beth Jordan?'

'None o' your business,' he grunted. 'I don't have to tell you everything I do. You don't own me.'

'Only when it suits you, Adam McIntyre!' Mary was getting quite het-up. 'I'm not daft, you know. I heard all about you taking that snotty bitch to the dance on Saturday. You never even asked me if I'd like to go. All you ever do is make use o' me!'

'Ach, c'mon, Mary,' Adam said placatingly. 'Beth asked me to take her, it would never have entered my head to ask her. You know you're my girl, Mary . . . '

His words had the desired softening effect. Mary sniffed, and she moved a bit closer to him.

Reaching out, he took her hand. 'We're the same, you and me. Beth's a snob. I know I'd have enjoyed myself better wi' you but she caught me on the hop and I said yes without thinking. Of course . . . ' he disentangled his hand, ' . . . if you don't want to see me anymore . . . '

For an answer Mary wound her arms round his neck and drew his lips to hers. 'Don't say things like that, Adam, you know how I feel about you. Look – I brought this for you to see . . . I'll have to put it back before it's missed, so you can only have a quick peep.'

Delving into her pocket she withdrew something round and shiny and handed it to him. 'I found this on Master Ralph's dressing table when I went to call him this morning. I saw him showing it to the Irish lad yesterday and

124

heard him saying he'd found it at the river the night Mr Mallard and Master Peter died. Do you know what that means, Adam?' she ended in a spectral whisper.

'No, what?'

'He was there that night and he maybe knows who killed them . . . so why doesn't he say anything?'

'Why doesn't he?' asked Adam blankly.

'Because he's too terrified, that's why. I think he knows who the murderer is but is too scared to say. He has nightmares all the time, I've heard him myself, yelling out in his sleep. I'm certain Master Robert thinks the way I do, the two o' them share a room and he hears everything. Yesterday morning he and her ladyship were speaking to Master Ralph, trying to get him to talk. He wouldn't say anything but later he showed this silver thing to Master Robert and said where he'd found it so it must be important. It could be a vital clue,' she finished grandly.

Adam turned the object over in his hand but had no time to examine it further for at that moment a groan came from near at hand, followed by another, and another.

Mary jumped, and the hairs prickled on Adam's neck. With bulging eyes they both stood transfixed, listening to the snapping of twigs, the eerie shufflings and creepings, the groanings and moanings coming closer. Something was crawling along the verge towards them, a creature that seemed neither animal nor human in the shadowed grey darkness.

'It's Sally McDonald!' cried Mary in horror as the figure collapsed and lay still just a few feet from where she was standing.

At her words Adam's heart thumped afresh. In all the happenings of the night he had forgotten Sally and the terrible things he had done to her. Now, it all came flooding back: the beating; the blood; that strange elation he had experienced while he had been hitting her.

Adam didn't feel elated now. In fact, as Mary rushed forward to drop to her knees by Sally's side, he felt sick as he wondered what had made him indulge in such cruelties, why he had felt as he did . . . just like his father beating Anna . . .

Slowly he went forward to stand staring at Sally, lying prone once more on the grass, her face a swollen blob, her tangled hair sticking to the blood and bruises on her eyes, her mouth . . .

Panic seized him. What if she were to die? He would be a murderer then – just like . . . Bile rose into his throat, he choked, coughed, tried desperately to control himself.

'Och, poor Sally,' Mary was saying, her voice full of concern, for, despite her underhand ways, she had a caring heart. 'I wonder who did this to her. She's in a dreadful mess.'

'We'll likely never know,' Adam said in a wobbly voice. 'She can't talk – at least no' enough to make herself understood.'

'No, but she'll put a curse on whoever did it if she recovers. Sally has her own ways o' getting back at people who do her ill.'

'A curse?' A wave of dread swept over Adam. 'She's too daft to do anything like that.'

'Don't you believe it. She has the gypsy in her, you only have to look at her to tell that.'

Lowering her voice, Mary went on cryptically, 'Look at old Mrs Dobie who lived in that lonely cottage near Coffin Pass. One night, Sally went to her house looking for a drink o' water. Instead o' giving her one Mrs Dobie threw a bucket o' water over her. A week later the old woman was found dead in Coffin Pass, no' a mark on her, nothing to tell how she had died. It all happened years ago, before you ever came to the glen, but nobody has ever forgotten it – and other queer goings-on whenever Sally has wanted to pay somebody back for being bad to her.'

'Never mind all that.' Quickly Adam changed the subject. 'What are we going to do wi' her? We can't just leave her lying here.'

'We'll take her to your house. It's the nearest and your sister will know what to do.'

'No, we can't take her there, Father hates all the McDonalds and wouldn't let her in the door. Nellie Jean's house is just up the road. We'll take her there.'

Between them they half-carried, half-dragged Sally to the widow woman's tiny cottage set into the boundary wall of the mill.

Nellie Jean's initial reaction was one of disbelief when she saw the state that Sally was in.

'Och, my, poor, poor cratur!' she cried in horror. 'Who did this to her? A wild beast by the look o' it. The glen is no' safe for anybody these days but for someone to attack a poor harmless soul like Sally.' She shook her tousled black head and took a swig of whisky from a flask in her apron pocket.

'Can you help her, Mrs Anderson?' Mary said anxiously as she and Adam held the limp body between them. 'She's freezing cold and might die if she doesn't get warmed up soon.'

'Ach, no, she'll no' die,' Nellie Jean declared emphatically, wrinkling her nose as the unsavoury smells of Sally's unwashed body assailed her nostrils. 'She's too tough for that.'

Sally groaned, her dark eyes fluttered open, and Nellie Jean's kindly heart melted. 'Och, bring her in and I'll see what I can do for her, fleas and all.' She gave a wicked chuckle and stood aside to let Mary and Adam carry in their burden.

'What the hell!' she cried. 'Dump her on the bed, I've had worse in beside me . . . ' She glanced at Adam and closed one eye in a shameless wink. 'Our young friend here can vouch for that, eh, laddie?'

Adam wriggled uncomfortably. He could take no more trouble that night and here was Nellie Jean letting the cat out of the bag, trying to see how far she could go in front of Mary.

But the Noble House kitchenmaid was too absorbed with Sally to listen to the clackings of Nellie Jean's drink-loosened tongue as Adam backed to the door to try and make his escape.

'Nothing that a good feed and a carbolic wash won't cure,' Nellie Jean was saying, stripping Sally of her clothes as she spoke, while Mary held her nose in disgust.

Adam reached the door, and without turning, he searched for the door handle.

'Wait for me, Adam,' Mary said hastily, 'I'll have to get back to make Molly's cocoa and Mr Baird will be mad if he has to stay up late to let me in.'

But Nellie Jean was having none of that. 'You'll do no such thing, my girl,' she said sharply. 'Just you bide here and help me undress Sally. Let the lad go, he'll only get in the way . . . though mind . . . ' A sly grin split her face, ' . . . he'll no see anything he hasn't seen already.'

Adam found the door handle. Turning it he fled into the night, never stopping till he reached the door of The Gatehouse.

He was about to let himself in when he remembered the metal object that Mary had given to him earlier. In all the turmoil with Sally he had forgotten to give it back to Mary. Taking it out of his pocket he turned it round and round before holding it up to squint at it.

The night sky was giving off a reasonably good light, and the thing in his hand glinted and gleamed. Something about it was oddly familiar to him . . . he felt he had seen it before somewhere . . .

Recognition came suddenly, the enormity of it hitting him like a thunderbolt. The object he was holding was no less than the hinged silver lid from a very fancy and very expensive pipe. He had only ever seen one person smoking a pipe like it . . . and that person was none other than Roderick McIntyre – his own father!

CHAPTER 13

A Journey

Anna and her brothers were rather quiet on the first part of the forty-mile journey to Kilkenzie.

It was a mild, dewy day, filled with the scents of pine forests and damp earth. Carpets of bluebells covered the woods, the perfume of them filling the air with their sweetness; the deep green basin of Loch Gorm reflected the rugged grandeur of the surrounding hills.

Every bend in the road revealed further splendours and Anna drank in every aspect, unable to stop the heartwarming feelings, despite the welter of darker emotions that churned inside her.

She felt as if she was being torn in two, one half of her longing to see her mother again, the other dreading the moment of meeting.

She had never thought it would be like this. Her childhood dreams had made everything so simple: she would see her mother, they would laugh, they would embrace, they would catch up on all the years that had been lost to them.

It was different now. She had grown up, her feelings were more complicated. It had been eleven long years! There would be changes, not only physical but – mental – emotional.

Beside her sat Magnus, silent, thoughtful, yet she could feel the strength of him touching her, giving her a sense of security.

The Reverend Alastair Simpson was sitting at the front

of the trap, more relaxed looking, the reins held comfortably in his hands, his appearance not in the least sombre although he was dressed in clerical attire.

His luxuriant, snowy locks were curling over his ears in a wayward fashion; his eyes were sparkling in his fresh, smooth face. He was obviously enjoying the journey and pointed out various things of interest: the little pleasure steamer known as *The Kelpie*, merrily chugging its way through the silken waters of Loch Gorm; the deep ravine of Coir an Tee where the Paper Cave was said to be situated. In this cave, according to history, the charters of the Clan Campbell had been hidden when the avenging men of Atholl had plundered the lands of the Campbells in the late seventeenth century.

Adam's eyes glinted during the telling of this tale and he began to prattle, asking questions which Mr Simpson readily answered.

The atmosphere grew lighter. Magnus's hand slid into Anna's, and a strange little emotion caught at her heart. His body was warm and hard next to hers; she could feel every small movement he made, even the vibrations of his heart. Something deep and tender surged in her veins. It was as if his love and his vigour were flowing into her body, fortifying her, making her relax and able to enjoy the day.

The horses trotted steadily, their hoofbeats ringing harmoniously on the road. One or two open coaches passed by, packed with sightseers who had made the trip on *The Kelpie* and were now heading back to the inn at the mouth of the loch.

Loch Gorm was left behind, they were now in Glenbranter. The horses were still in good fettle, as the wheels bounced on the stony road, over braes and down into hollows, past green and golden hills, through leafy glades and fields grazed by horses, cows and sheep.

'Whoa there!' cried Mr Simpson, applying the brakes as he guided the horses round the steep bend leading down to Loch Fyneside.

At that moment the sun broke through to glisten on the sparkling sea; amber-coloured seaweed waved lazily in the shallows; curlews were prodding long beaks into the rock pools; oyster catchers darted busily along the shore, scooping up mussels with their red beaks; seagulls screamed and jostled one another on the sandbanks and in the distance the hazy purple of faraway hills merged into the misted horizon.

'Oh, it's all so lovely!' The exclamation broke from Anna's lips. 'I can't help enjoying it.'

'And why shouldn't you, dear child?' Mr Simpson said serenely. 'It's a day for rejoicing in the beauties of nature. This is a wonderful place. I've often thought about bringing *Mrs Griffiths* over to Loch Fyne but I'm afraid she's much too cumbersome for me to manhandle her all that way on my own.'

'Mrs Griffiths?' Adam looked puzzled. He couldn't imagine the minister manhandling a woman of any sort, never mind one called Mrs Griffiths.

The minister laughed. 'Don't look so worried, Adam, *Mrs Griffiths* is what I call my boat. I named her after a Welsh cousin of mine who is very proud of her marital status and insists on being addressed accordingly. It took her a long time to hook a man, you see, and when she visits she talks incessantly about her husband in a loud, booming voice and eats large quantities of Mrs Simpson's cakes, with the result that she's rather a bulky sort of lady – just like my boat,' he finished with a mischievous chuckle.

At the hamlet of St Catherine's they stopped briefly at the staging post to change horses but were soon on their way again after a short walk round the village to stretch their legs.

The fresh pair were frisky and stepped out eagerly, easily covering the miles on the curving road to Inverary.

'We'll stop here,' decided the minister, bringing the horses to rest beside the lake. 'I must say I'm looking forward to this. It's a long time since I picnicked anywhere and the shores of Loch Fyne are particularly inviting on a day like this.' With Magnus's help he unharnessed the horses to allow them to feast on the juicy young grasses of the wayside.

The picnic hamper was unpacked and spread out in the sun. Anna had brought several packets of food, mostly plain fare that she had prepared under her father's eagle eye.

'No sweetmeats,' he had insisted in a surly fashion, his mood having been a black one ever since it had been decided that the children should visit their mother. 'They aren't good for you and besides, there's no sillar to waste in this house for nonsense o' that kind. Picnic indeed! Mr Simpson must be taking leave o' his senses to even think o' such a thing. You're going to see your mother, my girl; none o' you will find that much o' a picnic at the end o' the day.'

Mrs Simpson, however, had not stinted herself when she had heard her husband's plans for the young McIntyres. 'You must take plenty of food, Alastair,' she had told him. 'It's a long way to Kilkenzie and you won't have time to stop anywhere. Don't worry, leave it to me, I'll make sure that none of you starve.'

So saying she had rolled her sleeves to her elbows and had embarked on a baking spree, enlisting the services of Jean who had willingly scurried backwards and forwards when she had heard that Magnus was to be one of the recipients of the feast.

The result was a groaning hamper, filled with bread and ham, fruit of all kinds and enough cakes and scones to feed a dozen hungry people. At the last moment Jean had slipped in a large apple turnover, wrapped in tissue paper, Magnus's name scrawled on top.

'Well, well,' grinned the minister when he saw it, 'our wee Jeannie has certainly taken a liking to you, my boy. She must certainly believe in the old adage, "the way to a man's heart is through his stomach". Rachael – Mrs Simpson that is – has always quite spoiled me in that respect and wild horses would never drag me away from her – even when she's nagging me about my boat. Come on, don't let's waste any more time, I'm so hungry I could eat a horse!'

They sat on the rocks to eat, the sun beating down on them, the water gently lapping the shore just a few yards away.

For Mr Simpson it wasn't such a rare experience to be near the sea but for Anna and her brothers, living inland in Glen Tarsa, it wasn't an everyday occurrence and they were entranced by the novelty of it all.

When they had eaten Anna and Magnus went off together along the shore but Adam remained where he was, his chin on his knees as he gazed reflectively over the water.

He felt at peace with himself, with the world, a feeling that seldom touched him in the daily turmoil of living with his father.

But the sense of tranquillity didn't last long. Thoughts started crowding in on him. Sally McDonald for instance, the dreadful pain and anguish he had caused her. He hadn't meant to hit her so hard. Every time he thought about it he felt sick. Something had made him do it, something that had risen up inside of him, like a venomous serpent, poised, ready to strike . . . again and again!

And he had enjoyed doing it, every blow, every punch . . . He could have killed her! If it had been someone less tough than Sally they would be dead by now, so frenzied had been his attack, so fierce his rage. Luckily for him, she had survived or he would have had her on his conscience for the rest of his life. A murderer . . . like *him* . . . the face-less madman who had killed Andrew Mallard and caused the death of Peter Noble . . .

He swallowed hard and wondered – was he becoming as brutal as his father? Enjoying inflicting pain and misery on others? Loving the sense of power it brought?

Turning his head Adam gazed at the minister, sitting with

133

his specs perched on the end of his nose while he perused a church magazine. He had always regarded Mr Simpson as a stuffy old bird, good only for droning away in the pulpit and visiting housebound parishioners as ancient as himself.

Today he was seeing the minister in a new light, as somebody who was wise in the ways of the world, interesting, too, with his knowledge of the countryside and what went on in it – a sense of humour as well . . .

A thought entered Adam's head. Should he confide in the minister, tell him about the things that were bothering him? That silver pipe lid, for instance? He hadn't given it back to Mary and was still trying to decide what he should do about it.

At first he had thought to confront Roderick with it, see if he could profit financially by it. Blackmail in other words, something that his father understood only too well, going by the things Mary had told him about his father's dealings with Sir Malaroy. Then there had been that incident with Moira O'Brady, the postmistress, who, having filched some funds from the church, had suffered sorely for her sins through having to pay Roderick for his silence on the matter.

The idea of blackmail had been quickly rejected by Adam as being too risky. He had then toyed with the notion of telling Anna about the pipe lid, where and when it had been found and by whom.

After all, she was involved in all this. She had suffered the loss of Peter and must surely want to avenge his death. Ever since Peter had died Adam had seen her, looking at their father, watching him, something suspicious in her eyes, something terrible in her silent accusations, and there was an air about her of someone waiting, waiting patiently for the right chance to come along.

But it was only a metal pipe lid! It could have been lost days or weeks before the deaths! Yet that little runt Ralph had set great store by its discovery. Perhaps he had seen it falling from the killer's pocket during the struggle with Mallard. That would explain the importance that Master

Runty Ralph had attached to it. If so, it could easily lead to bigger things . . .

Locking Roderick away for instance, getting rid of him once and for all, allowing everybody some peace in their lives. The kind of wonderful freedom they'd had that time he had been sent packing to Canon Point to stand in for the manager.

'Is there something you would like to say to me, Adam?' The minister's voice cut into Adam's musings. Hastily, he shook his head. 'No, not yet, Mr Simpson, maybe some other time – except – I haven't said anything to Magnus or Anna – but I'm afraid o' seeing my mother again. Every time I think about it I feel like running away, and that place she's in – the loony bin! I don't really want to go there, I never ever wanted to, though I pretended I did. I didn't want my brother and sister to know how scared I was.'

'It's natural to feel as you do, Adam,' Mr Simpson said reassuringly. 'After all, you haven't seen your mother in a long time and there are bound to be some doubts in your mind. Don't worry, I'm sure it will all turn out well in the end. Don't forget, it's only an hour or two out of your life; your mother has to spend all her days locked away from the world, so surely she deserves the chance to see her family again.'

Adam nodded. He felt better, but even so he was loath to leave that peaceful spot by the loch. How lovely to linger, to just gaze and gaze at the water and perhaps feel again the peace of solitary places seeping into him.

But there was still a good distance to go, the minister hustled them back into the trap and they set off at a spanking pace.

Kilkenzie was reached at a little after four o'clock and the minister went off to arrange a night's lodgings in a homely looking inn by the shore. The horses were led to the stables and the travellers dispersed to their rooms to freshen up before dinner.

Adam and Magnus were sharing a room while Anna was overjoyed to discover she had one all to herself, even if it was connected to the boys' room.

At the door she stood for a moment to gaze round the tiny enclosure, so charming in its simplicity, with its pink walls and sloping ceiling. It smelled of camphor and lavender and fresh air; white muslin curtains billowed at the open window; the floor was so well polished, it reflected the colours of the walls.

Anna loved it. She had never known such privacy since her visits to Lady Pandora's home in England. A bubble of joy rose up in her. Throwing her bag on a chair, she skipped across the floor to the bed where she lay on top of the patchwork quilt and gazed around her appreciatively.

So different from the room she shared with her brothers at The Gatehouse, where she would hear the gurgle of the river swishing into The Cauldron and the sigh of the wind in the trees. Everything was entirely different near the sea. Here, she could hear the pebbles rattling on the shore, the lash of the waves against the rocks, seagulls crying as they rode the air thermals above the hills.

For several minutes she lay on the bed letting the enchantment wash over her till she remembered the reason for her being here.

Her mother, Lillian McIntyre, a woman who had once filled her life with warmth and love but who was now no more than a – the word crept unbidden into her head – stranger!

'No, no, not that,' she whispered and desperately tried to rid her mind of such disloyal thoughts.

She had longed for this day. With all her heart she had wanted it to happen. Now the moment was nearly here. In a very short time she would see her mother, speak to her, touch her . . .

She put her hand to her mouth and wished she didn't feel so – apprehensive . . .

136

CHAPTER 14

Lillian McIntyre

Anna barely touched her meal that evening and was glad that Reverend Simpson was hurrying them a bit, anxious as he was to get them to the hospital before the night routine began.

'It would have been better to have gone in the daytime,' he had explained, 'but we'll have to leave early in the morning if we're to get home at a reasonable hour. No need to worry though, you'll have plenty of time to spend with your mother if we get along there now.'

The inn was only a short distance away from the hospital and together they walked through the cool evening. To the west the sky was a sheet of flame which was reflected in the rippling waters of the loch and made dazzling jewels of the hills. Beyond the core of light everything was purple and blue and somehow secretive with the trees huddled into the shadows and little white houses snuggled into the hollows in the hills, half-hidden but for their windows which winked like big golden eyes in the light from the sky.

'I wish we could walk in the gloaming forever,' Magnus whispered to Anna, taking her hand and squeezing it comfortingly.

'Oh, so do I. Just wander on and on, following the sun, never stopping till we come to that magical land beyond the horizon, where there's no night and no cold, nothing but beauty.'

'Only thing is, there's a fair drop at the edge o' the world; we might fall off and never get back on again.'

She looked at him quickly. He was smiling, though the hazel eyes that searched her face were bright with anxiety, and she knew that he was doing his best to cheer her up, no matter how bad he himself might be feeling.

A pair of massive gates loomed ahead, and Reverend Simpson halted. They had arrived at their destination and Anna felt herself grow cold. All she wanted to do in those moments was to turn and flee. There, emblazoned in gold on the wrought-iron railings, were the words KILKENZIE ASYLUM FOR THE MENTALLY INDIGENT.

All through her childhood she had clung to the belief that her mother couldn't be as mad as everyone seemed to think and that never, never, could she really be in a place that others referred to as an asylum . . .

'Set a trap to catch a moose, your mammy's in the loony hoose!'

Her memories took her back, and the years slipped away. The childish voices from the past came floating into her mind to taunt and torment her.

Magnus, too, was staring, horrified, at the letters, his eyes big and disbelieving in the strained pallor of his face.

Only Adam seemed unaffected by it all. His expression was cocksure; his hands were buried in his pockets; his cap was set at a jaunty angle; a tuneless whistle was issuing from his lips. No-one could have told by looking at him that his stomach was turning over with nerves and that his bladder had filled up at sight of the forbidding words before his eyes.

Reverend Simpson pushed the gate open, and it squeaked and squealed on its hinges and clattered behind them with such a bang they all jumped, even the minister.

The building rose up in front of them, dark and forbidding. The main door opened, and nurses with unsmiling faces gave no welcome. Reverend Simpson muttered something to one of them and, nodding briefly, she led the way along a dimly lit corridor.

It was a cold, austere place, nothing homely about its

138

white unadorned walls and tiled floors, upon which their feet now clattered with alarming intensity.

Yet – it took a minute or two to sink in – there was about it a strange sort of peace. It was alright! No demented screamings invaded the night; no sounds of distress filled the stone halls with echoing horror, instead, an atmosphere of tranquillity pervaded the hospital. The rattling of dishes from the kitchen lent a touch of familiar domesticity to the sounds of the night; a large ginger and white cat came out of a doorway and made its way along the corridor, waving its tail in the air.

Reverend Simpson walked in front, leading the way, a solid, reassuring figure, his white hair shining like a beacon above his dark cloth, his footsteps soft but firm, as if he knew exactly where he was going, what he was doing, who he was going to see.

The nurse stopped at a heavy wooden door. 'You'll have to wait for a wee while,' she told the children, a smile suddenly curving her mouth, taking away its severity. 'Reverend Simpson did write to say you were coming but we weren't sure at what time. I'm so glad you made it – the people here seldom get anybody, even relatives who promise to come sometimes don't. I'll get a nurse to freshen Mrs McIntyre up a little and when she's ready, we'll put you into one of the side rooms to give you some privacy.'

Sympathy showed in her eyes at sight of the three strained young faces before her. 'Don't be afraid,' she told them kindly. 'I know this must be a big moment for you all and you're bound to be feeling a bit anxious. I must warn you though, your mother might appear not to recognise you, you have to prepare yourselves for that, but she'll be very pleased to see you, she loves young people.'

'What do you mean, might not appear to recognise us? Does that mean she knows people? Remembers them? That she's not completely without memory, even if she gives the impression that she is?' Magnus's voice was harsh with hope as the questions came tumbling out of him.

139

The nurse laid a conciliatory hand on his arm. 'We aren't completely certain what she retains in the way of memory. Occasionally there are small signs of recognition for those that she really trusts – like Reverend Simpson here for instance. She always *looks* as if she knows who he is but –' she shrugged her shoulders, '– We can't really go by that, because if you ask her his name she just shakes her head and won't speak . . . '

The nurse paused for a moment before going on slowly, 'Remember also, it's years since she saw her children. You have all grown up, if there are memories they are of her wee ones, the bairns she nursed on her knee a long time ago.'

Anna stifled a cry and the minister put a comforting arm round her shoulders. The nurse straightened, shook her head, smiled at them all again, before taking a key from her pocket to unlock a door which she shut carefully behind her, leaving them alone in the waiting room. The lock clicked home on the other side and that was when the first pangs of unease really touched them.

Mr Simpson read their minds. 'It's only a precaution,' he whispered. 'They have to do these things, you know, for the protection of everybody concerned, so don't look as if the big bad wolf is coming to gobble you up at any moment. Now . . . ' rising briskly from his seat he went on, ' . . . I have to leave you for a wee while; there are one or two people I want to see while I'm here. I won't be long, perhaps half an hour, that should give you enough time to be alone with your mother. I'll pop in to say hallo to her, too, so try to relax and enjoy your visit.'

As they watched him walking away along the corridor, each one of them felt deserted and afraid. Silently, they huddled together on a bench, none of them finding anything to say that might relieve the tension that clung round them like a grey cloud.

Anna sat very straight, her hands folded in her lap, to all appearances a picture of unruffled calm. Only her dark, burning eyes and a slight trembling of her chin gave away

140

the fact that she wasn't in as much control as she was trying to make out.

Magnus settled his broad shoulders against the hard wood of the bench. He felt cold and ill at ease and wondered if he had done the right thing bringing his sister here. Her fragility and vulnerability touched him as never before.

She sat with her brothers, small, fair and very feminine, trying hard to look strong and fearless, giving no voice to the doubts that he knew she was feeling. Other girls would have had plenty to say for themselves, Beth Jordan for instance, letting the world know exactly how she felt about everything while she paced restlessly up and down . . .

Magnus moved closer to his sister. She took his hand and held it tightly, her action dispersing some of his fears. He felt close to her, in mind, body and spirit.

Adam was hunched forward in his seat, as if he was getting ready to run. He was fidgeting, first with his thumbs, next with a lock of his hair which he began to wind and unwind round his fingers. When he grew tired of that, he started to play with the buttons of his jacket, incessantly pulling and tugging at them so that one or two were soon hanging on by just a few threads.

The building had grown quieter still. Sounds had become more intensified; footsteps echoed in unseen passageways; a tree branch clawed at a nearby window; an odd gurgling laugh came from behind a closed door . . .

Then they started, the sounds that the children had dreaded: a low, moaning wail drifting along the corridor, followed by another, cries of a terrible despair that might have come from a lost spirit condemned to wander forever the wastes of a half-life, neither of the earth nor of the heavens.

Adam's mouth grew tinder dry; his hands went clammily cold; the pupils of his eyes dilated; his heart pumped so rapidly it made him feel faint, and his bladder felt full to bursting. All he wanted to do in those fraught heartbeats of time was to get up and run away. For a desperate moment he thought he was going to wet himself.

'The lavatory!' he blurted through white lips. 'I must go to the lavatory! I'm bursting for a pee!'

He stood up, terrified that he was going to disgrace himself there and then.

A nurse came out of a door further down the corridor and Magnus grabbed his brother's arm and propelled him forward. 'Excuse me, nurse,' he said urgently. 'My brother – he has to go to the lavatory.'

The nurse glanced at Adam's contorted face and, smiling dryly, she said, 'Of course, follow me, young man, it isn't far, just along here.'

Magnus went back to where Anna was seated. At that moment a key turned in a door, a nurse appeared and they were ushered through, the lock clicking home behind them.

A jumble of impressions passed their eyes: a long ward in front of them; people pacing aimlessly or staring blankly at nothing; others re-enacting individual happenings in their lives; some holding animated conversations with people who weren't there . . .

'In here.' The nurse opened another door and they found themselves in a little room with bare wooden floors. The furniture consisted of a table and a few chairs. In one of them sat Lillian McIntyre, her bare feet enclosed in a pair of large, check booties that made her legs look matchstick thin. Her soft brown hair was brushed back from her brow and held in place with a pink clasp, and her recently washed face shone in taut brightness. She had the look of a small girl who had just newly emerged from a brisk bath. The scents of soap and talcum powder emanated from her in fragrant waves.

Lillian McIntyre was clean and tidy and ready to receive her visitors.

'I'll be outside if you need me.' The nurse turned back to the door. 'I'll get Nurse Saunders to watch out for your brother and send him in here when he's ready.' She raised

142

her voice. 'Mrs McIntyre, your visitors are here, Anna, your daughter, and Magnus, your eldest son.'

The door closed. Lillian McIntyre slowly raised her head, and her dreamy brown eyes lit up with pleasure. Both Anna and Magnus released the pent-up air in their lungs, their gasps of surprise combining together, for though eleven years had passed since they had last gazed upon their mother's face, there were no visible signs of ageing. It was smooth, and pink, beautiful in its childlike simplicity: the eyes were wide and trusting, the mouth tremulous and innocent.

It was as if, in excluding herself from the world and the cares of everyday life, she had turned her back on the ravages of time.

'Mother.' Magnus was the first to go forward. Dropping down on his knees he buried his face in his mother's lap, the tears falling unashamedly down his face, his strong shoulders shaking with emotion.

Anna stood as one transfixed, staring at the sweet face of the one she had so yearned for since that day of parting long ago. She glanced at her mother's hands, resting peacefully on the arms of the chair, and it seemed as if she felt again their loving touch, stroking her hair, soothing away all the little troubles of childhood.

'Mother,' she whispered and she, too, was on her knees, crying and laughing, murmuring, 'Mother. Mother,' over and over, as she had done so often in the endless nights of her lonely dreamings.

'Mother,' she whispered again.

'Anna.' Magnus's hand came out to clasp hers. Together they shared magical moments they knew would never be forgotten for as long as each of them lived.

CHAPTER 15

My Baby!

At first, Lillian McIntyre seemed uncertain of the situation she found herself in and for a few moments she sat as one mesmerised, bewildered, unmoving. Then she smiled and stretching out her hands, she laid them tenderly on the two young heads in her lap.

Rhythmically, gently, she began to stroke Anna's hair, letting the fair strands fall through her fingers, before turning her attention to Magnus, one finger playing with the thick brown tendrils at the nape of his neck.

And then she started to rock herself, back and forth, back and forth, snatches of a lullaby rising calmly and sweetly into her throat.

'Mother.' Anna raised her head. 'Don't you know who we are? Do you remember us at all? Anna, your daughter, and Magnus, your son?'

'Anna. Magnus.' Lillian repeated the names softly. With a secretive smile she reached inside her dressing gown to withdraw a china doll, dressed in layers of once frothy, pink muslin, now shabby and threadbare.

'Baby.' Proudly she held the doll aloft. 'My baby.'

Anna looked at the doll. She recognised it and sadness overwhelmed her. It was a doll from her own childhood, a favourite plaything with a pretty face and a row of pearly teeth showing between parted red lips.

Her mother had kept it, had smuggled it away with her when she had been taken away from her home all these years ago. In her lonely hours she must have snuggled it to her breast, a substitute for the little ones she had left behind . . . or – Anna's heart beat swiftly – a reminder of them?

'Mother,' she said gently, 'that was my doll, don't you remember . . . ?'

Lillian put the doll back to her breast. 'My baby,' she insisted, a slight frown creasing her brow.

Magnus threw Anna a warning glance and for a time they sat there in the tiny room saying nothing, because it seemed there was nothing they could say to the woman who had once listened to them with such patience and understanding.

Lillian appeared to have forgotten them. Her pose was quiet and peaceful; she was gazing dreamily into space and she gave the impression of having retreated, once more, into her own small world.

Then, quite suddenly, she turned her head to look at them and they saw recognition struggling into the deep brown pools of her eyes. 'Anna? Magnus?' Her lips formed the names, slowly, hesitantly, awareness making her voice tremble.

'Ay, that's right, Mother,' Magnus made his tone deliberately nonchalant. 'Anna, your daughter and Magnus, your elder son.'

'Elder son?' she repeated.

'That's me, and this is Anna, the wee lassie you used to cradle on your knee.' He stopped speaking and held his breath as he waited to see what kind of reaction his words would bring.

Very slowly Lillian brought her gaze to bear on Anna and reaching out with one exploratory finger, she traced the contours of the girl's face and ears before lifting up the strands of silken hair to once more play with them and finally press her lips to them.

'Anna – Anna Ban.' The name came out in a long sigh, her eyes fixed on Anna's face. Then her pupils darkened. 'My baby.' Her lip quivered, vehemently she shook her head. 'Not my baby . . . has . . . has my lady found her baby?'

'Mother, what do you mean?' Anna said softly, but Lillian had drawn her hand away. Sitting back in her chair she murmured again, 'Not my baby. My lady must find her baby.'

Unable to bear such a rejection Anna's eyes filled with tears. Magnus shook his head at her and looking straight at his mother he said carefully, 'Your younger son, Adam, he's your baby, it's him you want, he'll be along to see you in a minute.'

'Adam,' she said the name unwillingly, the little frown back on her brow, a strange expression on her face. 'Adam,' she said again but without feeling, as if what she was saying meant nothing to her.

Adam took his time in the lavatory, sitting for ages on the wooden toilet seat while he fought to contain the emotions that were seething within him.

He was terrified of seeing his mother again. Ever since Magnus had told him that Reverend Simpson was arranging for them to visit the asylum, every fibre in his body had rebelled against it.

He had no desire to see the tortured, mad creature that his mother had become. Magnus had said she wasn't like that at all but he didn't believe him, it was contradictory to what their father had told them.

He had maintained that she was a raving being, possessed of the devil. Adam's friends said she must be mad or she wouldn't be locked away in a lunatic asylum.

Lunatic! The very word chilled him to the marrow. Why should he visit a lunatic? It wasn't fair to make him go. He hardly even remembered what this mother of his looked like.

It was so long ago. She was just a shadowy memory with no substance. She belonged to the past. She had no place in his life now. He didn't want her in it. Why couldn't they

146

all just forget about her and be done with it? She could never be a mother to any of them again. Not a real mother.

They had managed without her all these years and she didn't deserve to be remembered when she had done nothing to give them a happy childhood. It was her fault that they'd led such miserable lives with their father. She should have stayed and protected them from him. She was weak. She shouldn't have gone off her head in the first place.

A lot of people said her mind had just snapped, that it had been her way of escaping the harsh realities of her life. Well, many's the time he would have liked to escape, too, but he'd had to stay and face the music and go on living with things he didn't like. He knew why, of course. He was strong. Strong and bold. And one day, when he was older and able to fend better for himself, he would just up and leave Glen Tarsa and all the folk who had ever been mean to him.

Though mind, there was Beth to consider, he didn't want to leave her, not just yet, he was having too good a time with her, and with Mary, and Nellie Jean would likely want him again. He was young and strong and next time he'd be able to satisfy her – now that he knew the ropes . . .

Iron Rod was past it, she'd said so herself, and what a feather in his cap to know that he was making it with Nellie Jean behind his father's back.

Oh ay, he'd get even with the old sod, somehow, some way, and there was still all that murder business to be sorted out . . . If he could get to the bottom of that it could be the best trump card he'd played yet . . . No, he couldn't leave Glen Tarsa just yet, best wait awhile and let things develop a bit more . . .

Leaning back against the cistern Adam stared unseeingly at the wall in front of him. Perhaps if he told a nurse he was feeling ill she might advise him against seeing his mother. He could wait outside in the fresh air and watch the colours of the sky mirrored in the rippling water.

147

He wouldn't be lying. He did feel ill. A kind of sick, heavy feeling in the pit of his belly, churning, churning away. It was normal to be afraid in such circumstances though boys were supposed to be brave all the time, never to show their fears.

Anna wasn't a boy but she was brave, Anna had always been brave. She and Magnus seemed able to do things that weren't always nice to do, the sort of things that made women of girls and men of boys.

But he was too young yet to be a man – though how could he ever tell anyone that when he was always trying to prove just how manly he was?

A spurt of bravado seized him. 'Bugger it! I'll show them!' he vowed through gritted teeth. 'I'll show them all – even her!' Buttoning his fly he made his exit from the toilet and went marching noisily along the corridor.

Nurse Saunders saw him coming and had the door open, ready. His show of boldness faltered when he saw the long ward stretching away in front of him . . . All those mad people, staring at him, cackling, coming to get him . . .

He gulped, held back, but the nurse laid a hand on his arm and guided him towards the side room. His nerve returned. Straightening his shoulders he followed the nurse and prepared himself for his first glimpse of *her*.

Adam's entry into the room was boisterous and showy.

He made a hasty appraisal of the scene. Anna and Magnus, sitting there, talking quietly to her! His mother! A harmless looking, fine-featured woman, with eyes that might have belonged to an innocent child and a face as sweet and as fresh as a dewy morning.

His façade fell from him like a mantle; weakness pervaded his limbs; an unexpected rush of tenderness enveloped him . . . His mother. His flesh and blood. Not the raving lunatic of his darkest imaginings, but a real human being . . . looking at him, saying his name, as if she remembered who he was . . .

148

Slowly, he went forward, a well-built lad going on sixteen, his muscular frame filling the room, making it seem as if it had shrunk in size and that the walls were somehow closing in.

Lillian McIntyre watched his approach. All at once the innocuous expression in her eyes was replaced by one of horror and disbelief. Wordlessly, she shook her head, and panic spread over her face.

'No,' she whimpered. '*No! No! NO!*'

Her voice was rising till soon it became a crazed shout of protest. Slowly, she rose to her feet, knocking her chair sideways in her anxiety to escape. 'Take him away! Take him away!' she yelled. 'I don't want him here! He's mad! Mad!'

She began sobbing and screaming while she stumbled backwards across the room to take refuge in a corner where she crouched like a trapped animal. 'He'll hit my lady's baby! Please don't let him do it! My lady must find her baby! God help me! God help me!'

'Mother!' Magnus made to go to her but she cowered lower, her face contorted. No more was she the Lillian McIntyre they remembered, a mother gentle and kind, instead she had turned into the demented creature of their worst imaginings.

Her screams were growing in volume, now, spewing into the room with such ear-splitting intensity they struck nameless fear into the hearts of Anna and her brothers.

Then the ravings began, the ravings of a madwoman, more petrifying than anything they could have conjured up in their most ghastly nightmares. Saliva was drooling from her mouth, she was clawing at the walls, as if trying to dig herself away from her own hellish fears, her bloodied nails raking ragged furrows in the plaster.

Nurses came running, behind them Reverend Simpson. Without a word he hurried the children from the room, out into the passageway, where they all stood looking at one another, white-faced with shock, the yells and shouts of their mother pounding in their ears.

From the ward in front of them came a monotonous drone as someone sang off-key; a cackling laugh split the night; a long, low sobbing from a helpless, lost soul went on and on and on . . .

'Come away from here.' Mr Simpson hustled the children towards the second door but it was locked and no nurses were available to open it, all of them being too busy with Lillian McIntyre.

Adam's eyes were black with terror. 'I knew she would be like that,' he whispered, then turning to the minister, he went on accusingly, 'Why did you bring us here? To this madhouse? You should have known what she was like! You should have known better! She's crazy! Father was right. She's possessed o' the devil.'

'Stop that, Adam!' Magnus sharply told his brother. 'You weren't there to begin with. You didn't see her as me and Anna saw her. She was fine then, sweet and gentle.'

'Ay, she was – Mother.' Anna spoke in a daze. 'The mother I remembered, with hands that were warm and eyes so kind . . . ' Her voice broke into a sob and she couldn't go on.

Mr Simpson shook his head. 'I don't understand it. I simply do not understand it. I've never seen her like this. I would never have brought you here if I had thought –'

A nurse came out of the room. 'I'm sorry, I must ask you to leave,' she said firmly. 'Mrs McIntyre is very upset. We'll have to get her to bed and give her something to quieten her down.'

Magnus's mind was whirling with a hundred questions and when he spoke his voice was harsh with worry. 'If you don't mind, nurse, I'd like to see a doctor. We've come a long way and I want to know more about my mother, we all want to know.'

The nurse looked at him quizzically. 'The doctor isn't here. He's already explained your mother's case to Mr McIntyre. We do all we can for her, the rest is really up to her. I personally sense a great deal of awareness in her, as if

150

she knows full well what's going on round about her but feels safer ignoring it. Only time will tell which way it goes for her.'

Her tones were laden with sympathy and Magnus stared at her. She knew what was going to happen to him! To Anna! To Adam! She didn't need to say anything. It was all there, in her eyes, in her voice. She was sorry for them. God! No wonder! Their father had been right after all. Madness awaited them in the dark years ahead. The same kind of insanity he had just witnessed.

He'd die rather than face that! At least there would be peace in death. How could he live with it? How could any of them live with it?

He passed a hand over his eyes and staggered slightly. Beside him Anna shivered and drew in her breath and glancing at her face he saw the same kind of dread in it that was turning his insides to jelly.

Pulling himself together he put an arm round her shoulders and led her away, Adam following hastily on their heels.

Reverend Simpson turned to the nurse. 'What happened, Nurse? I wasn't in the room at the time. Has she been like this before?'

The nurse regarded him for a long, considering moment before saying slowly, 'Yes, Reverend Simpson – several times. Mr McIntyre doesn't visit often but when he does – her behaviour is similar to what it was tonight. We have told him that it might be better if he doesn't come again.'

'But, this evening, Nurse, with her own children? What sort of thing could have triggered off such a reaction?'

She shook her head. 'I really don't know, Reverend Simpson, everything was fine at first. Her daughter and son were with her and she seemed pleased to see them. Then . . . the boy came in . . . and that's when it started.'

'I see. Strange, very strange. Oh well, mustn't keep you, Nurse, thank you for everything, you have been most kind. Goodnight. I'll come back to visit Mrs McIntyre whenever I can. It may not be for some time but – we'll see.'

As he walked slowly towards the heavy wooden doors where the young McIntyres were waiting. Mr Simpson's thoughts were very deep. Roderick McIntyre and Adam! Adam and Roderick McIntyre! A father and son so alike in manner and build that people often commented on it.

Tonight, Lillian McIntyre had mistaken Adam for Roderick. In the son she had seen the father and the results had been terrifying. Words she had once spoken came back to Mr Simpson. 'Don't let him come near me. Pray God, keep him away!'

It was clear that Lillian McIntyre feared and loathed her husband and would do anything to keep him at bay. Because of him she had cocooned herself from a reality so dreadful she would rather spend her life in seclusion than face it again. She would fight tooth and claw in order to protect herself from Roderick McIntyre.

Reverend Simpson sighed as he came to the conclusion that he didn't know Lillian McIntyre as well as he would have liked. No-one had known her all that well in the village. Before coming to Glen Tarsa she must have led a mysterious, stormy, and disturbing life, one that had eventually caught up with her and had culminated so tragically in mental illness.

Mr Simpson sighed again and wished he could do more for the young McIntyres. As it was, his good intentions had turned sour on him. It was with a heavy heart that he gathered up his charges and led them out into the bracing air of the moonbathed evening.

CHAPTER 16

Like Father . . .

It was good to get back to the homely little inn after the forbidding severity of the asylum. Even so it did nothing to cheer the travellers from Glen Tarsa. They went early to bed, weary of mind and spirit, each with their own thoughts to carry them through the long night hours.

Before going to his room Magnus had spoken privately to Anna in an urgent, hurried manner. 'Listen, Anna, I can't say too much just now, but as soon as I can I'm taking you away from Glen Tarsa. It's getting too dangerous for you to bide much longer in that house wi' him. His temper's getting worse, he's becoming more violent. On our own we can at least be at peace wi' one another and, whatever's in store for us, we can face it together.'

He had hurried away before Anna got the chance to speak and for a long time afterwards she had sat by her window, feeling lonely and dispirited, going over in her mind the things he had said, wondering what was going to happen to them all in the future.

But it was her mother that she thought about most, seeing in her mind's eye that dear, familiar face, remembering the touch of those warm and gentle hands.

It had been so peaceful . . . then something had happened to turn it into a nightmare, a horrific experience that Anna knew she would never forget.

Her mother's violent reaction to Adam was a puzzle to her. The questions ran round her head in circles but there were no answers.

Slowly, she undressed and got into the strange bed. It was soft and comfortable. The sheets and the pillowcases smelt of lavender.

As she lay there, sounds of the night came drifting into the room. Outside her window the sea murmured, ceaselessly, pleasantly, rhythmically; laughter rose from the rooms below; coach wheels rumbled on the road. The laughter was nearer now; footsteps padded on the narrow, twisting stairs, followed by the opening and closing of doors further along the passageway. A soft little whinnying snort came from the stables; more footsteps on the stairs accompanied by muffled voices; a light laugh rang out to be quickly smothered.

Comforting sounds, all of them, nothing threatening or sinister there. The laugh reminded Anna of Lady Pandora and she wished she was back once more in Noble House, doing all the lovely things that had made her life so sweet.

She remembered the portrait she had been painting. Would she ever finish it now? She had enjoyed doing it, though there was one thing she could never get quite right. The eyes. Lady Pandora's eyes . . .

She sat up in bed, excitement catching in her throat because suddenly she knew what she had been doing wrong. She had been trying to paint the eyes the way they were in the picture above the fireplace in Noble House, mysterious and rather sad.

The secrets had now gone from those fascinating eyes. They were open and clear and laughing and Anna knew that these were the expressions she had to try and capture in the painting – if she ever got the chance to finish it.

Lying back on her pillows she thought about the different ways that her ladyship smiled: sometimes teasing, occasionally petulant, usually with a radiance so bright it uplifted everyone who saw it. Then there was the wistful smile, so filled with tenderness that to look upon it was to feel becalmed on a sea of love.

154

To Anna it was like a caress, she knew it so well, it seemed to be reaching out to her now, like a light in the darkness, so brilliant it dazzled her senses and gave her a small measure of comfort.

Her mind turned to the visit she had paid old Grace the day before. The old lady had told her how Lady Pandora had gone to Corran Kirk to look for her. 'Och, but she wasny herself, no' herself at all,' Grace had proclaimed, with a shake of her white head. 'She had heard about your father's cruelty towards you, my lassie, and when I told her you weren't being allowed out o' the house because o' it she just upped and flew out o' the kirk, her hanky to her eyes and her poor face like death.'

'My lady,' Anna whispered now, her heart twisting with pain. 'I'll never leave you . . . never . . . but what am I to do? What can I say to Magnus? He wants what's best for me, he worries about me, I worry about you.'

The problems seemed insoluble. It was as if she was being torn apart, one half of her longing to run away with Magnus, the other half wanting only the chance to return to Lady Pandora.

Anna felt cold and very alone. Curling into a ball she closed her eyes. The murmur of the sea was like a lullaby: hush, hush, it went against the shore; lap, lap, it went against the rocks. The wavelets were washing the pebbles, she could hear them chuckling as the wind whispered down from the hills, sighing over the loch . . .

A voice came to her, from dreams, from imaginings? She didn't know but quite plainly it said, 'Not my baby. Has my lady found her baby?' The tears rolled down Anna's face. 'I am your baby, Mother, please don't shut me out . . . '

She awoke with a start, feeling dazed and disorientated, not knowing how long she had been asleep. It might have been hours or minutes – if indeed she had been asleep at all. She hadn't been aware that she had drifted off . . .

155

Someone was in her room, a looming shadow that seemed to float towards her and hold out its arms to her as if to envelope her.

Her heart thudded. Was she still asleep? Was this ghostly grey creature part of the night and the dreamings . . . ?

'No, no, no,' she sighed. 'Please go away, I don't want you in my dreams, I only want to sleep.'

'Wheesht, Anna,' Adam's gruff voice spoke at her side. 'It's only me. I'm sorry I woke you but I couldn't settle. Oh, Anna, please let me talk to you, I'm lonely, I miss you beside me. At home I always rest easy, knowing you're there in the room with me. You're like her, like Mother, like she used to be before she went off her head. I'm frightened, Anna, I'm so lonely and frightened.'

His voice broke, and Anna tried to still her wildly beating heart. This was Adam, the brother who had teased and tormented her ever since she could remember, childish things to begin with, progressing to more serious and threatening behaviour when he had begun developing sexual urges at an early age.

Anna had never trusted him in the same room as herself and now here he was, sneaking through the connecting door in the middle of the night . . . just to talk to her!

Yet he sounded so sincere – and there was something about the dreadful, lost despair in his words that touched her deeply. He was sitting on the edge of her bed, shivering, a vision of abject misery.

Her heart melted, she wanted to reach out and touch him, but her mistrust of him held her back. The old unease of being alone with him gripped her and she, too, shivered.

With Magnus it was different. They had always been able to communicate, to discuss their hopes, dreams, and fears. The love she had for Magnus had grown stronger with every passing year till now she loved him more than she loved anyone else in the whole world.

Too strong! Too deep! The warnings had been with her a long time now but sometimes she couldn't help ignoring them. That strange breathlessness she often experienced whenever he looked at her, the warmth that invaded her being when his body was close to hers . . .

Love! Nothing wrong with love. He was her brother, she loved him, it was as simple as that. When she was with him she felt warm and safe and good, none of which she had ever felt with Adam.

Adam wrought apprehension in her, there was a wildness about him, fathomless depths that she couldn't reach. His was an undisciplined nature, changing from one mood to another without warning. Often she wasn't sure if she loved him as a sister ought to love a brother and she would ask herself why – when all the time she knew the answer.

She mistrusted him because he was too much like Roderick. She could sense his cruelty, his selfishness, his attitude that he could take what he wanted from life without thought for others.

Anna shuddered. She didn't want him here beside her, she didn't want him in her room. It had been a relief to get away from him, to enjoy some privacy for a change, but now he was sitting on her bed, a pale, ghostly figure in his shapeless nightshirt, sniffing and shaking, his head in his hands, his emotions completely out of control.

'Help me, Anna,' he muttered bleakly. 'Tell me why my mother hates me.'

'Hates you? Och, c'mon, Adam, that's putting it a bit strong, Mother doesn't hate anyone, she's too kind . . .'

'Stop it!' he said passionately. 'You're lying. You know! You saw! She was fine wi' you and Magnus but when I came in she went crazy. Everyone saw it. She was afraid o' me! Why should my own mother hate and fear me? She went mad wi' terror and I don't know why, Anna. I wish I'd never come! Nobody likes me, no' even my own mother.'

Anna's heart turned over. Pulling him towards her, she put her arms around him and he curled against her like a little boy.

'Wheesht now,' she soothed, stroking his hair and rock-ing him gently. 'You mustn't think these things. Mother didn't know who you were – she didn't know any o' us. I think she just got a fright when you barged into the room like an elephant. You frighten me sometimes, the way you charge about. Don't cry anymore, we'll be home tomorrow and everything will be back to normal.'

'Will it, Anna? Will you sing around the house the way you did before father knocked the stuffing out o' you wi' those bloody great fists o' his? I hated him for that. I wanted to pay him back but I – I didn't have the nerve.' There! It was out! He'd admitted something to his sister that never, never, would he have told anyone else.

'Och, don't think any less o' yourself for that,' she said comfortingly. 'We're all afraid o' things and it would be a gey strange body indeed who had no twinge o' dread when faced with Iron Rod in a rage.'

'Ay, you're right there, Anna,' Adam said in some won-derment. 'The sight o' those bloodshot eyes o' his and his mouth all twisted and snarling would terrify Goliath himself.'

Anna laughed. For the first time in her life she felt an empathy with her younger brother and it was a good, warm feeling. He snuggled in a bit closer and said softly, 'Promise me you'll be happier and laugh the way you used to when we get home.'

'Alright, I promise.'

'That's good. I wish we were home right now, at this very minute. I don't like it when you aren't in the same room as me. I feel safe wi' you, even when you don't speak.'

He was quiet for a few moments then he went on thoughtfully, 'Anna, do you like living in Glen Tarsa?'

'I love the glen,' she replied readily. 'It and the folk who live there, in fact everything about it.'

'Would you ever leave it?'

For a moment she wondered if he had heard something of the conversation between herself and Magnus but decided, no, his question was innocent enough.

'Only if I felt I really had to.'

'Me too. I would stay there always if it wasn't for him. I wonder what made him bring us to The Gatehouse. I know I was just a tiny wee lad when we came and I don't remember any other place. Do you know where we came from? Where we were born?'

'Somewhere in England. Mother told me. She left Scotland as a young girl and found work as a nanny there. That's where she met Father. He had come from Scotland and was in a job in England and then he moved us all back North when he was made under-manager of the powder-mill. We were all very young at the time and I feel as if Glen Tarsa has always been my home.'

Adam had stopped shivering and was nuzzling his face into her neck. 'You smell nice, Anna, all soft and warm like toast. Remember when you were little? How you used to let Magnus into bed beside you? I never, ever told Father about that, Anna, not even when I told him you had been to the Hallowe'en party at The House o' Noble. I used to get jealous o' Magnus and wished it was me in there with you.'

'Let me sleep wi' you tonight. We'll keep each other nice and warm.' He was cuddling in tighter and a chill washed through Anna, even though his behaviour was no more threatening than that of a small boy seeking a measure of comfort . . .

Unpleasant memories began piling in on her. She recalled the winter nights of her growing years, the feeling that eyes were watching her as she undressed, Adam's eyes, leering into the darkness, trying to get a glimpse of her developing body . . .

Beth had known about Adam too. Words that she had spoken long ago floated into Anna's mind. 'He'll grow up to be like your father, looking at girls' bosoms . . . anything with a skirt on . . . '

'Go back to your room, Adam,' Anna's voice sounded hollow. She tried to untwine his arms from her neck but

159

they only gripped her harder and his mouth was on her cheek, pressing in hard.

'Do you know how to kiss boys, Anna? Properly, I mean, like this.' His lips closed over hers.

She tried to push his face away but his hold on her grew stronger. His hands were on her breasts, roughly kneading them, bruising the soft flesh.

He had been labouring in the mill since the age of thirteen, and his muscles were like iron, his chest broad and hard and deep, his legs sinewy and powerful. Added to his physical strengths, his control over his lustful desires was practically non-existent, his opinions about his prowess with women were bloated, and he felt it was not only his right to have who he wanted but that he was doing a great service to womankind in general by giving them what they wanted . . . himself.

He began panting now, his breath fanning Anna's face. Fumbling with his nightshirt he pulled it up to his waist and rammed his pelvis hard against her.

'Come on, Anna,' he pleaded hoarsely. 'It doesn't matter that you're my sister. Other people do it. Danny Black told me about a brother and sister who sleep together in the same bed and do it all the time. No-one will know but you and me. It's good, Anna, you'll love it. Put your hand down and touch it, it's a big one and it's all for you. I know girls like them big and angry and bursting. Let me get in there, Anna, I can't wait, I never can wait when I'm worked up like this!'

Anna's throat had constricted, so tightly she was unable to make any sound, let alone cry out for help. The room was spinning round, the walls began to close in on her. Adam was frenziedly tearing at her nightdress, she could feel his nails scraping her skin. The weight of his body was crushing her into the mattress, his knees forcing her legs apart.

She took a deep, sobbing breath, and terror gave her a sudden burst of strength. Power returned to her rigid limbs and she began to fight back. Struggling and kicking she caught him off guard and threw him away from her.

'Get out o' here this minute!' she panted tearfully. 'You're mad, Adam McIntyre! Mad! Mad! Mad!'

The words were out before she could stop them and she clamped her hands to her mouth, as if by so doing she could take back what she had just said.

A thought spiralled like a whirlwind into her brain. Father was right! He was right! It's happening, already it's happening!

As her declaration unleashed itself into his ears all the fire seeped out of Adam and he crumpled in utter dejection. 'Don't say things like that, Anna. It isn't true. You know it isn't true!'

Falling down on his knees by the bed he buried his face into the blankets and wept. 'I'm sorry, Anna, I'm sorry.' His voice came out in muffled sobs. 'I never wanted to hurt you. I didn't mean it, something came over me. Don't tell Magnus – or Father. Oh, please, say you won't tell Father. He wouldn't believe you anyway, you know that, don't you, Anna? He's always listened to me. He wouldn't like it if he thought you were telling tales about me.'

'Ay, fine well I know it,' she returned bitterly. 'If I'd had to rely on him to fight my battles I wouldn't be here today. I don't need him and I don't need you. Go away now and never dare lay a finger on me again.'

Head downbent he got up and went to the connecting door but, before he turned the knob, he paused for a moment. 'Forgive me, Anna,' he begged and his voice was dull and lifeless in the silent darkness of the room. 'I – I love you and I couldn't bear it if you were never kind to me again.'

She made no answer. She couldn't. It was too soon for her to make any promises of that nature.

The door opened and closed softly and she lay back on her pillows, cold and stiff with shock, her heart pounding dully in her ears.

She felt sick, afraid. She seethed with loathing and revulsion for her brother, yet, for all her miseries, she was unable to understand why a feeling of compassion engulfed her when she recalled his last words.

'I love you, Anna, I couldn't bear it if you were never kind to me again.'

Though he was gone the echoes of his voice seemed to linger on in the silence.

'Oh, Adam,' she sighed, 'you're so lost, so alone. I will forgive you, I will, but not yet, not for a long, long time.'

She lay in the unfamiliar bed, wide-eyed and wakeful, aware of the night and the shadows, alert to every sound, every flicker of movement, and she wished only for the morning that she might be delivered from her thoughts and her fears and her imaginings.

CHAPTER 17

Roderick Alone

It had been a busy and demanding day for Roderick and he was weary and disgruntled when he finally sat down to the cold supper Anna had prepared for him before her departure to Kilkenzie.

That afternoon William Jordan had had words with Roderick over his mean handling of the mill employees.

Jordan was all for treating them with tact and respect. Respect! Roderick sneered at the very idea. Who the hell did Jordan think the workers were? Gentry? People who ought not to be spoken to with authority? College nancies who shouldn't be allowed to get their hands soiled?

It had all come about because he had shouted at Davie McDonald for dropping a barrel-load of gunpowder. The whole buggering lot had rolled away down the riverbank but had fortunately remained undamaged when it had finally come to rest in the undergrowth.

But that had not been the end of the matter. The barrel had wedged itself between two trees and no amount of hauling and pulling would free it. In the end it had taken two men to cut it loose and all the while the daft, deaf bugger who had been the cause of the trouble had gone about with an inanely triumphant expression on his face, as if he was glad he had been the perpetrator of all the upset and bother and wasn't in the least sorry for it.

Well, of course, Roderick couldn't let an incident like that go, without having some say in the matter. He was, after all, the man in charge, and valuable time had been lost all through the incompetence of that sly swine, Davie McDonald, with his foxy face and his shifty eyes.

So he had let loose on the man, giving him a piece of his mind and a bit more besides, and through it all Davie had stood there, as meek as a lamb, not giving anything away . . . except for that muscle twitching in his jaw and his fists clenching at his sides . . .

Roderick knew all about that muscle. It was a sign that the man was having a job holding back his temper, and those fists . . . small and insignificant looking but as hard as rocks just the same.

Davie's strength was legendary: he could lift and shift things that men twice his size could barely budge, yet he looked as puny as an ill-nourished cat.

The combination had always worried Roderick, though never by one word had he ever given Davie wind of his feelings. Far better that he was never allowed to forget who was boss around the place.

It didn't really matter anyway what anybody said to him. He was supposed to be hard of hearing and unable to take in much of anything . . . Though mind, a lot of folk had expressed doubts about that. Here Roderick went cold, since he himself had always harboured a suspicion that it was all an act, and that Davie could hear as well as the next man.

All in all, Roderick was never slow to seize on any opportunity to hurl abuse into Davie's ears, and today Roderick was in a worse mood than usual. His temper had been on a short fuse ever since Mr Simpson had offered to take the children to Kilkenzie and it had become worse than ever when they had set out that morning on their journey. Even Roderick, for all his huffing and puffing, couldn't suppress a shiver of fear at the thought of what that daft bitch, Lillian, might say to them.

All day he had been simmering with suppressed rage and he had been more than ready to unleash his vitriol on Davie, taking a positive delight in spewing out the vindictive words, the threats, the taunts.

Too bad Jordan had chanced on the scene and had heard everything. Browbeating he had called it. Browbeating a daft, deaf sod who couldn't hear a word Roderick was saying!

'The man needs discipline,' he had growled. 'He's lucky to be in a job o' work at all. No other place would take him on.'

'Davie's a damned good worker and well you know it, McIntyre,' William Jordan had retaliated, his blue eyes flashing, his jaw jutting aggressively into the under-manager's face. 'I've watched him doing the work of two men and you standing by, allowing it. Never let me hear you speaking to him in that manner again. He isn't a dog. He's a human being like the rest of us and you see you treat him with a bit of respect in future.'

'Respect! It's discipline the bugger needs!' Roderick had roared, his eyes bulging with chagrin. 'It's a pity you don't exercise a bit o' that in your own family, Jordan! That wee madam o' a daughter o' yours would have been all the better for a damned good hiding now and then!'

William Jordan's nostrils had flared at this. 'Watch it, McIntyre,' he had said warningly. 'You have no damned right to bring personal affairs into this, but, as you have, I'm glad you brought the subject up. I take your point about Beth, an occasional slap might have done her some good and when I say occasional I mean just that.

'We're of the extremes you and me. I never laid a finger on my girl while you just about killed yours . . . and still attempt to do so, from all I hear. Only a bully and a coward would do that to a lass like Anna. It's as well that Magnus is able to stand up to you now – a boy after my own heart, always has been. I can hardly say that about your other son, a good worker, I'll grant you, but deceitful, would rob his own granny if he thought he could get away with it. I've had to pull him up once or twice for acting suspiciously in the changing sheds, rifling through the pockets, no doubt. There have been one or two reports about personal items going missing.'

'You keep Adam out o' this,' Roderick had snarled menacingly. 'He's a good boy and I'll thank you to keep your snide remarks to yourself.'

'Oh, I'd be glad to keep him out of it, if I thought he would do me a favour and stay away from my family – from my daughter in particular. One hears things, McIntyre, I believe he's been seen pestering Beth, and I for one have no doubts whatsoever as to what the young stag has in his mind.'

'Pestering your daughter! More like her flaunting herself at my boy! She's a hot piece o' goods and no mistake, and from all I hear it doesn't matter if they be from cot or castle! She isn't fussy, just so long as there's a lively romp in the hay for her afterwards!'

The two stood glaring, daggers drawn at one another: tall, sandy-haired Jordan, the manager of the mill, immaculate in his dark coat and pin-striped trousers; thick-set, crudely hewn, Roderick, equally smart in his well-pressed suit, his watch chain hanging elegantly from his pocket.

William Jordan was the first to recover himself. 'I'm not here to argue with you, McIntyre,' he said with admirable composure. 'Especially about our respective offspring. But I am telling you this, watch your step with the workers, and that goes for all of them – and don't let Davie lift such heavy loads in future – and I mean that. I will not have him chastised just because he has a handicap.'

His voice had held slightly threatening overtones, a hint for Roderick to go easy – or else. Watch his bloody step indeed! Jordan was the one who should be doing that. It was high time he was knocked off that buggering God-Almighty pedestal of his!

He wasn't infallible. Anybody who could put on a snobby accent and display a bit of brass neck could do the job Jordan was doing . . . both of which doubtful assets Roderick owned in full measure.

*   *   *

166

A bully! A coward! The words that William Jordan had spoken festered in Roderick's mind as he sat at the table eating his lone supper.

Viciously he dug his knife into his boiled mutton. The house was very quiet; the clock ticked; a blackbird trilled in the rowan tree outside the window; the sheep bleated from the hills; the river sang over the stones; a bumble bee buzzed on the window ledge, a frantic rasping of sound that got on Roderick's nerves.

Tibby the cat had knocked the bee down with her paw. Like a statue she sat there, watching it whirling round in frenzied circles, every sleek hair in her body bristling with interest.

The sight of the cat's self-satisfied contentment enraged Roderick. Damned moggy! Fooling idly around with buggering bees! As if that justified its place in the home!

The cat had been Anna's doing. 'She'll earn her keep, Father,' she had declared, her words tripping over themselves in her eagerness to extol the animal's virtues. 'Old Grace's cat had kittens and this is one o' them. She'll be a good mouser like her mother.'

'Is that so?' Roderick said now to the empty room. 'We'll soon see about that.'

He rose from the table, knocking over the milk jug in the process. It clattered to the floor and the cat was immediately on the alert, for she hated the bully who kicked her whenever he got the chance.

With the intention of throwing the animal out of the house Roderick's big, meaty fist shot out to grab her by the scruff of the neck.

She crouched low, spitting and snarling, making an agile twist out of his clutches to cower against the window panes, ears pinned back, lips drawn to reveal sharp glistening fangs.

'Want to play games, eh?' Roderick sniggered, tormenting the little creature by wriggling his fingers about in front of her face.

A warning growl rumbled deep in her throat, and the smiles left him. 'Come here, you smelly brute!' he muttered savagely, and made a lunge forward.

He got to within an inch of the cat's face before her unsheathed claws tore at his flesh, ripping it apart, leaving a trail of ragged, bloody streaks on the back of his hand.

'Filthy, dangerous brute!' Roderick stared at the scratches, as if unable to believe that any living creature should dare to attack him in this way.

The cat, sensing the danger of her position, gave a pitiful little, squeaky meow which only served to heighten Roderick's rage. 'Begging for mercy, eh? Well, I'll soon show you who's boss around here!' Without another word he grabbed her round the neck with both hands and began squeezing, squeezing, tighter, tighter, releasing all the pent-up venom he had been bottling up all day.

The cat struggled and kicked for a few moments, her paws frantically flaying the air in a fight for life, she made a gurgling sound, then she went limp, her eyes staring, her pink tongue protruding from the froth of saliva that had filled her mouth.

'Christ!' Roderick stared at the furry little bundle dangling from his big hands, as if surprised that she had died so quickly.

With a shudder he went quickly outside to the ashpit, made a hole with his boot, threw the lifeless body into it, and covered it over with ashes.

He stood for a moment, gazing down at the dusty grave, then, with a shrug, he hooked his thumbs into his waistcoat and lifted his eyes to the hills. Taking a deep breath, he muttered, 'Too bad, it shouldn't have been buggering about wi' that damned bee, it was asking for it and it got what it deserved!'

Turning abruptly on his heel he went into the byre to seize a bucket from a hook on the wall. Going into Clover's stall he began milking her, his body balanced awkwardly on the tiny milking stool, his big, bull head resting on the cow's flank.

'This is a woman's work,' he grumbled moodily, pulling at Clover's teats as if they were made of rubber, his inexpert handling of her tender parts making her roll her eyes and kick out protestingly with her back legs.

The pail tipped over, and the dribble of milk it contained went trickling down through the straw bedding and into the dung-filled trench.

'Bitch!' Spitefully he slapped her rump. 'Stay still or I'll leave all your damned milk in your udder and see how you like that!'

But the cow was heavy with her summer calf and he was too money-conscious to risk anything happening to the beast. Forcing himself to take his time, he worked the teats more gently till the bucket was half full and feeling pleased with himself, he placed some hay in the manger and carried the milk into the cool larder.

For ten more minutes he pottered about outside before going back into the house. He ignored the untidy table and didn't bother to wash up his supper dishes. Let Anna do that when she came back. It was her job. She ought to be here now to see to the house. This business of gallivant-ing off to Kilkenzie was a piece of nonsense, though of course he hadn't said that to the minister.

He wondered about Lillian again. The last time he had gone to see her she had ranted and raved at him. God, she was mad alright! Nobody could tell him otherwise. She couldn't even converse as well as a mentally retarded child.

Rubbish! Just meaningless rubbish!

Let Anna and Magnus get a taste of that and see what they thought of their precious mother.

But Adam – he didn't want Adam to see it. He hadn't wanted Adam to go, only it would have looked odd trying to keep him away. Favouritism. A lot of whispers of that nature went on behind his back . . .

He sat on the sofa and puffed furiously at his pipe as unsavoury memories paraded through his mind . . . that look in his wife's eyes last time he had seen her. Wild! Idiotic! Terrifying!

He rocked in his seat. 'Oh, God help me,' he said aloud. 'Don't let it happen to Adam! Oh please, God, help me!'

He got up and paced, his movements jerky, his legs feeling unsteady. This had happened to him before, a feeling of weakness and a staggering when he walked which made Nellie Jean laugh and say he was getting so past it he could even get drunk on water.

She had never been the same towards him since he'd got rid of Boxer Sam. He didn't see nearly so much of her now and when he did all she could do was ridicule him. Bitch! Just let her try and make a fool of him in front of other people and he'd soon show her he wasn't known as Iron Rod for nothing!

He wondered what she was doing for a bedmate these days. He had only clapped eyes on her once since that humiliating business more than a fortnight ago, when he had let her down in bed. His face reddened as he recalled the highly insulting remarks she had made about his diminishing sexual abilities, blaming it on too much drink and other self-indulgences over the years.

The awful thing was, he hadn't been in the least drunk at the time, he just hadn't been able to do it, to satisfy her in the way Nellie Jean liked to be satisfied.

The whole episode had worried him a good deal and he had tried to console himself with the thought that it all owed itself to the row he'd had with Lady Pandora over Anna.

That was enough to put any man off his game, even one as resilient as he was.

He stopped pacing and gazed unseeingly at the mantelpiece, wishing that Nellie Jean would stop by tonight. He was feeling better. His shaky turn had dispersed. He felt ready for her again but earlier that day, when he had drawn her aside at the mill and had mentioned a get together, she had told him that she would be 'otherwise engaged' that evening.

Hmph! Otherwise engaged indeed! She wasn't getting any younger and should think herself lucky to get invited into his bed at all. Still, he had to admit, she was good, damned good . . . perhaps if he went along to her cottage he might find her in. With the children away it was an opportunity not to be missed . . .

Taking out his watch he looked at it. Almost half past nine. The night alone in the empty house stretched bleakly ahead. He missed the children. It was no use trying to deny it even to himself. Oh, God, yes, he missed them! They made the house a home. No matter how quiet they were they gave the place life.

He didn't like this feeling of loneliness, he hated being alone.

Ay, he would go and see Nellie Jean, take her some eggs, cheese, and a drop of his whisky. The bitch would like that, he had never known her yet to turn up her nose at a dram. It made her more hot-blooded than ever and when she'd had a few, she became clingy and affectionate and could hardly wait for him to get his trousers off . . .

The thought made him lick his lips with anticipation, and his mind meandered pleasantly on. She might make him some supper. He had hardly touched his cold dinner and now he was feeling hungry. They could eat and drink together and then . . .

A light knock at the door interrupted his thoughts. He cocked his head, listening. Who the hell was it? Few people ever came to his door, and when they did, it was usually the children they wanted to see . . .

The knock came again, a little louder this time . . . could it be Nellie Jean? Feeling as lonely as he was? Perhaps with the same kind of thoughts in her head that had been in his?

He rubbed his hands together. This was more like it.

Her coming to him. It wasn't right that he should go cap-in-hand to her. When all was said and done, he was boss around here and it was only fitting that she should be the one to do the running.

Roderick smirked. Closing the lid of his watch with a snap he strode to the door to wrench it open and almost fainted with surprise as he beheld his visitor. Never, in all his wildest imaginings, could he have believed a moment such as this would come to him.

It seemed that all his dreams were about to come true. Feelings of power swept over him. It was as it should be. After all he was Roderick McIntyre, a man not to be trifled with – by anybody.

CHAPTER 18

Surrender

Lady Pandora stood on Roderick's doorstep, a shadowy figure who didn't move or speak at the rude opening of the door. In her stillness she seemed an ephemeral creature, one who might disappear at any moment into the silence and vastness of the darkening hills.

The tiny entrance hall of The Gatehouse was shrouded in gloom but Roderick's eyes quickly adjusted to it as he stared at his visitor. She was real alright! A being of elegance in her green silk dress and velvet cloak. A presence who permeated the very air with light and life and being.

Without waiting for him to speak, she brushed past him and made her way into the kitchen, leaving him to close and bolt the door.

A smile of triumph lifted the corners of his cruel and sensual mouth. He had won! She had capitulated! He was used to getting his own way with people but he hadn't expected it to be so soon with Lady Pandora.

But then, she was a woman who liked to get her own way too – only she hadn't quite managed it this time. Roderick held the trump card. He had made her sweat and worry and wonder and the waiting had been too much for her.

She wanted Anna back. She wanted that very badly indeed. She was pining for the girl – why else would she be here now? In his house? Ready to do business with him.

Roderick's smile deepened. Going over to the hall mirror

he stared at his reflection. The dimness was kind to him: his florid face was free of lines, he looked younger than his forty-four years.

'Mirror, mirror on the wall . . . ' he murmured with a snigger. Sobering, he regarded his image intently. You'll do, my lad, he thought smugly, Ay, by God and you will! You're a catch for any woman, gentry or otherwise! Straightening his shoulders, he tugged his waistcoat into shape, smoothed his sideburns with a wetted finger, took a deep breath, and strode into the kitchen.

The lamps hadn't yet been lit, and the room had that strange air of mystery about it that comes with the gloaming, faintly illuminated by pearly light, yet cloaked in a filmy dark veil that pushed everyday objects into obscurity.

'I waited till nightfall,' Lady Pandora spoke from the shadows, her voice low and husky and somehow defeated. 'I didn't want anyone to see me coming here. Sir Malaroy has gone to Glasgow for the night – I knew the children would be away . . . '

Roderick rubbed his hands briskly together. 'Fine, fine, just let me light the lamps and make things a bit more homely. Not a grand place like yours, my dear lady, but my little castle just the same.'

He applied a match to the wicks, light sprang up, scattering the shadows. Spinning round on his heel he looked at her and was quick to note the dark smudges under her eyes, the hollows under her cheekbones, the slight trembling of her mouth.

She looked aloof and unobtainable, the way she looked whenever he had reason to visit Noble House. It was an expression that had always maddened him, now it excited him, he was the one in command, she was here, in his house, for one reason and one reason only. The thought turned his knees to water. All this time of waiting for her and now . . .

The perfume of her wafted to him, delicate, provocative. God, she was beautiful! That neat little nose of hers

174

uptilted; her breasts rising and falling; her head held high with pride even though she knew she must soon lose it . . .

He forced himself to behave normally, to keep up the pretence of the polite host for a while. 'Your cloak, my lady, let me take it. Sit down and make yourself comfortable. Can I get you anything? A glass o' port wine perhaps?'

She remained standing and looked him straight in the eye. 'You know why I'm here, Roderick. It will be better if we are honest with one another. I've come about Anna – as you very well know. I am aware that she has suffered because you and I argued the last time we met. The knowledge of that has been very difficult for me to bear. I haven't been able to get her out of my mind and – and that is why I'm here tonight. I'll do anything – anything you will of me – if you'll unbend and allow Anna to come back to me.'

'Anything – dear lady?'

'That is what I said.'

'But not against your will, my lady. Whatever you may think o' me I am first and foremost a gentleman. You must be willing, you understand, you must be willing.'

She closed her eyes to shut out the sight of his lecherous eyes devouring her body. 'I am – willing.'

He cleared his throat. 'Grand, grand, then allow me a few moments to draw the curtains in my room. My bed is very comfortable. You won't be disappointed, I can assure you. Although I am a man o' modest means there are certain things I consider necessary to someone o' my standing. Pray, be seated. I won't keep you waiting long, you can be sure o' that.'

Hastening to his room he tidied away some of the jumble he had left behind that morning, annoyed that Anna hadn't had time to do it for him in her hurry to leave the house.

Nevertheless, once he had drawn the heavy cream-coloured drapes across the window, the room looked extremely cosy and tasteful.

Intimate! That was the word for it! He stood back to admire it, his gaze going from the elegant marble-topped washstand to the dresser with its array of expensive toiletries . . . and the bed. Oh ay, the bed! draped over with blue chenille, everything about it soft and inviting.

How many times, he pondered, had he visualised Lady Pandora lying there, her skin gleaming white against the blue coverlet, her golden hair tumbling about her slender shoulders?

He didn't allow his thoughts to go any further. Soon, very soon, his dreams would be a reality.

The thought brought him out in a sweat, a pulse throbbed in his groin. Turning to the mirror again, he made another swift appraisal of his appearance. His heavy face was glowing, his eyes were brilliant with excitement.

'Hmm, not bad, my lad,' he told his reflection smugly. 'In fact, very handsome, ay, very handsome indeed.'

He knew he wouldn't let her ladyship down. God no! he could hardly wait!

He was master of himself again. The sensation of unsteadiness that had seized him earlier was gone, and he felt strong and fit, every faculty in perfect working order.

Lowering the lamp to a peep he took another glance round the room and nodded with satisfaction. It looked peaceful and mysterious – only the bed, with its rich blue covering, stood out in all its tempting splendour.

Retreating into the parlour he paused for one more minute to gather himself together before making his appearance in the kitchen doorway.

'Come now, my dear,' he said smoothly. 'Everything is ready, you will not find yourself wanting for anything.'

Slowly she moved towards him. He seized her hand, and it lay in his like a piece of ice. Quizzically, he raised his bushy brows. 'Why, you're freezing, my lady, like a little bird without a nest. Och, well, don't worry your pretty head about that, I'll soon warm you up, my trousers are on fire wi' heat – and it's all for you.'

176

His laugh was as coarse as his words and she shuddered, hating him, hating herself for what she was about to do – and all for Anna – for the companionship of a child she had first met on a country road; for a little girl who had fled in terror of recognition from Noble House on a Hallowe'en night four years ago; for a sweet waif who had filled her childless life with happiness for the past wonderful year.

But could she go through with this? Even for Anna? Now that she was here, in the home of Roderick McIntyre, face to face with him, listening to him, every instinct within her made her want to turn and flee from everything that he stood for . . .

'Roderick,' she heard herself saying, 'you must understand that I can only stay for an hour or so. The servants have eyes in the backs of their heads and see everything that goes on. I managed to slip away without being seen, but Baird has ears like a fox and seems to hear all the comings and goings when the house has quietened down.' Her voice sounded hollow and unconvincing even to herself and nervously she moistened her dry lips as apprehension seeped into her very marrow.

'Nonsense, my dear Pandora,' Roderick spoke with jovial intimacy. 'Servants only know what you wish them to know and I can safely guess that you pleaded a headache and let it be known that you were going early to bed. I want you to bide the night wi' me, we can be a solace to one another in the lonely hours – far safer that you go home later when everyone is abed and you won't be noticed stealing indoors.'

Pandora stood there loathing him. The man was a devil. One who was capable of anything. She could sense the evil in him, reaching out to envelop her in its ruthless embrace . . .

'Come now, dear lady.' Placing a hand under her elbow, he steered her through to his room. 'You won't be cold in here, warm, nice and warm.' He had lowered his voice to a rough whisper, as his lips brushed her ear, his fingers caressed her arm.

'Undress for me, Pandora, slowly . . . I want to enjoy every moment o' our time together. I've waited patiently for this to happen and I'm going to make the most o' it.'

Mechanically, she began removing her garments, her cold fingers fumbling with buttons and hooks.

'Put some effort into it, woman!' he barked. 'I've seen more life in a corpse! Pandora . . . ' His tone grew softer, ' . . . surely you must know the effect you have on me. When I'm near you things happen to my body that I can't control. Willingly, you said that, Pandora. Give yourself to me in all freedom or you can just bugger off back to that fancy house o' yours . . . and things will be as they were regarding Anna.'

She forced a laugh. 'Of course, Roderick, freedom, abandon! Am I not renowned for both!' With a flourish she stepped out of the remainder of her clothing and Roderick staggered backwards as if he had been struck.

Never, in all his flights of wildest fancy, had he pictured such perfection of womanhood. Her skin was creamy-white, her figure that of a young girl, innocent and pure yet wantonly desirable.

She stood there, amongst the jumble of her discarded clothing, her head tilted, her golden hair framing her perfectly honed face, a goddess who embodied everything attributed to the Greek Eve: all gifts, all powerful, all the qualities that promised heaven to mortal man.

A strange and unfamiliar emotion seized Roderick. He felt that to violate that perfect body would be one of the greatest sins he could ever commit. She looked so pure, so young, so chaste. Her breasts seemed newly sprung, with the nipples pink and child-like, the muscles taut and firm. Surely that tiny waist, those smooth rounded hips, belonged to a girl? A virgin? One who was untouchable, a beautiful creature to be kept virtuous at all costs.

* * *

178

But his fanciful notions didn't last long, swept away as they were by such a tide of longing he felt the pounding of his heart deep inside his chest.

'Unpin your hair for me, Pandora,' he ordered in a gruff whisper.

Unwillingly, she did as he asked and her hair cascaded downwards, a cloud of honey-gold threads that swirled about her naked shoulders.

He advanced towards her, ripping his braces down over his arms, tearing off his shirt to expose his broad chest with its thick furring of black hair.

She closed her eyes to shut out the sight of him but she couldn't shut away the feel of him, pawing her, his thick lips closing over her mouth, his breath blowing down his nostrils, the violent impatience of him struggling out of his trousers.

His hands travelled over her breasts, her thighs, her legs, his loathsome panting filling her head. She felt herself being lifted, thrown onto the bed, then his weight was upon her, pinning her down on the bedclothes.

Everything went black around her as his big bull head shut out the light: the giant shadow of him cavorted on the ceiling; the sweat of his body soaked into hers. Tears blinded her, nipped her eyelids, she turned her head on the pillow and stuffed her fist into her mouth to stop herself from screaming aloud in disgust.

'Pandora,' he gasped harshly, 'I know now why men want you. You're a temptress . . . a temptress, and tonight you belong to me. I warn you, it will be twice, thrice, before I'm satisfied . . . Oh, the feel o' you, your breasts, your belly! I thought I had it all, now I know – I – was – wrong.'

He was contorted in his strivings, bestial in his demands, and while he used her body as an instrument of pleasure, she tried to make her ordeal bearable by saying to herself, over and over, Forgive me for my sins, God, and please, I pray, never let Malaroy find out about my betrayal of him. I love him, with all my heart I love him, but he could never give me the children I wanted. I love and need Anna, the child of another man, this man who lies with me now and offends every one of my senses . . .

Some hours later, when Roderick had at last fallen asleep, she slipped from the bed and began to dress, shivering with fatigue and cold. Her skin was bruised, her muscles ached, but worst of all she felt soiled beyond measure and could hardly wait to get home so that she could bathe herself.

Roderick grunted and turned. 'Not going, my sweet seductress, surely? Come back to bed – once more before you go – my nap has refreshed me.' His tones were slurred with the dregs of sleep but even so she knew that he was still quite capable of further carnal acts.

'Please,' she murmured, not looking at him. 'I am – my body is aching – you are not a gentle lover, Roderick.'

This delighted him, he lay on his back and laughed. 'Gentle? Gentle? With you? If you ask that o' any red-blooded man you ask the impossible . . . my dear little mistress.'

'I am not your mistress!' she flared at him. 'Don't dare even think such a thing!'

But he was feeling utterly contented and merely chuckled at her words. 'What shall I call you, then? My wench? My Jezebel? It matters not, you are all o' these things to me now, whether you like it or no. You have lain wi' me and lusted wi' me. I have a part share in you, whether it suits you or doesn't.'

White-faced, she said quietly, 'How long, Roderick? How long do you think you can go on using people? One day someone will turn on you – from what I hear you have made quite a few enemies in your time.'

'Enemies!' he sneered. 'Weaklings more like. I'm a strong man, Pandora, tonight you saw that for yourself, but there are other ways for a man to prove himself, make no mistake about that, and woe betide anyone who crosses me, be they cat or king!'

He stared at her and grinned mockingly. 'You are an intelligent woman, Pandora, and I can see that you get my meaning. Enough o' this foolish chatter, I want to know when I can see you again.'

'Whenever there is a safe opportunity, I can't promise more than that. Sir Malaroy must never suspect, I want you to understand that. If you lay one finger on me in his sight then everything is finished between us. I love my husband, he is everything to me.'

'Not quite, my dear lady, or you wouldn't be here now. He couldn't give you the one thing you really wanted, bairnies, the wee people you've hankered after all your life.'

'No, he couldn't give me children,' she said huskily. 'But he has given me his love and his loyalty and done things for me that I can never repay . . .'

'Ay,' Roderick interrupted rudely. 'Money can't buy everything, eh, my poor little rich lady?'

'You're despicable,' she returned bitterly. 'Money might not be able to buy everything but it has certainly been your idol all along.'

She laid some guinea pieces on the dresser. 'You won't need any second bidding to accept these. They will ensure you get someone in to keep house for you and so release Anna from your clutches. I'll expect to see her when she gets home. No doubt she will wonder why you are allowing her to come back to me, but I'm sure she must be used to you and your changes of heart.'

She paused for a moment then went on, 'I wonder how the child found her mother after all these years of being parted from her.'

Roderick laughed mirthlessly. 'She will have found her as I did on my last visit to the asylum – insane.'

'You are an unfeeling man, Roderick McIntyre. I hear no compassion in your voice for the woman who shared your bed and bore your children. I can't recall her very well, perhaps because she was never seen very much outside the house. What was she like? Was she pretty?'

181

'A bonny enough woman in her way but she had no strength o' character, none at all. The responsibilities that marriage and motherhood thrust upon her proved too much for such a weak woman.'

'Don't you feel anything for her?'

'Go home, Lady Pandora, there are some things that are best left unsaid. Anna will be along to see you at the first opportunity. You have paid well for the privilege o' her company, a pity the little madam will never know how valuable she is – eh, my dear?'

Anxious only to make her escape Pandora did not deign to answer him and slipped gladly out of the house.

It had been raining but now the clouds had vanished. The glen was cool and peaceful in the sleeping hours of night, all silent except for the rustling of the trees and the burns tinkling down from the hills.

Thankfully Pandora lifted her face to the slumbering bens and to the stars twinkling in the vast reaches of the sky.

The pure air of wide spaces flooded her lungs, cleansing them, purging her blood, clearing her head.

She wished that it was as easy to wash the guilt out of her heart but that was something that she knew would live with her forever now.

She walked on, her thoughts in a turmoil. How could she continue with an arrangement that the beastly Roderick believed was going to go on . . . and on . . . and on . . . ?

She shuddered at the very idea. She was on the edge of a filthy bog of deceit and lies. One foot was already in, she couldn't, she just couldn't allow herself to sink any deeper.

But what could she do against an unscrupulous rogue like Roderick? He was merciless and evil and she knew he would stop at nothing in his greedy need to extract as much as he could out of anyone he thought might be useful to him.

Then an ungodly notion struck her. What if he were to die? Some sort of accident, anything, to be rid of him. He

182

deserved to die, he deserved nothing but pain and sorrow in return for all the unhappiness he caused . . .

Her mind raced on even as she whispered in horror, 'Oh, God, forgive me, and I ask you to please rid me of such ugly thoughts.'

God seemed very near in the timeless beauty of dreaming Glen Tarsa and by the time her footsteps brought her in sight of the reassuring solidity of Noble House she felt better.

Feeling like a thief in the night she turned her key in the lock of the scullery door and stole inside, all the while praying that she wouldn't be seen flitting through the corridors or heard ascending the stairs to the waiting haven of her bedroom.

CHAPTER 19

Pointing the Finger

Lady Pandora paused, one foot on the stairs, listening. The sound of raised voices came to her and inwardly she groaned. It seemed that she wasn't to be allowed to go unnoticed after all. The household wasn't asleep, people were up and about and obviously very wide awake.

Warily she went on up, her mind grappling with a dozen excuses as to why she should be abroad at this hour after telling everyone she was going to bed with a headache.

Reaching the landing she saw that the door of the boys' room was wide open and that pandemonium seemed to have broken loose inside.

Robert was there, wrapped in his dressing gown, as was Michael Dick who was looking positively grim.

Everything in the room had been turned upside down, pillows and sheets were topsy-turvy, drawers had been pulled out and the contents scattered everywhere.

In the middle of the commotion was Ralph, on his knees as he scrabbled through the jumble on the floor, looking very different from the self-composed lad that everyone knew, his face afire with temper, his hair standing on end, his eyes wild and staring.

'It's here! I know it's here!' he was shouting. 'I put it here myself! Who's taken it! Who's been at my things?'

'Aunt Dora!' Robert turned a relieved face as Lady Pandora entered the room, not batting one eyelid at the sight of her standing there, fully dressed. 'Ralphie is going daft altogether! See if you can calm him down for I've tried

184

everything short o' knocking him on the head with a brick!'

'Ralph, what is it?' cried Lady Pandora. 'What is it you have lost?'

But Ralph was too enraged to listen, he just went on rummaging through the drawers, turning back the rugs, rifling through the pockets of trousers and shirts.

'You won't get any sense out of him, my lady,' said Michael Dick in a wheedling voice, taking off his glasses for the umpteenth time and wiping them on his sleeve. 'No sense at all. I've tried to talk to him, believe me I've tried, but he won't listen, he just won't listen. If you ask me he's gone berserk, it's plain for all to see.'

Lady Pandora ignored him. Going to the boy, she put a soothing arm round his shoulders and leading him to the bed, she made him sit down. 'Ralph,' she said softly, 'we can't help you unless you tell us what it is you're looking for. Take a deep breath and try to relax. Come now, I want to help, you know you can trust me. You've always been able to talk to me, Ralph.'

Ralph took a deep, shuddering breath. The sound of his aunt's voice was like balm on troubled waters. Aware of the comforting warmth of her hands through his night-shirt, he felt himself responding to the steadying influence of her nearness.

Distractedly he ran a hand through his hair. His dark eyes flashed. 'It wasn't anything important, Aunt Dora, I'm sorry I made a fuss, I didn't mean to lose my temper like that.'

'Nothing important!' exploded the tutor. 'Nothing important! You get us all out of bed in the middle of the night and tell us it's nothing important! Really, Ralph! Your quirks of nature are getting worse. I've never come across anything like this in all my days of teaching. I'm disappointed in you, Ralph, I thought you were learning to control your rages. Yes, very disappointed indeed.'

'Mr Dick, please,' Lady Pandora's voice was icy, the look of warning she threw at the teacher made him feel small.

'I'm sorry, my lady,' he said deferentially. 'I just thought . . . '

'We all know what you thought, Mr Dick, but if you will just bear with me we might hear what Ralph has to say, after all, it's his welfare we are interested in at this moment, don't you agree?'

'Oh, yes, of course, my lady, yes indeed. Please forgive me.'

'It was only a pipe lid,' Ralph spoke up suddenly. 'A silver pipe lid I found some time ago. I put it in my dressing table and now it's gone.'

'That pipe lid?' gasped Robert. 'The one you showed me?'

'That one,' agreed Ralph in guarded tones.

'It's that Mary, I bet she's taken it,' Robert decided. 'She's always snooping around, listening at doors, seeing things she shouldn't be seeing.'

'Boys.' Lady Pandora looked from one to the other. 'What is going on?'

Both boys looked uneasy.

'It's nothing, Aunt Dora,' Ralph said evasively.

'I told you, I told you!' Michael Dick couldn't hold his tongue a moment longer. 'Nothing! And here we all are, roused from our beds, upset, worried and anxious, and all you can say is "Nothing, Aunt Dora," as if that solved the matter and we can all go back to sleep pretending that nothing had happened.'

'It really isn't good enough, Ralph,' Lady Pandora said slowly. 'This past year you have been behaving strangely – all those bad dreams you've been having and none of us able to get a word out of you. Can't you tell us, Ralph? At least, can't you tell me, if you speak to me alone?'

A look of fear flitted over Ralph's face and his temper returned. 'No, Aunt Dora!' he shouted. 'I can't tell you anything, there's nothing to tell. I can't speak to anyone, not even you! Why can't you just leave me alone, all of you!'

'If you're really sure, Ralph,' Lady Pandora said, a frown marring her forehead.

'I'm sure, I'm sorry I got you all out of your beds. It's over now, I'm fine.'

'Come on, Ralphie.' Robert put his hand on the other boy's arm and led him back to bed. 'You'll be fine now, it's myself that's here beside you, I'll keep an eye on you – if I can keep it open long enough that is.'

'"I'm fine. I'm fine." As if that's any consolation to us.' Michael Dick viciously tugged the cord of his dressing gown and went out of the room, muttering under his breath.

Lady Pandora turned away also. In all the upset no-one had noticed that she was dressed or had asked where she had been and she went gladly to her room to shut the door and lean against it.

Weariness was making her bones feel like lead. She wanted only to sink into bed and sleep forever, but first she had to wash . . . to scrub and scrub the feel of Roderick McIntyre from her body, to rid herself of his smell, his touch, his lust . . .

But he would always be there, in her awakenings and her dreamings, she would never be free of him now – and she had allowed it to happen – for Anna, for the love of a child who had touched her life with joy . . .

'Anna,' she whispered into the darkness. 'Come back to me soon.'

When finally she got into bed she lay awake for a long time, thinking about Anna, wondering how she was getting on at Kilkenzie, how it had been for her seeing her mother after so long.

How strange was life, she thought, Anna without a mother all these years, me without a child.

'But we have each other now, Anna,' she murmured. 'We need one another. In our different ways we've yearned for things that couldn't be ours – until now.'

She turned over and looked out of the window. She had drawn back the drapes so that she could lie there in bed and see the stars. The sky was purple-blue, peaceful, deep, infinite. The sound of the river gushing through the trees was like a lullaby, soothing, healing.

Her eyes closed. She remembered the scene with Ralph. Such a strange boy, brooding, secretive, unhappy.

She wondered about him, the secrets he kept, the fears he harboured, the things he dreamt about . . .

She wondered about him very much and she fell asleep, still wondering.

Adam had made up his mind! He was going to see Ralph Van Hueson and he was going now! Before he could change his mind. Though that wasn't very likely. Not now, not after he had found Tibby in the ashpit, her neck broken, her once-agile little body all limp and still, her beautiful soft fur grey with dust.

Adam had liked Tibby, he had liked her very much indeed. When no-one else would speak to him she had always been there to welcome him home, her tail waving in the air as she came towards him, her warm, sleek body wrapping itself round his legs, her little pink mouth opening up to meow her greetings to him as she craned her neck to peer up at his face.

He had killed her! That murdering swine who strutted about like God Almighty, thinking he could do what he liked to anybody and anything! He had murdered a little cat who had never harmed a soul. He had taken her in his brutal grasp and had twisted her neck till she died. A tiny wee thing like that.

And he had the nerve to call himself a man! An upright citizen! A God-fearing Christian! A buggering coward more like! Adam thought bitterly, it's high time somebody put a stop to him!

He went to seek out Anna and explained everything that he intended to do, finishing up by showing her the pipe lid. 'It's his, Anna, and it was found at the riverbank – near where Peter and Andrew Mallard were killed. Dark-horse Ralph found it, but he's too scared to say anything else.'

188

Anna stared at the object lying in the palm of her brother's hand. Her heart went cold in her breast. In her mind she saw Peter's face again, his smile, his joy when they met, his arms outstretched to lift her high before the warmth of his mouth met hers.

'I'm going to see Ralph, Anna.' Adam's face was taut with determination. 'I'm going to make him tell the truth – and I want you to come wi' me.'

Anna backed off a little. She hadn't forgotten what had happened between herself and her brother in the inn at Kilkenzie. Since their return home she had been avoiding him as much as possible. Now this – confiding in her, asking her to accompany him to Noble House to confront Ralph.

She didn't want to go anywhere with Adam but this was different. It was about Peter, and Andrew Mallard, and she had to know the truth, she had to know who had killed them . . .

'Alright, Adam,' she said quietly, 'I'll come with you. But what about Magnus? Shouldn't we tell him what's going on?'

Adam shook his head. 'Not yet, I only asked you to come wi' me because o' Peter. Let's just see what Dark-horse Ralph has to say before we do anything else.'

When they arrived at Noble House the next afternoon, Adam wasted no time. At the door he demanded of Baird the butler where he could find Ralph.

'Upstairs, in the schoolroom,' Baird said woodenly, but as Adam made to barge inside, he protested, 'Just a minute, young man, you can't . . . '

'Oh ay, but I can,' grinned Adam and, suiting action to his words, he shoved Baird aside and strode boldly into Noble House.

Lady Pandora was coming downstairs. 'Anna!' she cried. 'I was wondering when I would see you. Oh, my dear child, how are you, I've missed you so much.' She enveloped the girl in her arms.

189

Anna felt the tears springing. It was so good to be back, so good to hear the warmth, the affection, in the older woman's voice.

Pandora held Anna at arm's length and they both laughed with the joy they felt at seeing one another again.

'I'll be back properly tomorrow,' Anna explained. 'When we came home from Kilkenzie Father told me it was alright for me to come here again.' She frowned. 'I don't understand what made him change his mind.'

Lady Pandora looked away. 'It doesn't matter, Anna, what matters is that you're back and I hope you'll be staying with me for a very long time.'

Anna thought about Magnus, the plans he had for them to leave Glen Tarsa. But she couldn't say anything to Lady Pandora. Not yet, when her violet eyes were sparkling and her face glowed with happiness.

'Adam and myself have come to see Ralph,' Anna spoke quickly. Adam was growing impatient and had begun ascending the stairs. Anna took her ladyship's hand. 'I'll see you tomorrow, just now I have to go with Adam.' She rushed away before any awkward questions could be asked.

Adam was in an excitable state and he was standing no nonsense from anybody. He went marching straight into the schoolroom without so much as a tap on the door to announce his arrival.

Mr Dick's head jerked up at the intrusion, and the boys looked up from their schoolbooks in surprise.

'I've come to see you, Ralph,' Adam came straight to the point. 'And I think it might be better . . . ' he swung round to the teacher, ' . . . if you could leave us alone for a while.'

'Impudent upstart! I'll do no such thing!' spluttered Mr Dick. 'And I'll thank you to get out of here before I have you thrown out.'

Adam ignored him. Turning to Ralph he held out his hand in which reposed the silver pipe lid. The boy turned white. 'Where did you get that? It's mine!'

190

'Oh, no, it isn't, it's my father's, though I think you know that already.'

'Mr Dick,' Robert spoke up. 'Would you be allowing us a ten minute break while we deal with this?'

'Ten minutes, no more,' grudgingly the teacher conceded. He left the room and Adam spoke once more. 'Listen, you two, I don't like you and you don't like me. But I want the truth about this pipe lid.' He stared straight at Ralph. 'You saw Mallard being murdered and you know who did it. Now you're going to tell us. You've been a buggering coward for too long and it's time you spoke up.'

Ralph's eyes were black blobs in his white face. Terror, stark and ugly, oozed from every pore.

'I don't know what you mean!' he whispered. 'I don't know anything.'

Adam grabbed him by his collar and leered into his face. 'Ay, you do, it was my father, wasn't it? He killed Mallard, didn't he?'

'Adam, stop that!' warned Anna. 'You don't have to maul him like that.'

But Ralph crumpled suddenly. Sinking into a chair he put his head in his hands and sobbed. 'That night – the night of the murder, Mr Mallard wanted me to stay in and finish my homework. But I was bored and I sneaked out and went for a walk to the Rumbling Brig. That's where I saw it happen, your father pouncing on Quack Quack, knocking him senseless, tying a noose round his neck and hauling him up into the trees.

'I thought he must have been mad at that moment to have the strength to do what he did. I was hiding in the bushes, but as soon as McIntyre left I went to see if I could get Quack Quack down. But it was no use, it was muddy and I kept slipping and I knew he'd be dead by that time anyway. That's when I found the pipe lid. I didn't see what happened to Peter, because I just ran and ran all the way home. I didn't tell anyone, I was too scared, I thought if

191

McIntyre found out I had seen what I had, he would come and kill me, too.'

There was a terrible silence in the room. Anna felt ill. At last, the truth was out, but it didn't make her feel any better. Hearing Ralph talk had brought everything flooding back: the horror of Peter's death, the grief that followed, the anxiety of not knowing what had really happened. Now, the thing that she had suspected all along had just been confirmed and she felt sick at heart. Her father, her own father, was responsible for the death of the boy she had loved. In these moments of terrible truth she wanted to die herself. Roderick would pay for this – somehow, sometime, he would pay for it.

She glanced at Adam. He was pale and strained-looking, but there was a strength about him that had never been there before and she found herself admiring this unpredictable brother of hers, a devil one moment, an advocate of justice the next.

Robert coughed, his keen eyes searched Adam's face. 'I'm thinking it's a strange thing to be sure, you so anxious to have your father's guts for garters.'

A crooked little smile touched Adam's mouth. 'He killed our cat, that's why, no' to mention the years o' bullying and fear he doled out to us all. He deserves to be punished, so just you come down to the police station wi' me tomorrow, Master Ralph, and we'll get the whole matter sorted out.'

Ralph gulped. 'The police station?'

'Ay, the police station, that's the right place to go to report a murder. Will you do it?'

Ralph nodded. 'I'll do it, but not if you're not there.'

Robert grinned. 'Oh, yes you will, Ralphie, because you'll have me to support you and I won't be letting you down.'

'I don't want Aunt Dora or Uncle Malaroy to know,' Ralph stipulated. 'They'll just complicate things and start asking a million questions. They'll find out soon enough.'

'A deal.' Adam held out his hand.

Ralph hesitated for a moment then took it.

'Tomorrow morning,' Adam decided. 'Eight o'clock, the sooner the better. You can get Neil Black to take us in the gig. Alright?'

'Alright.'

Robert threw his arm round Ralph's shoulder. 'Well done, Ralphie. I'm proud o' you, and once this is over with you'll maybe stop all that blabbering you do in your dreams and let me get some sleep at night.'

Mr Dick was hovering in the doorway, his face tight with annoyance.

Anna and Adam took their leave and for once Anna didn't mind when her brother's hand crept into hers. They were both shattered by Ralph's disclosures. Their father was a murderer, and they both needed comfort and reassurance in these, their blackest moments.

CHAPTER 20

Waiting

The stillness in the house was laden with suspense, the atmosphere so tight and heavy it was like a living thing, waiting to pounce from the shadows.

Outside the window a blackbird was pouring out its evensong, the notes soaring ecstatically into the stillness of the summer gloaming, a sound of freedom and delight that found no echo within the walls of The Gatehouse. Rather it only served to emphasize the feelings of tension that had been growing in everyone ever since Roderick had entered the house and they had all sat down to eat their evening meal.

Roderick was in a black mood. He ate and drank in total silence, all the while scowling down at his plate as if it was going to rise up and bite him.

Anna was aware that Magnus was watching her with a puzzled look in his eyes. She hadn't had an opportunity to tell him about the things that had happened earlier, but she was longing to pour her heart out to him. Of all the people in the world he was the one she could rely on for strength and support. She wished Adam had taken Magnus into his confidence instead of just blundering off to Noble House in his headstrong fashion. Magnus would have taken time to plan it all differently, he would have been calm and rational and much more realistic.

As it was it was all too airy-fairy and secretive. She didn't like the idea of Ralph's decision not to say anything to Sir

Malaroy and Lady Pandora and wondered if he had done it to safeguard himself against a change of heart.

She met Magnus's eyes and smiled softly at him, but he didn't smile back. He knew something was going on and he was wary and watchful.

Adam toyed with his food. He was beginning to feel sick, the burst of courage he had experienced that afternoon was fast deserting him.

He glanced at his father's sullen face and broke out in a sweat. Each tick of the clock made him realise the enormity of the thing that he was about to do. How could he ever have been so stupid as to think he could get the better of Iron Rod? It was only Dark-horse Ralph's word against that of a man who had moulded a secure niche for himself in Glen Tarsa. The Noble lad was a newcomer, a nobody, an unlikeable one at that. He wasn't the sort to make the kind of friends who would believe in him.

As for that pipe lid. It meant nothing. Roderick could have lost it anywhere. Anyone could have found it. Daft Donal, for instance, he was always picking up shiny objects and losing them again through the holes in his pockets . . .

Adam gulped and tried to fight down the feeling of nausea that was threatening to overwhelm him. A coil of steel seemed to be tightening in his belly. He clenched his fists and forced himself to think of other things, Beth for instance – he had arranged to meet her at the usual place tonight, a good thing too, if anybody could take his mind off himself, she could . . .

Roderick was not in the best of spirits, but for reasons that were very different from those of his family. He was wondering when he would see Lady Pandora again. The lovely bitch had very successfully evaded him when he had last gone to Noble House on a business pretext.

She had better watch out or he could make life very awkward for her, ay, very awkward indeed! Surely she didn't think she could go on avoiding him? Playing with his feelings like this! Buggering him about as if he was no better than cow dirt . . .

Besides all that he wasn't feeling too good these days. Headaches. Dizziness. He had far too much to cope with in his life. Too much work and no play. He glared at his plate. It seemed to be floating in front of his eyes, everything was swimming, the table was wobbling about like a jelly . . .

Glancing up he saw Adam's face, his eyes big and dark, watching him, like a snake trying to hypnotise its prey. Why was he watching? Why were they all so silent? As if they were waiting to pounce on him like a pack of wild animals . . . hunters going in for the kill.

Was that it? All of them in league with one another, ganging up on him because they sensed that he wasn't up to the mark? Well, he would show them that he was still top dog in his own home! He would show them all!

Reaching across the table he caught Adam's hand and dug his fingers into the boy's wrist. 'Eat your food, lad,' he growled. 'I've told you before, there's no room for waste in this house. Do you think sillar grows on trees? Is that it? Is it, Adam?'

'No, Father.' Adam kept his eyes downcast. 'I'm just not hungry, that's all.'

'That's all! That's all!' Roderick's face was reddening, his eyes were beginning to bulge. 'And why aren't you hungry? You that's normally got the appetite o' a young lion. Is it because you've got something on your mind? Something you don't want me to know about? Things other than whoring and drinking and fighting!'

Adam's heart thumped, he felt his gorge rising. Getting up hastily from the table he muttered something unintelligible and rushed outside to be sick.

Roderick folded his lips and glared meaningfully at Anna and Magnus. 'Would you two like to join him? Get rid o' the poison you're bottling up inside yourselves, because I tell you this . . . ' Standing up he leaned over the table to tower above them, ' . . . you can't fool me! You ought to know that by now. The minute I walked in that door tonight I knew something was in the wind and I demand to know what it is – *NOW!*' He banged his fist down on the table, making the crockery rattle and the cutlery bounce.

Anna felt faint, she couldn't speak or make a single sound. A feeling of panic seized her. Roderick knew something terrible was going to happen and she wondered if she could go through with her part in it. This was her father after all. What if Ralph was wrong? He might have made a mistake in thinking that Roderick was the person he had seen on the night Andrew Mallard and Peter had died. It had been getting dark at the time; everything looked different at dusk; the changing light played tricks with the eyes, made everything seem unfamiliar and strange. Shapes became shadows, shadows merged into shapes, nothing was as clear cut as it was in the daylight.

She shuddered and turned her face away so that she didn't have to meet Roderick's blazing eyes.

A muscle was moving in Magnus's jaw. The expression on his face was contemptuous, his gaze unwavering as he looked at the looming figure above him. 'Sit down, Father,' he directed evenly. 'Nothing's in the wind, you're imagining it.'

'Don't you dare order me about, you bloody little upstart!' roared Roderick. 'This is my home and I'm the boss in case you've forgotten!'

'No, I haven't forgotten, you make damned sure o' that by reminding us at every opportunity. But it's our home as well, and if we feel like being quiet, we will be, and if Adam's ill it's maybe because he's been upset ever since we came home from Kilkenzie and found our cat lying strangled in the ashpit. Remember the cat, Father? A tiny wee thing that used to meet us at the door and never did any harm to anybody?'

197

Roderick subsided like a deflated balloon. Without another word he got up and stomped through to his room.

He stared at himself in the mirror. He looked haggard and void of colour after that little episode with Magnus. The boy was getting above himself, lording it over him as if he was God Almighty!

He'd better watch out! They'd all better watch out . . .

He had arranged to meet Nellie Jean at The Munkirk Inn that night. Mechanically he began to get ready, his movements slow and jerky and strangely lacking in coordination.

As soon as their father had left the room Magnus turned to Anna. 'What's going on, Anna? Adam sick? You acting as if you'd like the floor to open and swallow you up?'

Anna jumped to her feet and began clearing the table. Her face was pale, her eyes were big and anxious looking. 'I'll tell you later, when Father's gone. Hush . . . ' She put a finger to her brother's lips. 'Don't ask any more questions – just – wait till the house is quiet.'

Adam came back into the room, wiping his mouth with the back of one unsteady hand. His hair was rumpled, his shirt-front soaked. Going to the table he lifted the milk jug to his mouth and gulped noisily.

'Are you all right, Adam?' Magnus asked with a puzzled frown.

'Ay, as fine as I'll ever be. I've got to change, I'm going out.'

Half an hour later he was striding down the road, lost in thought, hands deep in his pockets as he stared unseeingly ahead. He had changed his clothes and brushed his tightly-curled brown hair; the colour had returned to his crudely handsome face; the glow of whisky warmed his belly.

He had taken a half-bottle from the cupboard in the parlour where his father kept his supplies. The old sod might miss it, but it didn't matter. Nothing seemed to

198

matter as much as it used to. He thought about tomorrow: Neil Black arriving with the gig; the journey to Munkirk; the police house with its tiny office; Dark-horse Ralph looking at everyone with those scowling brows and brooding black eyes of his.

What would he say? How would he begin? How did you start to explain a murder that you had witnessed a year ago but had been too scared to mention at the time?

Old Size Twelve McGregor would stand there like an ancient monument, his big, sheeplike face more serious than usual, licking his pencil, his hairy brows would knit in concentration, he would hum and haw and shift his feet, because his shoes nipped no matter how much damp newspaper he stuffed into them.

The whisky bottle was heavy in Adam's pocket. Taking it out he held it to his mouth and gulped down a large quantity of the fiery liquid.

His innards burned, and he felt light-headed, but a sensation of well-being flowed through him. He felt much better. Out of his father's sight he was his own man again and was no longer worried about tomorrow. Let it bring what it would. Meantime, he was going to enjoy himself with Beth. The hot little bitch would be waiting for him with her drawers down and her knees up!

He smiled to himself. If old Ma Jordan knew what her daughter got up to on the quiet she would blow up and burst with rage.

Lately she had been glaring at Adam in a suspicious sort of way, as if she suspected that he and Beth were up to no good, but they had been careful. Adam frowned. Too careful, perhaps. He would have liked to have taken Beth out properly, to be seen in public with her, but she wouldn't hear of it.

His frown turned into a scowl. Not good enough for her. He was only Adam McIntyre of The Gatehouse. She wanted something better than him – Lucas Noble, no less. Money, position, power, these were the things Beth wanted from life and knowing her she would get her way, right from the start Beth had always had things her way.

For a few minutes Adam battled with his bitter thoughts then he cheered up. Having her to himself like this was better than nothing. It might not last, but he was going to enjoy it while it did – and he could always fall back on Mary to comfort him if the going got rough. Mary worshipped him. She would do anything for him.

The whisky was having its effect. Adam felt optimistic and ready for anything. Holding the bottle once more to his mouth he threw back his head and drained it, before tossing it into the undergrowth at the side of the road.

Beth would smell the drink off him. She would nag and scold and tell him he was getting like his father but she would soon change her tune when he showed her the physical evidence of what he had in store for her.

He smirked. She could never get over the size of his willy. 'And you only fifteen,' she would gasp in pretend shock even while her eyes danced in delight and she licked her lips in anticipation.

Digging his hands into his pockets Adam pursed his lips and began to whistle, his steps jaunty as he made his way across the road to the gentle slope that led up to the woodshed behind the quarry.

Roderick had taken his leave of the house some time ago, now it was just Anna and Magnus, sitting together in the inglenook, reaching out to one another as Anna finished telling him of the events that had taken place that afternoon.

'Anna,' he murmured huskily, taking her in his arms to stroke her hair and hold her tightly. 'We've all got to stick together now, you, me, Adam. It took some guts to do as he did and we've got to help him to see it through.'

Her hair was silken under his hand. He lifted the strands and let them glide between his fingers. 'My babby,' he whispered, 'this is terrible for you, but you've got to be

200

stronger than you've ever been before, for Peter Noble and for Andrew Mallard. The old man must pay for what he's done, somebody has to put a stop to him. He's getting worse, he isn't in control of himself any more. That temper o' his, it's frightening.'

'It was the cat,' Anna spoke almost to herself. 'It was the cat that was the last straw. Adam couldn't get over it, when he found her, lying dead and cold among the ashes. Something just snapped inside of him and I was proud o' the way he marched up to Noble House and demanded to see Ralph.'

'Ay, Ralph,' muttered Magnus thoughtfully. 'I've often wondered about him, he isn't like the other lad, the Irish one called Robert. He's open and honest and full o' the blarney, but Ralph, a dark horse if ever there was one.'

'That's what Adam calls him, especially now, keeping a secret like that all this time. He says he was too terrified to talk and I can't blame him for that. If I had seen what he had I would have felt the same.'

'Ay, but you would have wanted justice done, Anna, for Peter. You couldn't have held your tongue. Some things have to be said, even if it is our own father who's involved. He's done some evil things – to all o' us – and it's high time he was punished. God knows how he treated our mother when she was here. Something terrible must have happened to make her want to shut the world away.'

Anna shivered. 'Mother,' she murmured. 'Our mother, so kind and gentle. Things could have been so different for her, she could have known happiness here in this house with us – if it hadn't been for him.'

'It isn't too late, Anna,' Magnus said quietly. 'I don't think she's mad, just bewildered, and she could still come back here to us. When all this is over, we'll go and see her again, let her get to know us a bit better. I spoke to Mr Simpson about it and he said to wait awhile but that he'd take us whenever we felt ready.'

Anna's face lit up and she hugged him to her. He was

201

warm and hard and strong. 'I – love you, Magnus,' she told him, her voice vibrant with feeling. 'I always have and I always will. I wish we could be together forever – just like this, peaceful and close and caring for one another.'

His deep dark eyes looked into hers. 'We can be, Anna. I told you I was going to find a place for us, somewhere that you'll be safe and secure. I'll look after you, just as I've always done, right from the beginning.'

'I know you will, Magnus, but I can't give you my answer just now, there's so much happening and I'm too mixed up to think straight.'

She got to her feet, still holding onto his hand. 'I promised Miss Priscilla I would see her at McDonald's cottage tonight. She's trying to teach Sally to read and she thought I could help.' She glanced around the room. It was chilly and cheerless and lacking in homeliness. 'Come with me, Magnus. I can't go off and leave you on your own, not tonight. We need one another, but not here in this house.'

He, too, got to his feet. 'Ay, I'll come. Who knows, Miss Priscilla might be able to teach me a few things. I was never very good at learning when I was at school.'

She looked up at him 'All you need to know is here . . . ' She placed her hand over his heart, '. . . and it was there long before you ever went to school and always will be, for as long as you live.'

CHAPTER 21

Silenced

It was an oddly reassuring feeling to have Miss Priscilla in the house. So Davie thought as he settled his gaunt frame in a rickety chair by the smoky fire to stare in his moody fashion into the uncertain flames.

Not that he had always felt that way about the advent of the schoolteacher into the tiny, filthy hovel that he and his brother and sister called home.

Very few people had ever crossed over the front doorstep. Davie's hostile manner, his suspicious nature had very effectively seen to that. He hated the idea of anyone poking their nose in and had thought the same of Miss Priscilla when she had courageously come to inquire about Sally's welfare after the attack.

On that first visit Davie had not allowed Miss Priscilla into the house. He had been surly and rude to her and after a few minutes had all but closed the door in her face.

But Miss Priscilla was made of stern stuff and was not prepared to be put off so easily. Davie's attitude only served to make her more determined than ever to see Sally, whose cruel beating had shocked and sickened the entire neighbourhood.

'You're surely no' going back there,' Ben McLeod had told his sister when she had voiced her intention of returning to the McDonald house. 'Yon Davie's a dour, stubborn cratur, he'll no' thank you for making a nuisance o' yourself.'

'I am not making a nuisance of myself and of course I'm

going back. Somebody has to concern themselves with the two weaker McDonalds, and that someone is going to be me,' Miss Priscilla had declared, with a determined folding of her lips. 'Stubborn he may be, but he'll find that I, too, like to get my own way when I put my mind to it.'

'Amen to that,' Kate McLeod, Ben's other sister, had said with feeling, adding with one of her big cheery smiles, 'Ach, stop glowering down your nose at me, Priss. I've just made a batch o' scones. Take some with you, and a pot o' jam, the McDonald bunch could be doing with a good feed.'

In no time at all Miss Priscilla proved herself to be 'just the boy' to wear down Davie's defences and soon she was a fairly regular visitor to the McDonald household.

To her way of thinking the eldest and youngest McDonalds were far too idle for their own good, the result being that they were wont to wander the glen at all hours, getting into mischief, inviting trouble on themselves. In her opinion the answer lay in learning and so she set herself a daunting task, that of teaching Sally and Donal to read.

Armed with big coloured picture books, slates, chalk and crayons, she marched along to the cottage whenever she could and got to work.

At first neither Sally nor Donal would apply themselves to the written word, but with dogged perseverance, Miss Priscilla got them gradually interested till soon they were looking forward to her visits with eager enthusiasm while Davie was inclined to view the whole thing with dark ingratitude.

One day Kate, too, had gone along, bearing a large basket of food and another of cleaning materials.

Fortunately Davie had been out at the time or he might have exploded altogether. So, Kate had a free hand. Setting down her baskets she briskly chased the hens out of the house and was soon blithely sweeping the filthy floors, brushing away the cobwebs, clearing out the choked grate, and fixing clean muslin curtains at the freshly washed windows.

When Davie came home he found Kate snoring in one of the lumpy chairs, the fire leaping merrily up the lum, a pan of soup bubbling on the hob, and Miss Priscilla at the table with Donal and Sally, chanting out the alphabet which they were repeating, parrot fashion.

Davie's face blackened, his fingers curled, a muscle began to twitch in his thin cheek. With a backward thrust of one hobnailed boot he kicked the door shut behind him. It crashed against the ancient timbers, shattering the peace, bringing fear to Sally's black eyes, and waking Kate who shot bolt upright in her chair. The action had caused one of the springs to shoot out of the sparse padding of the seat and into the small of her back. She arose hastily, flustered for a moment, till she saw Davie standing at the door, glaring round the room.

She didn't give him time to talk. 'Davie,' she acknowledged with one of her beaming smiles. 'Come right in and sit yourself down. Everything's ready. There's soup and tatties and apple tart for afters. Ben, my brother, loves my apple tart. A man needs a good feed after a hard day's work. When we were bairns my mother always had our father's tea waiting and I've just followed her example.'

Davie's eye fell on the cheerful grate, the savoury aroma of lentil broth wafting to his nostrils. The contrast of the homely scene with the dirt and chill he was used to, hit him forcibly.

He softened. He sat down, he tucked in, and after that day he made no objection to either Kate or Miss Priscilla in his home, rather he began to look forward to their visits with as much enthusiasm as Sally and Donal, though never by one flicker of his pale blue eyes did he give the fact away.

Tonight he was feeling vastly contented. Miss Priscilla was here, she had brought with her jam and butter, a loaf of new baked bread, oatcakes, a batch of floury soda scones and a pile of fluffy pancakes. A pan of broth was simmering on the hob, keeping hot till the reading lessons were over with and they could all gather round the fire to eat supper together.

When the door opened to admit Anna and Magnus, Davie's eyes flickered, he half rose from his chair, but a few seconds later he subsided. Of all the McIntyres these were the ones he trusted and liked. They had never shown anything else but kindness to him and his family . . .

It was the other two that he hated, Adam with his taunting and cowardly accusations! That filthy swine Roderick! Tormenting him, causing trouble for him in the mill. And that terrible night some time ago . . . when he had violated Donal's innocence with his evil acts of indecency. Davie's face twisted at the memory of that episode. He had made the swine pay for what he had done. Too bad he had lived to see another day. He would get him in the end though . . . one day he would get him . . .

Davie glanced at his sister and remembered the time, not so long ago, when Nellie Jean had brought Sally home, bruised and beaten to within an inch of her life. The marks of that night were still on her, scars that would take a long time to heal.

Davie scowled into the fire. A McIntyre was behind it all, he was sure of that, even though Sally had been too shocked by her experiences to name the bastard who had hurt her. She had hardly uttered a single word since then, and it was only now, with Miss Priscilla coming to the house, that she was slowly beginning to communicate again – if communicating was the word to use for her slurred, almost unintelligible, speech.

With the arrival of Anna and Magnus the tiny room was suddenly filled with life. Anna, with her flaxen hair and glowing appearance, was like a ray of sunshine in the dingy surroundings, Magnus, with his aura of strength, seemed like a rock holding up the place.

Anna went straight to the table to join Miss Priscilla and Sally, while Donal, who had grown tired of the reading lessons, grinned happily at Magnus and taking him by the

206

arm, led him to the chair opposite Davie and made him sit down.

'I've brought you something, Donal.' Magnus searched in his pocket and withdrawing a pocket knife and a piece of wood he immediately began to whittle away at it.

Donal clapped his hands in delight and squatting on the floor in front of Magnus, he watched with open-mouthed fascination as the carving slowly began to take the shape of a little mouse.

It was an extraordinarily homely scene. Davie couldn't help but be affected by it and, before long, he became just as entranced as Donal as Magnus's deft fingers moulded pieces of wood into different animal shapes.

At suppertime everyone gathered round the fire to eat buttered bannocks and piping hot soup. Davie had never felt like this before, peaceful and contented instead of watchful and suspicious. It was like having a family round him, the kind of family that he had never known and for once in his life he allowed himself to relax and even to add an occasional word to the conversation.

He was genuinely sorry when the time came for every-one to depart and he stood at the door with his brother and sister, watching in a rather mournful silence as Miss Priscilla went walking away along the road with Anna and Magnus.

Long after they had become just blobs in the gathering dusk he stood at the door, puffing at his pipe, thinking about the evening and how much he had enjoyed it. With a sigh, he knocked out his pipe on the step and went back into the house.

Donal had gone to bed but Sally, excited and wakeful, was over by the table, jabbing one long, dirty finger at the big coloured letters of the alphabet that Miss Priscilla had left behind.

As soon as Davie stepped back into the room, Sally rushed over to grab him by the arm and lead him over to the table, a string of garbled words issuing from her mouth.

Davie, however, conditioned to a lifetime of her speech difficulties, was able to understand her to some extent, though he was in no mood then to listen to her. He was fast returning to his old self and with an impatient grunt he shook off her restraining hand.

Sally's eyes darkened. A wild expression came into them; her mouth was slackening, saliva drooling from the corners. Davie recognised the signs, he had witnessed them often enough. Something was disturbing her, she was growing more and more agitated, any moment now she would start screaming and raving and shouting.

Davie knew of only one way to stop it. Raising his hand he was about to bring it down on her face when he saw something that made him freeze the action in mid-air.

Moaning and grunting, Sally was pointing to certain letters of the alphabet, sounding them aloud as she went along. 'A – D – A – M,' she pronounced laboriously. 'A – D – A – M.'

She repeated the letters over and over then suddenly she balled her fists and began beating them off her chest, her face twisted, her eyes glazed as it all came back to her, the terror, the pain, the dread that she had suffered.

Davie stared at her. He froze. The message was clear. He had been right after all. His sister had just told him everything he needed to know. That cowardly little runt, Adam McIntyre, was the one.

Davie's logic was simple, he had his own set of rules. Tit for tat, an eye for an eye.

Davie put his arm round his sister's shoulders and led her to the pile of threadbare blankets that was her bed. He then went to the kist under the window where he kept his few personal belongings. From beneath an ancient deer-stalker hat he extracted a bottle of whisky and holding it to his mouth, he swallowed the contents greedily.

He didn't need anything else. His fists were his weapons,

his cunning was his ally, acquired through years of spying on the movements of those who were the enemies of himself and his family.

He knew where Adam would be. He had been watching the bastard for a long time now, swaggering, whoring, drinking . . .

Davie took a last swig from the bottle and straightened. He was ready.

Going to the door he looked out. A steady drizzle of rain was sweeping over the countryside, and the mist was rising up from the river. The rain made no difference to him – he was used to being out in all weathers. He smiled slyly to himself – he was savouring the idea of Adam McIntyre lying helplessly on the soggy ground – perhaps ending up with pneumonia – or worse!

With the stealth of a cat he let himself out of the house and cut up to the road, keeping to the bushes, hiding in the shadows, not so much as the snap of a twig giving away the fact that he was there . . .

Adam hadn't enjoyed himself as much as usual with Beth. She had been in one of her superior moods, boasting away to him about her friendship with fat old 'Yuffie' Smythe; the quaint people that haunted Deerfield House: 'Simply hilarious, so different from Mother's stuffy old dears.'; how she was learning to ride 'With Yuffie alongside.'; the wonderful stories that Yuffie told, 'Such a dear – and she adores me, we have so much in common even though she's a hundred years older than me.'

Beth had then gone on to talk about Lucas, how much she was missing him, saying that it was only a matter of time before he came back to her.

'I know him, you see. He won't put up with that little milk-and-water goody-goody for long. Lady Yvonne Marchmont indeed! More like Lady Chastity Belt if you ask me. Lucas is far too passionate for the likes of her and I should know what I'm talking about.'

Beth had been bored with Adam that night and wasn't at all impressed by his lovemaking. She had nagged him because he had smelt of drink and in the end she had rolled away from him to tidy her clothes and complain that she was cold.

She had made no arrangements to see him again and he had left the woodshed in the huff, hunching his shoulders against the rain, pulling his collar around his ears.

Once or twice he slipped on wet leaves as he made his way down the slope. The rain was hissing down harder, he could see nothing in the misty darkness, only the shapes of trees rising up out of the gloom. And then a shadow rose up from the bushes, one darker, more menacing than the rest.

Adam drew in his breath. Instinctively, he recoiled, but he couldn't evade a fist that was like iron and which knocked him senseless in one ferocious blow.

Anna and Magnus, unwilling to go home to the unwelcoming atmosphere of The Gatehouse, had stopped off at Moss Cottage to visit old Grace. She had been delighted to see them, ushering them inside, sitting them down at the fire and plying them with tea and biscuits even though they protested that they had just eaten a hearty supper with the McDonalds.

Grace, of course, had wanted to hear all about Miss Priscilla's reading lessons, shaking her head and looking sad when she spoke about Sally and saying she didn't know what things were coming to in the glen when it wasn't safe for folks to leave their own houses anymore.

'When I was a lass,' she went on, hoisting her beloved cat onto her knee, 'we could wander about in safety and freedom at all hours. The glen was a good place to be in those days but something terrible has happened to it this while back, something evil . . . '

She paused cryptically and looked at her young visitors. They looked at one another, their eyes saying more than words about the things they knew that Grace didn't, the evil things she spoke about – and much, much more.

When at last they took their leave of Moss Cottage the clouds had piled up over the hills and the rain was teeming down.

Magnus took Anna's hand and together they ran home.

As they neared the house Anna tripped on a sodden bundle lying at the side of the road.

'Magnus!' she half-screamed in fright. 'It's a – a man – I'm sure it's a man!'

Magnus stooped and turned the bundle over. 'It's Adam,' he said in horror. 'Half-dead. Maybe he was hit by a carriage, or else – somebody's knocked the hell out o' him.'

Between them they tried to lift their brother but, in his helplessness, he was a dead weight.

'Wait here,' Magnus told Anna. 'I'm going over the road for William Jordan. If anybody knows what to do he will.'

The lights of Corran House still glowed in the windows and it was William Jordan himself who answered Magnus's frantic pounding on the door.

Beth emerged from her room to hover at her father's shoulder, and Mrs Jordan appeared on the stairs, wrapping herself in a silk dressing gown as she came down to see what all the noise was about.

'Beth, go back to your room,' she ordered in her most authoritative manner, and, seeing Magnus standing on the step in the pouring rain she added, 'Come inside at once, William, you mustn't concern yourself with other people's affairs. You can't allow yourself to bring trouble on your own family.'

'Go back to bed, Victoria,' he said firmly. 'This is none of your business. Wait there, Magnus, I'll just get my coat and I'll be right with you.'

William Jordan wasted no more breath on useless words. Between them he and Magnus carried Adam into the house to set him down on the sofa, where he lay, deathly-white, his nose and mouth congealed with blood, red weals criss-crossing his face where it had been torn on tangles of thorns growing at the roadside.

'He's in a bad way,' William Jordan said grimly. 'Somebody's made a good job of punching him senseless. There's been far too much of this in the glen of late and I'm going to do something about it. I'm going for the doctor – the lad needs medical attention – and the police. I'll get Robertson to help me hitch up the gig and I'll be back in no time.'

He went off, leaving Anna and Magnus to stoke up the fire and swing the kettle over the flames so that there would be hot water for the doctor when he came.

Roderick was in a worse temper than ever when he left The Munkirk Inn. Nellie Jean had been in one of her teasing moods. She had unashamedly flirted with every man in sight and had talked in a loud voice about Boxer Sam, further taunting Roderick by waving a letter in his face.

'It's from Sam,' she had laughed, her ripe, red mouth opening wide with enjoyment. 'He's been writing to me ever since he got the boot from the mill. His fortunes are on the mend now, though, he's got a good job in England – and you know what, Roddy? He says he'll be coming back one day and that he'll get the swine who did for him!'

The look of chagrin on Roderick's face had amused her greatly. The other men had nudged one another. Roderick had stood it for as long as he could, then he had left the inn to make his way to a backstreet pub in the village where he spent the rest of the night with a glass of ale, since he didn't feel like drinking anything stronger.

Now he was on his way home, stone cold sober, the rain and the chill washing over him, the rumble of cartwheels under him. His horse was trotting along, needing no tug of the reins to guide him on a road he could have traversed blindfold.

Roderick's teeth began to chatter. By the time he reached the Rumbling Brig he was feeling really ill – his hands and feet felt strangely numb, as if tiny pinpricks were prodding his flesh. His head felt queer, too, everything swimming, nothing in his control anymore. The trees, the hills, the fields, sailed silently by, as if they were made of cardboard, nothing real, everything strange. Even the horse seemed to be gliding along like a creature driven by clockwork.

Then all was motionless, all was still, except for his head which felt as if it had left his shoulders and was riding on by itself towards the lowering hills.

The horse had stopped, and Roderick got down. Magnus or Adam could put the beast away, he was tired, too tired . . .

He staggered into the house, his legs like jelly under him. At the living-room door he stopped. There, like figures in a tableau, were Anna and Magnus, their faces turned towards him – and on the couch was the huddled figure of Adam, bleeding, bruised, unmoving.

Roderick's mouth opened but no sound came out. He took two steps forward, his hands held out in front of him, like a blind man feeling his way. He got no further. For one long moment he stood quivering from head to foot before he crashed to the floor to lie in a crumpled heap, his walking cane flying from his grasp, his hat rolling from his head, spinning across the room before it came to rest on its crown beside the table.

Roderick the invincible had fallen, like a mighty tree struck down by lightning in a storm.

CHAPTER 22

A Decision

When Doctor Alistair Minto arrived at The Gatehouse it was to find two patients waiting for him instead of the one that William Jordan had told him about.

P.C. Murdoch McGregor came too, otherwise known as Size Twelve McGregor because of his enormous feet. Roused from his bed he had dressed hastily: his collar was awry, only three buttons held the material of his jacket over his portly stomach, and he had forgotten to insert his false teeth, an omission that made his long face seem thinner and more mournful than ever.

Doctor Minto, who was stubby and square with keen blue eyes and a shock of grey hair, wasted no time in his examinations, first going to Adam, lying prone on the couch.

'The boy's taken a bad hammering, somebody must have had it in for him,' he announced in his soft west-coast accent. 'His jaw's broken, I think his ribs may be cracked, and there are multiple bruises and cuts. He'd be better off in hospital for a day or two where we can keep an eye on him. We'll arrange all that once I've had a wee look at your father.'

When he disappeared into Roderick's bedroom, Beth turned a tragic face to Anna. She had arrived soon after her father had departed for Munkirk, turning a deaf ear to her mother's orders to 'Go at once to bed.'

'I might be able to help, Mother,' she had said defiantly. 'You yourself have told me often enough to love my neighbour as myself.'

'I was quoting from the commandments, Elizabeth, this is a different matter entirely, surely you must see that.'

'Och, Mother, I'm not exactly stupid, you know,' Beth had returned sweetly. 'But I really do feel we should make allowances in this case. According to Father, Adam's been badly hurt. Lately, I've been getting to know Adam a bit better and I've been finding out that he's not as bad as everyone makes him out to be.'

'Yes, Elizabeth, I am quite aware of your liaisons with the McIntyre family. Just what you see in them is beyond me. As for the younger boy, I can only hope that you haven't been getting to know him rather *too* well,' Victoria Jordan spoke with a dangerous glint in her eye. 'One hears things, you know, and I would hate to think that a daughter of mine was associating herself in an intimate manner with the likes of Adam McIntyre.'

'Oh, come now, Mother,' Beth said with a show of utmost innocence. 'You should know better than to listen to the gossips. What they don't know they make up, it's the way of things in the country.'

Before her mother could say another word she had hurried away.

She was now proving herself to be more of a help at a sickbed than anyone could have realised. She had fetched and carried for Anna and had taken it upon herself to bathe Adam's wounds and had spoken to him soothingly till the doctor arrived.

She was genuinely sorry for him and meant it when she said, with round-eyed concern, 'Oh, poor Adam, I do hope he'll be alright. He won't like it when he wakes up and finds himself in hospital. I'll go to visit him tomorrow. Mother won't think much of the idea but she'll just have to put up with it. I'm old enough now to please myself.'

Magnus said nothing. Beth had been pleasing herself all her life. Her mother could talk herself blue in the face for all the good it would do or ever had done. Beth was Beth, an entity unto herself. She would go her own way regardless and never mind how many people she used for her own ends.

She had been using Adam. Magnus knew that full well. He also saw that she was really concerned about him now and he admired her for that. Like her mother she could easily have ignored the situation but there was something in Beth that wasn't in her mother. She had grit, spirit and determination, and though she could be sly at times, she was possessed of a peculiar kind of honesty that laughed at convention and loved the unusual.

Her mother had laid down a strict set of rules and guide-lines for her daughter. Beth followed them when it suited her, when it didn't she simply did as she wanted, if she hadn't she would have lost her individuality. Magnus appreciated that fact and at her words he took her hand and squeezed it hard. She smiled into his face, all rancour against him forgotten, her big, pale blue eyes showing her affection for him in those small moments of closeness.

During the doctor's absence Size Twelve McGregor produced a notebook and a stubby pencil and wrote down some details, his tongue sticking out from the side of his toothless mouth, his serious, sheep-like face set into lines of frowning concentration.

'The lad canna speak, your father canna speak,' he said at last and with comical satisfaction. 'There's no' that much for me to go on in that respect, so in the meantime, I'll just . . . ' He made a mark in his notebook. ' . . . have a word or two wi' you three young folks. Now, Miss . . . ' he gazed at Beth expectantly.

'Elizabeth – Elizabeth Ellen Jordan of Corran House.' Beth was putting on her best style.

'Ay, and how did you come to be involved in all this, my lass?'

Beth took her time with her replies. Much as she was sorry for Adam she wasn't going to implicate herself in any way with his misfortunes.

'Magnus and Anna found Adam lying unconscious at the side of the road,' she began carefully. 'Magnus came over to our house to ask my father for help and I thought I should come over too in case I might be of some use.'

'Aha,' proclaimed the constable, as if what Beth had just said was of prime importance. 'Go ahead, young lady,' he directed, pencil at the ready. 'And, by the way,' he wet his lips with the tip of his tongue, 'wi' me leaving my house in such a hurry tonight I didna have a chance to make myself a cup o' tea. I don't suppose . . . ?'

Anna took the hint. Fetching the teapot from the hob where it had been keeping warm she poured out a large cupful and laid it on the hearth, conveniently near the constable's side.

He nodded his thanks. He sipped the hot tea and, with a sigh of contentment, he stretched his legs to the fire and applying the point of his pencil once more to his notebook, he waited for Beth to continue.

When Doctor Minto appeared out of Roderick's room he folded away his stethoscope, closed his bag with a snap, and turned to Magnus. 'Your father's had a stroke. It's impossible to say at this stage just how serious it is but he's going to need constant attention over the next day or so. I'll come back tomorrow to see how he is . . . '

His keen gaze fell on Anna. 'Well, young lady, do you think you'll be able to manage to look after him? It may be weeks or months before he recovers, it's difficult to say in these cases. He's going to need a lot of nursing if he's to get well.'

A terrible sense of trepidation seized Anna. Nurse her father! How could she after all that happened! It had been different that last time, when he had been found in Stable Lane, half-dead with exposure. That had been before Peter's death, before all those dreadful things that Ralph had revealed.

All she wanted was to see her father pay for his murderous

deeds and now it looked as if he was going to get away with everything. He had played his final trump card, he was having the last laugh. She had no doubt that he would recover – a man with his constitution didn't go under so easily – but she couldn't nurse a murderer, she just couldn't.

She caught Magnus's eye and knew that he was thinking and feeling the same as she.

'It would be better if we got someone in to look after him.' Magnus spoke up. 'We were leaving here anyway, it's time for us to make a new start somewhere else, away from . . . ' He glanced around him ' . . . this place. Anna has wasted enough o' her life looking after other people, she has to think o' herself now.'

The doctor's eyes flashed. 'You can't just go off and leave your father and brother to fend for themselves at a time like this! Your place is here, with your family!'

Anna's mind was whirling. Taking Magnus aside she spoke to him quietly. 'I am going to stay here and look after him,' she said decidedly. 'Hush, oh, hush, my dearest Magnus. Don't you see? The sooner he's better the sooner justice will be done. When the time comes, Ralph can still tell the police what he saw, it's just going to take a little longer than we thought.'

Magnus gripped her hand and looked into her eyes. 'Are you sure, Anna? You'll have to – touch him, feed him, wash him . . . all the while knowing what he did.'

'I'll get Nora McCrae in to help. I want him to get well again, Magnus – I – I want him to pay for what he's done.'

'Alright,' he conceded huskily. 'He's won again – next time it's our turn, it's got to be.'

The doctor was watching them, waiting for their decision. Anna turned to him. 'Alright, Doctor,' she said, and her voice was clear and firm and strong. 'I'll look after him, he'll get the best o' attention, you can be sure o' that. I – all o' us – want nothing more than to see him up on his feet again.'

'Good, good,' the doctor studied her for a long moment. She was very young, fragile-looking, with her big eyes, her slender figure, and her mass of flaxen hair falling about her shoulders – yet in those moments there was an indestructible quality about her that was oddly unnerving.

The doctor knew that he would remember those impressions of her for a long time afterwards. He coughed, and turned away to speak to Beth. She nodded and went to fetch her father and Robertson, the man who saw to all the odd jobs in and around Corran House.

A short while later Adam was on his way to hospital and soon Glen Tarsa was quiet again, with only the patter of the rain to disturb the silence.

CHAPTER 23

Escape!

Ralph tossed and turned in his sleep. He was dreaming again, only this time the dream was different. He was in a long, dark tunnel and Roderick was chasing him, an ungodly black phantom of a man, floating towards him at great speed, mouth stretched wide in a hideous leer. Then the creature began laughing, a loud, cruel derisive laugh that bounced off the walls of the tunnel and echoed in Ralph's head. Back, back, into the depths of the tunnel the laughter rang, round and round it whirled, all the while growing in volume till Ralph felt he would go mad with the clamour of it.

He couldn't run fast enough. The phantom that was Roderick rushed towards him, catching him, crushing him, squeezing the air from his lungs, enveloping him in a darkness that was blacker than night, more silent than space.

Ralph knew it was the final, all-consuming embrace, the one that would kill him, the one that was – death . . .

He whimpered in his sleep and awoke with a start, gasping for breath, heart pounding, lungs bursting.

He lay quite still for several moments, disorientated, sweat pouring from him. And then he saw that he was safe. He was in his room at Noble House, everything calm and peaceful around him. Robert hadn't wakened, he was lying on his back, blissfully snoring, his hair tousled on the pillow.

Ralph stared at the ceiling, recalling the dream, snatches of it vividly alive in his head. He was afraid, more afraid than he had ever been in his life before.

He had always been afraid, ever since he could remember. Before Aunt Dora had taken him under her wing he had spent some years in a boys' home and had hated every minute. The other boys had tormented him unmercifully and had called him names.

'Sissy, sissy, yellow pants, sits down to pee! Sissy, sissy, yellow pants, on his nanny's knee!'

He could still hear the taunts and the jeers and, to this day, he felt the shame of not having fought back, of having taken it all without sticking up for himself, of running away and hiding when it had all become too much for him.

'It's because you're such a dolly mixture, Ralphie,' Robert had teased. 'If you were just plain old Irish like myself you would have no worries at all in your head, none at all.'

For all that he could be annoying Robert didn't rile Ralph the way those other boys had. Robert could say things and get away with it. There was no badness in his laughing remarks and though they often tussled with one another it was done in a good-natured manner and they always shook hands afterwards.

Ralph turned his head to gaze at the huddled figure in the next bed. Robert was the first real friend that Ralph had ever known. He was staunch and loyal and strong and Ralph liked and admired him with all his heart. He wanted desperately to be like Robert, to be happy-go-lucky and likeable, but he knew he never would be – ever. He was too suspicious of everything, too shy, too withdrawn. People didn't take to him the way they took to Robert: one look at his dour dark face made them turn away and they seldom approached him again.

Robert, on the other hand, positively glowed in company. He could draw people to him like a magnet and had the knack of making them laugh with his outrageously funny chatter and droll sense of humour.

Ralph moved restlessly. He was wide awake and knew he would never get back to sleep now, not after that dream, that dreadful state of the subconscious mind that had seemed so real with Roderick chasing him, throttling the life out of him . . .

He shuddered and wondered if it had been some sort of omen, a warning for him not to go with Adam to the police tomorrow. For the first time Roderick would be aware that a witness had been present that terrible night at the Rumbling Brig. He was capable of anything and in the end he would get his revenge, he would come for him and he would – kill him . . .

Unable to bear his dark thoughts a moment longer Ralph threw back the covers and got dressed quickly and silently. It was a quarter past three in the morning. The first glimmering of dawn was showing through the window.

He crept downstairs and through the sleeping corridors, letting himself out of the tradesman's entrance at the back of the house. It wasn't the first time he had done this. Quite often, when he wasn't able to sleep, he had gone out for a walk and had been back in bed without anyone ever knowing.

He had always enjoyed these lone wanders when the world was new and sweet and seemed to belong only to him. He liked the evenings too, fragrant and sleepy, waiting for night to descend over the quietening countryside – only he didn't go out on his own anymore in the dark – not since Mallard and Peter had died – not since he had lain there quiet and unmoving in the bushes, watching it all happening, feeling as if he, too, was dying because he was too afraid to move or speak or afterwards, to say anything that would incriminate Roderick McIntyre of The Gatehouse.

Slowly he wandered along, his steps taking him towards the river. Everything smelt fresh and clean after last night's rain, the birds were starting to sing, blackbirds and thrushes, spilling their notes of purest delight into the dewy morning.

It would soon be midsummer. Ralph wondered if Robert and he would go fishing again, as they had done last year because Robert had said a good catch on a midsummer's day meant a bountiful harvest in the months ahead.

Robert was always coming away with things like that. 'Blarney,' Molly the Cook, called it, an indulgent smile on her face, her hands folded over her stomach, as she listened to Robert's tales.

'The Irish in him,' Aunt Dora would say, all smiles and dimples, waiting to see what was coming next.

Ralph wished he had the Irish in him; he wished he had lots of things in him that he hadn't but he knew he would always be the same as he was now, stubborn, deep, and difficult.

'It's the way you're made, Ralphie,' he could hear Robert's voice inside his head. 'A leopard can't change its spots, if they could I'd have knocked a few o' me own off years ago. You've got lots o' things I haven't: you're clever and good at lessons, old Dicky Bird likes you for that and hates me because I'm such a dunderhead. If you could maybe learn to speak a bit more you'd get by. Also, you might try smiling at folks instead o' gnashing your teeth and glowering at them from under your eyebrows. When I'm in the doldrums I think o' fat ladies dancing in the garden in their birthday suits. You'll find yourself laughing in no time at all and everyone else will laugh, too, even though they don't know what it is you're finding so funny.'

Ralph smiled to himself as he remembered those words of Robert's. He had never seen a fat lady in her birthday suit and doubted if Robert had either. But he had imagination, that was another of his assets, he could imagine things so vividly his descriptions of them made you draw in your breath and look about you to see if a dog with two heads really was coming to get you or if a nun in a fig leaf was wandering up the leafy lanes looking for dragonflies.

223

It was ridiculous! It was hilarious! Ralph felt better. He had reached The Overhanging Rocks above The Cauldron and he stood on the edge, looking down. The rain had filled the river to overflowing, it thundered along in peaty brown swirls and eddies, foaming over the rocks, covering the many potholes, gliding in giddy circles round and round the whirlpools.

When the river was like this it excited Ralph. He enjoyed its wildness and its splendour and he could sit for hours just staring at it, being mesmerised by it, feeling the tremble of it beneath his feet, hearing the roar of it in his ears, smelling the freshness of it pouring down from the hills.

Some way distant, through the lacy canopy of the trees, he could see the chimneys of The Gatehouse and he was reminded afresh of the promise he had made to Adam yesterday. Depression swept over him again. The moment that he dreaded was just a few hours away. He swallowed hard, panic seized him . . .

A movement on the opposite bank caught his eye, a dark broad figure was moving about in the bushes, making its way through the trees towards the river . . .

Roderick! He knew it was Roderick! He would know that thick-set bull of a man anywhere. Somehow he had found out what was going on! Adam must have said something, given out some hint of there having been an eyewitness at the scene of Mallard's murder . . . !

Ralph stood up. His nightmare was about to become reality, Roderick was coming to get him! The dream had been a warning after all – an omen of what was to come . . .

The man was coming nearer, creeping insidiously closer, he was wearing a hat, his face was in shadow – which made him seem all the more sinister and threatening . . .

Ralph began to back away from the edge of The Overhanging Rocks. He knew, now, what he had to do – but first . . .

With a swift movement he removed his cap and peeled off his jacket. Tying them up in a bundle he tossed it over the rocks and, with bated breath, he watched as it went whirling down, down, to the waiting waters churning below.

Then he took to his heels, never once looking back, intent only on putting as much distance as possible between himself and all the nightmarish things that had happened to him during his time in Glen Tarsa.

Jimmy Johnson, the head gamekeeper for the Leanachorran Estates, was intent on examining his rabbit snares. The roar of the river pounded in his ears, the greenery that surrounded him was thick and heavy. Although he was a big burly man Jimmy was as stealthy as a cat in his movements, much to the sorrow of the local poachers who had nicknamed him The Pouncer.

Pausing for a moment, Jimmy sniffed the early morning air with appreciation. He liked this hour, the mill still and silent, not a soul to be seen for miles, just himself and God, that was how he liked to think of it.

Taking his pipe from his pocket he stuffed some tobacco into the bowl and pushed it down with a stubby finger, then he went on his way, feeling at peace with himself and the world.

In order to escape the prying eyes of the local community, Miss Primrose Pym and Michael Dick had taken to rendezvous-ing with one another in the mornings, before the rest of the glen was up and about.

To herself Miss Pym described the meetings as lovers' trysts and was greatly thrilled by the idea.

Michael Dick's notions were less romantic. He had discovered that she had a tidy little nest-egg tucked away and his interest in her was of a more practical nature. He wanted to escape the mundane routine of his life and for a long time he had secretly harboured a dream to travel the world. In this rather dowdy woman, with her buck teeth and squat figure, he saw the answer to his prayers.

225

Ever since their first meeting it had become obvious to him that she was starved of male companionship and was ripe for adventure of a marital nature.

In no time at all she had been panting after him like a bitch in heat and, though he was anything but attracted to her he was prepared to put up with her shortcomings to further his ends. Foreign lands beckoned to him and who knew what excitements loomed for him beyond the horizon.

He had wooed Miss Pym and he most certainly had won her and even if his intentions were somewhat calculating, it mattered not – the woman was happier than she had ever been in her life, if her breathless giggles and starry eyes were anything to go on.

They strolled along by the riverbank, arm in arm, her wispy head on his shoulder, her whole being filled with a wondrous contentment.

'Oh, look, Michael, down there,' suddenly she pointed. 'I can't really be sure from here but – there's something lying among the rocks?'

'I do believe you're right, Primrose,' he agreed and together they scrambled down the bank, he omitting to give her a hand in his hurry, she forgetting to be helpless and ladylike in her equal anxiety to get to the little bundle lying at the edge of the river.

'It looks like clothing!' cried Michael Dick, tentatively turning the garments over with his foot. His face turned white. 'These are Ralph's things. I'd know them anywhere.'

Stooping, he picked up the sodden cap and stared at it in disbelief. 'Look. I was right! His name is on the inside of this hat – I remember her ladyship had it done when he and Robert kept getting their things mixed up.'

'Oh!' Miss Pym's hand flew to her mouth. 'But what are they doing here? And where is Ralph? I hope he hasn't fallen into the river.'

'We'd best get back to Noble House and report this,' Michael Dick decided firmly. 'Whatever has happened must have taken place this morning, since the boy was in bed when we all retired last night.'

He glanced about him. 'I wonder if anybody saw anything . . . perhaps . . . ' As if on cue, Jimmy Johnson appeared, a clutch of rabbits swinging from one meaty fist.

'I say, Johnson,' Michael Dick called imperiously. 'Be so good as to come over here. Something very odd has occurred.'

Jimmy came bounding forward and stood listening attentively to the tutor. When he had finished speaking Jimmy rubbed his chin and looked thoughtful. 'Strange, very strange indeed, Mr Dick,' he hazarded in his slow, careful manner. 'I was out early this morning, right enough, checking my snares, but I canny say that I saw or heard anything out o' the ordinary. Mind you, I did see Master Ralph on other occasions, up wi' the lark and wandering about in that lonely way he has. He had a particular liking for the rocks over yonder. I would see him, standing at the edge, gazing down into the water in a fascinated sort o' way.'

'Thank you, Johnson,' Michael Dick dismissed the gamekeeper with a nod of his head. 'We'll get back with these things. No doubt the police will have to be called. It's a nasty business, very nasty indeed.'

'I think I'd better come with you,' Jimmy was bristling a bit at the tutor's curt manner. 'I said to Molly I'd hand her in a rabbit or two and I'd like to be there when the police come. They'll want to look for the lad and will need the help o' every able-bodied man they can get.'

It was an odd little procession that made its way along the bridle path: the muscular gamekeeper striding along, with his clutch of rabbits; Michael Dick following, holding the wet tangle of clothing at arm's length as if he were afraid he would catch some sort of illness from it; Miss Pym at the rear, holding up her skirts as she picked her way along, her stringy hair falling out from under her hat.

227

They hadn't gone far when she said in a breathless voice, 'I think I should get back, Michael, they'll be waiting for me at breakfast and I can't have Mrs Jordan looking at me in a knowing fashion while Beth stands by making cryptic comments.'

'Yes, yes, that would be best,' the tutor replied distractedly. 'I don't know what's going to happen here, the whole routine will be disrupted and I won't know if I'm coming or going. These boys – really . . .'

His voice tailed off into obscurity and Primrose Pym turned away, just a weeny bit disappointed that he hadn't said anything that could be construed as a fond farewell. Then she shook herself. How could she! Poor Michael. He had enough to worry him with all the unpleasant happenings of the morning.

Lifting her skirts she hurried along, praying that neither Beth or Mrs Jordan would see her slipping into the house with her hair undone – she'd never hear the end of it!

CHAPTER 24

A Free Man

At half past six Anna woke from a restless sleep and immediately her mind filled again with everything that had been in it the night before.

Hurriedly she got dressed and going to the kitchen she glanced out of the window. It was a beautiful morning after the rain of last night: everything was green and fresh looking, pearly wisps of vapour clung to the hills, splashes of pink campion and yellow buttercups brightened the long grasses surrounding the mill buildings.

She saw some people moving along the bridle path on the opposite bank but the greenery was too thick for her to see who it was and she turned away, wondering who could be abroad at this early hour.

But she had other matters to occupy her mind. The doctor had sent word that Adam wasn't as bad as he had at first feared and with him being 'as strong as a horse' he would be on the mend in no time.

Now, it was her father who was uppermost in her thoughts. She would have to go in and see him, talk to him, tend to him. The doctor had said he would need constant attention and she felt sick at the idea of having to look after him.

She had to force herself to go to his room. Turning the handle she went in. He was lying there on the pillows, grey and haggard looking, his eyes closed, his breathing shallow, his mouth slack, saliva oozing from the corners.

She shuddered. She couldn't go near him, never mind touch him, talk to him . . .

His eyes opened suddenly. He stared straight at Anna, and the expression she saw in them made her heart go cold in her breast. Fear, stark and naked, looked out from those eyes, something that she had never seen before in him. He thought he was going to die! He couldn't move, he couldn't speak! He could only make desperate grunting sounds and scrabble one hand on the blankets, his nails scraping on the wool as he tried to reach out to her.

She felt faint with the strength of her dislike of him. Because of him Peter had died, because of him she had been robbed of a happiness that had filled her life with light and love and laughter . . . all gone, finished, dead . . .

'You are not a good man, Father,' she heard herself saying and her voice was cold and pebble-hard. 'You don't deserve any mercy because you have shown none to anyone else. Just the same, I'm going to look after you. I want you to get well so that you will pay for all the terrible things you have done in your life. It would be too merciful if you were to die now, so I'm going to nurse you till you are well and able to face up to reality.'

She couldn't tell if he fully understood her or not. He just kept staring at her, his eyes dry and unblinking, his mouth trembling, small sounds of helplessness issuing from his throat.

'I know you can hear me, Father,' she went on, in a breathless voice. 'You're going to be listening to me a lot over the next few months and I'm going to start off by laying down some rules o' my own.

'I can't nurse you and look after the house so I'll be bringing Nora McCrae in to help me. In my spare time – ay – I'll be making sure I have some o' that – I'll go and see Lady Pandora whenever it pleases me. Magnus and myself – Adam, too, if he wants it – are planning to see a lot more o' our mother and will go to Kilkenzie whenever we can. Mr Simpson is only too willing to take us and who knows, there

230

might come a day when Mother can come home to us and we can all be a family again – only this time we'll make sure that no harm comes to her. We aren't bairns anymore, and it's time you realised that for yourself.'

His eyes kept on staring at her, only now they registered his frustration at all the emotions he felt but couldn't convey. The hand on the blankets seemed stronger now, the fingers gripping the folds while the sounds from his throat were growing in volume with every passing second.

Anna stumbled from the room, weak with her reaction to her father, her head spinning, her heart racing.

Magnus was up and he had lit the fire. He turned to her and she went to him. He asked no questions, instead he stroked her hair and soothed her with his words of comfort.

'I said terrible things to him, Magnus,' she whispered. 'I – it didn't seem like me saying the things I did and him too ill to fight back.'

'Wheesht, wheesht, my babby,' Magnus said gently. 'He had it coming, ill or no; the time had come for you to speak your mind – no-one knows that more than him so don't worry about it anymore.'

All of that day the police had been out in force, searching the river, combing the countryside, but no further trace of Ralph did they find. By evening all those concerned were coming to the conclusion that the boy had run away.

'But why, why?' Lady Pandora cried in grief and bewilderment. 'Oh, I know he had been in turmoil for some time and was afraid of something or somebody, but I thought he felt safe here.'

Turning to Robert, she spread her hands in appeal. 'Of all people, Ralph trusted you. Have you any idea why he went off on his own like that? So early in the morning, without a word to anyone?'

Robert did have an idea, but he didn't say anything. Ralph had been a victim of his own fears and imaginings.

231

He had been unhappy and frightened for a long time, now he had taken himself off, a terrified boy who hadn't been able to face up to the dreadful burden of exposing a murderer.

Now, it was over and fate would do what it would to Roderick McIntyre and all that he stood for.

By the time September came Roderick was getting around with the aid of a stick. By October he was almost back to normal, except for a slight speech impairment. By Christmas he was getting out and about, as hale and hearty as ever, paying goodwill calls to his neighbours, looking and feeling like a man who had never been touched by illness or trouble of any sort.

'I've never known anything like it,' Doctor Minto told Anna. 'I know you nursed him with the utmost dedication but even so, he must have the constitution of an ox to have recovered as well as he has. What's his secret, I wonder?'

'There is no secret,' Anna said quietly. 'He's Roderick McIntyre, he's strong and he's determined and he seems to be indestructible but, odd as it may seem, he is also human and no one is immortal – not even him.'

She sounded calm but there was something in her voice and in her words that made Doctor Minto suck in his breath and look at her strangely. But she had turned away and he never saw the darkness that touched her lovely face nor the tears of sadness that drowned her eyes. Everything seemed so hopeless. She had pinned her faith on Ralph's confession to the police. Now he was gone, what chance had she left of bringing her father to justice? Nothing made sense any more and she felt lost and afraid.

Doctor Minto didn't know anything, he was only an onlooker, one who saw without seeing and listened without hearing, no matter how hard he tried.

A lot of people seemed to be leaving Glen Tarsa at once. Beth was soon going off to her school for young ladies

232

in England. Before she left, she came to say goodbye to Anna. 'Nothing's the same here anymore,' she said peevishly. 'Miss Prim and Mr Slick Dick are going to be married. Can you imagine it! She won't know what to do with him once she gets the ring on her finger. As for their wedding night, I'd love to be a fly on the wall. I imagine he'll wear gloves and she'll swoon on the spot when she sees what he's got to offer! Not that it'll be much, he's always struck me as being a bit wet behind the ears, though no doubt it will keep her occupied for a while. After all, she can't really compare him with anybody else, can she, her being a daughter of the manse with a very strict upbringing and a father who's dead, God rest him.'

At this both girls burst out laughing and Beth's eyes were rather misty when she said pensively, 'Oh, Anna, I am going to miss you. We have had some good times together and I just know I won't meet anyone else like you, no matter where I go.

'It's as well to get this school business over with. Mother has a bee in her bonnet about making a lady of me though I'll never be like that beastly little Miss Chastity Belt. She seems to think that she owns Lucas but I just know he'll come back to me in the end.'

At that point her eyes gleamed. Just recently she and Lucas had enjoyed a lusty romp in the hayloft in the grounds of Noble House, almost under the snobby nose of the 'real little lady', much to Beth's triumph.

'Oh, yes,' she continued thoughtfully, 'he'll come back to me, I've always known what Lucas needs and he can never resist the kind of things I can give him.'

Sure of Lucas, Beth felt able to be suitably sorry for Adam. 'I'm glad Adam's fully recovered from the beating he took. He's not so bad when all's said and done and I was truly sorry about what happened to him. Pity they never found the one who did it but the police here are just a lot of old women who ought to take up knitting.'

Pausing for breath she searched her friend's face with her big, round, critical eyes. 'You look tired, Anna, and no wonder, running after that horrible father of yours all these months. Why don't you leave home? He doesn't deserve you.'

'I'm not staying for him. Lady Pandora needs me, she's lost Peter and Ralph's gone and I can't leave her now.'

'Of course, she always did have a soft spot for you, didn't she? Nevertheless, you have your own life to lead, Magnus too. I wonder he doesn't go away also.'

'He stays to be near me, Magnus has always looked after me.'

'I know, you're very close, aren't you, even for a brother and sister?' There was a nuance of sarcasm in her voice together with an underlying hint of accusation but before Anna could speak she went on, 'It doesn't matter, time will tell all, meanwhile I must fly. Mother wants to take me to Larchwood to be fitted for a new dress – one that will befit a proper little schoolgirl!' With a giggle she hugged her friend and went off in a flurry of rustling silk and satins.

Robert, too, was being sent away to school, for several reasons, one being that he had been lonely without Ralph, the other because Michael Dick was leaving.

He came to see Anna to say goodbye. 'Aunt Dora is sending me away,' he grinned in his cheeky fashion. 'She thinks it will be good for my mind and might rid me of all the Irish that's in me. As if anything could ever do that, I was born with the blarney stone in my mouth and swallowed it with me first breath.'

Seizing her hand he grew suddenly serious. 'I'll be back, Anna, one day I'll be coming back to see you, though a lot o' my holidays will be spent in Ireland with some long-lost relatives that Aunt Dora has managed to dig up. She believes I need blood kin to make me really happy, but I feel that my home is here now, in Glen Tarsa – with folks I have grown to know and love.'

His blue eyes were shining in his handsome sparkling face. Bending his head he kissed her, full and square on the lips, then standing back he said, 'There, that will do you nothing but good, it's what you've been waiting for all o' your life . . . ' He stepped back a pace. 'I'll never forget you, Anna,' he murmured softly and then he went quickly away, leaving her to gaze after him with tears in her eyes as she wondered when she would see him again.

But he had said he would be back, he was Robert Shamus O'Connor, a loyal, laughing Irish lad who always meant what he said.

Slowly she wandered along the glen road, her steps taking her to the wild and wonderful countryside that surrounded Noble House. Pausing by the drystone dyke, she pulled her shawl closer round her shoulders while her eyes searched the wintry landscape. And then she saw him, the boy who was a man now, the one she had always cherished just as he had her – right from the beginning.

Magnus,' she whispered, gazing at him as he strode through the frosty fields, guiding the plough, his head downbent, the tall, lithe figure of him, strong and sweet and filling the morning with life. Her morning, the morning she would always know with him, the days she would always share with him.

He was her brother but somehow she knew he was much, much more. She had so much to learn yet, mysteries of the past to unearth, if she was to have a future at all with the people she loved most.

'Magnus!' she cried, her voice echoing over the fields.

He stopped, he looked up. 'Anna!' he called back, his voice winging to her over the distance that separated them.

She began to run towards him and the light in her eyes found its reflection in his as he waited to welcome her to him with open arms.